Michelle Perry
Cain & Abel

Jewel Imprint: Emerald
Medallion Press, Inc.
Florida, USA

Dedication

For Quinton, Chase and Selena

Published 2005 by Medallion Press, Inc.
225 Seabreeze Ave.
Palm Beach, FL 33480

The MEDALLION PRESS LOGO
is a registered tradmark of Medallion Press, Inc.

If you purchased this book without a cover, you should be aware that this book is stolen property. It was reported as "unsold and destroyed" to the publisher, and neither the author nor the publisher has received any payment from this "stripped book."

Copyright © 2005 by Michelle Perry
Cover Illustration by Adam Mock

All rights reserved. No part of this book may be reproduced or transmitted in any form or by any electronic or mechanical means, including photocopying, recording, or by any information storage and retrieval system, without written permission of the publisher, except where permitted by law.

Printed in the United States of America

Library of Congress Cataloging-in-Publication Data

Perry, Michelle.
  Cain and Abel / Michelle Perry.
    p. cm.
  ISBN 1-932815-03-1
  1. Family violence--Fiction. 2. Runaway wives--Fiction. 3. Abused wives--Fiction. 4. Tenessee--Fiction. I. Title.
  PS3616.E7935C35 2004
  813'.6--dc22

                                                      2004028347

Acknowledgements:

For your invaluable help and encouragement with this project, I'd like to thank Theresa Gaus, Rebecca Miller, Sally Apokedak, Cat Brown, Barbara Hughes, Charlina and Mavis Adams, Diana White, the WWCG gang: Patsy Phillips, Kate MacNeil, Julie Jones, Eric Kregel, Nicole Service, Carrie Smoot, Lori Saltis, Glee Bohanon, Caryl Harvey, Karla Bran, Angie Blanco, Marie Disbrow and Carole Suzanne Jackson.

Thanks to my family and friends for your support.

Chapter 1

If he looked up, she was as good as dead. Jessica was afraid to move, afraid to breathe, afraid he would hear her heart slamming into her chest from across the room.

How had Cole found her?

She watched him eat his hamburger and marveled at his casualness as he sipped his iced tea.

Was it possible that he didn't know?

It had taken five years for her to stop looking over her shoulder. Five years to reach the place where a ringing phone or a knock at the door didn't terrify her. The idea that he might've crossed her path again by mere chance staggered her.

But the late Mrs. Cole Ramsey, as she humorlessly considered herself, had never been much of a believer in chance.

Fear coiled in her stomach like a thick, cold serpent. She wiped her sweaty palms on her slacks and clutched her purse. As she gauged the distance between herself and the door, Jessica tried to suppress the whimper that rose in her throat. Her habit of always seeking a back table may have gotten her killed.

To get out, she'd have to walk right by him, and she didn't think she could do it. She looked around the room, searching for any means of escape, any help. Nothing. Then she glanced back at Cole and nearly screamed.

He was staring at her.

Her furiously pounding heart nearly skidded to a stop as his pale blue eyes locked on hers. Then Cole did something extraordinary, something that frightened her more than if he'd pulled a gun.

He smiled.

With a strangled cry, Jessica jumped up and toppled her chair. It banged against the gray marble floor like a gunshot. Conversation at the neighboring tables ceased, and the other customers seemed to fade away until there was nothing left but Cole and her and the ragged sound of her own breathing. Cole's smile flickered and died and was replaced by a look of confusion.

Was it possible he hadn't recognized her?

The thought seemed ridiculous, even though she'd tried to alter her appearance. Her long blond hair was now short and mousy brown; her green eyes were hidden beneath a pair of brown contact lenses. She no longer looked like Jessica Ramsey, the trophy wife of a wealthy businessman. She was Emily Jackson, a shy woman who worked at Mid-Tennessee Realty and hid behind thick bangs.

Cole looked over his shoulder, then back at her, as if trying to spot the cause of her distress.

Jessica's stomach lurched. He hadn't recognized her. She'd just blown it.

Cole wiped his mouth with a napkin and pushed away from the table.

Panic freed her feet, and Jessica sprinted past him.

Cole shouted something, but the roar of the pulse in her ears drowned it out. Propelling herself out the door, Jessica slammed into a beefy man in a business suit. His briefcase went flying as he staggered and nearly fell. It skidded off the sidewalk and landed underneath a nearby car. As the man scrambled for it, Jessica darted around him. She ignored his indignant cry as she scanned the street.

Where could she hide?

Jessica cursed herself for walking to lunch. Her car was five blocks away in the real estate office parking lot. It might as well have been on another planet.

The bell above the restaurant door chimed and blindly, she ran. Her low heels clicked against the pavement as she wove through the midday crowd, trying to put as many people between her and Cole as possible.

Jessica fell in with a group of shoppers crossing Duncan Street and tried to make herself disappear in the middle of them, but her terror wouldn't allow her to keep their relaxed pace for long. She broke from the pack and took a sharp left down a side street.

As Jessica leapt off the curb, her heel caught in a grate. She sprawled forward onto the asphalt and cried out as the rough surface bit into her palms and ripped through the knees of her slacks. Blood made her fingers slippery as she tried to work her heel free from the grate. The navy pump was wedged in tightly and, in her desperation, Jessica abandoned it. She yanked the other one off as well and raced off in her bare feet.

Her knees stung but she ran as hard and as far as she could before the familiar tightening started in her chest.

Oh God, not now!

A bout of coughing wracked her body. As Jessica stumbled into an alley, the warm, fragrant scent of fabric softener assaulted her. Stunned, she leaned against the gray slate of Michaelson's Laundromat.

Had she really run seven blocks?

The exhaust from the dryers pushed air through the vents on the side of the building. Lint particles danced in the warm air. They tickled her throat, and her coughing grew steadily worse. She had to get out of here, but she was too terrified to move. Terrified that Cole would seize her if she stepped into the open.

He was out there somewhere; Cole never gave up.

To her horror, she began to wheeze. The high-pitched hissing seemed obscenely loud in the enclosed space, and Jessica felt a flash of anger at her body's betrayal.

Pain stabbed through Jessica's knees as she hunkered

behind a chipped, green garbage bin and fought for her next breath. She fumbled at her purse with stiffening fingers, leaving a sticky crimson smear across its shiny black surface. Her shaking hands nearly dropped the .38 as she jerked it out and laid it across her lap. She let her purse slip to the ground as she pulled out her inhaler, shook it and took the first puff. She held her breath for a seven count, waiting for the steroids to hit her bronchial tubes.

Maybe she had lost him. Maybe . . .

Through the crack between the dumpster and the wall, Jessica watched Cole enter the alley. She dropped the inhaler in her lap and clutched the gun with both hands.

"I saw you run in here," he said casually, and walked right past her hiding place.

Jessica nearly lost her footing on a discarded bread wrapper when she lurched to her feet. Something clattered to the ground, and she realized an instant too late that it was her inhaler. For a split second, she took her eyes off Cole to watch it roll underneath the dumpster, and jerked her gaze back to him when she realized her mistake.

Oh God, she wasn't ready for this. Another stupid mistake like that and he'd kill her.

"Stay back!" she growled.

Cole raised his hands as Jessica trained the gun on him. She hated the way her hand trembled. She feared the man standing before her more than she did the devil himself. His handsome face was just a mask.

"Let me walk away," she managed.

Spots danced before her eyes as she tried to hold the gun steady.

"Easy!" he said, his blue eyes widening in alarm. "I'm not going to hurt you."

"No, you're . . . not," she wheezed. "Not . . . this time."

The look in those eyes surprised her, a mixture of confusion and compassion. Nothing like the icy blue gaze she expected. A coughing fit rendered Jessica momentarily helpless, and she lost her aim. Cole took a step toward her. She straightened her arm, pointing the gun at the center of his chest.

"You're bleeding," he said.

Involuntarily, she followed his gaze and stared down at the ragged knees of her slacks. Blood soaked through the tan fabric, and the sight of it made her dizzy. She forced back a wave of nausea.

"Put the gun down. I only want to talk. Can we do that?"

He sounded so calm, so innocent, but she hadn't forgotten the things he was capable of doing. Memories of the beatings, memories of psychological torture flooded her brain, and her finger tightened on the trigger.

Then she thought of Joe.

"Stay away from me," Jessica whispered, dismayed to hear that scared little girl voice she thought she'd left behind when she'd escaped from Cole.

How she hated that voice and the helplessness she felt right now.

Jessica backed out of the alley and onto the sidewalk.

Bright sunlight flashed in her eyes, nearly blinding her as Cole took another step toward her.

"Stay back!" she hissed.

Intent on watching Cole, Jessica stumbled off the curb.

"Watch out!" Cole shouted, just before her world exploded in a cacophony of blaring horns and screeching brakes.

"Are you okay? Talk to me," a voice commanded.

Jessica looked up, struggling to see through the red haze that clouded her vision. Cole's face loomed above her, and she tried to scream, but all she could manage was a moan.

"Help is on the way. Hold on."

What was wrong with him? Why didn't he just kill her? Confusion warred with pain as she slipped in and out of consciousness. His hands moved behind her head, and Jessica closed her eyes, expecting him to snap her neck. She dared to take a glance at him and cried out when he eased his hands free.

Instead of striking her, he tugged his white T-shirt over his head and gently pressed it to her forehead to stanch the warm flow she felt streaming down her face.

The gun. Where was her gun?

It rested beside Cole's leg. Jessica glanced at it, then at Cole. Her desperation must have shown on her face, because his eyes widened. She lunged for the gun, but he was quicker. He jerked it away from her and tucked it in the back of his pants.

An elderly woman appeared in her peripheral vision. Jessica wanted to shout, "Run! Run before he kills you too!"

"I never saw her!" the woman cried as she knelt beside Jessica. "Is she okay?"

"She's going to be okay," Cole said, not looking at the woman, but staring into Jessica's eyes. "You're going to be okay," he repeated. His voice was quiet and calm and, amazingly, it almost lulled her.

She stared at his broad chest and frowned. Something was wrong, something was . . .

"Where . . . what happened to your tattoo?" she asked.

He lifted his eyebrows. "Tattoo?"

Jessica frowned again, and felt some minute shift of reality. The sudden, terrifying thought flashed across her mind that she was going crazy. Was this even real? Was *he* real?

"Cole?" she whispered.

A black curtain fell over her eyes before she heard his answer.

Alex stared down at her, stunned. How did this woman know his twin? Cole was two thousand miles away in Los Angeles. What was going on here?

An icy feeling gripped him as he watched her body jerk with ghostly, hitching breaths. This situation felt so desperately wrong. The terror he'd seen in her eyes unnerved him. Her asthma unnerved him. Who was this woman?

Alex thought about Jessica, and one of the last times he'd phoned her before her death. Caught up in one of her asthma attacks, she'd asked him to call back later, but her rattling gasps had scared him so badly that he'd insisted on staying on the line until he was sure she was okay. Until it was almost time for Cole to arrive home.

Could this woman be some relation?

Sirens screamed down the street and an ambulance screeched to a stop in front of them. The doors opened, and two paramedics scrambled to her side.

"What happened?" one of them asked, and the elderly woman started crying.

"She walked out in front of me. I never saw her."

Alex stared down at the bloody T-shirt he still pressed against her head and felt a little queasy.

"Excuse me," the other one said, and Alex scooted out of his way. He shakily climbed to his feet and watched them work on her. As his mind struggled to connect the dots, he remembered that she'd had a purse. He slipped through the gathering crowd and reentered the alley.

The black purse lay on its side beside the dumpster. Alex picked it up and poked through the contents. Nothing unusual. A roll of Lifesavers, a set of keys, an ink pen with Mid-Tennessee Realty imprinted on the side. Alex took out her billfold and flipped it open to her driver's license.

Tennessee license, number 78065624. Emily Jackson.

The name meant nothing to him, but he used her pen to write the number on the back of his hand. Jessica had mentioned a sister somewhere, but Alex couldn't recall her name. All the other plastic photo sleeves were empty, as were the credit card slots. The wallet contained a total of forty-seven dollars.

Alex stared long and hard at the DMV photo, then closed his eyes as he tried to compare that image with the mental picture he had of his late sister-in-law, which was dim, at best. Although they'd talked on the phone several times, he'd only seen her in person once, when he'd stood in that tiny room at St. Anthony's and stared down at her sedated form after her nervous breakdown.

He'd seen her wedding pictures, though, and that smiling image was the one that came most readily to his mind. Jessica Ramsey had been a knockout, a bronze California beauty with flowing blond hair and sparkling green eyes.

The pale, gaunt-faced brunette he'd just met, although pretty, showed none of that vitality. Her DMV photo was as grim and unforgiving as a mug shot. She looked tense, almost defiant. But yet there was something . . . the line of her jaw, the curve of her cheek . . . something that made him realize he couldn't let this go without knowing who she was and why she'd reacted to him like she had.

Alex tucked the billfold back into the purse and carried it out of the alley with him. The police had arrived. One uniformed officer stood close by, talking to the elderly lady, while the other spoke to the paramedics outside the ambulance. Alex walked up to the nearest one and tapped him on the shoulder.

"This is hers," he said, and handed him the purse.

"Ramsey, is that you?" the other barked, and Alex twisted his head to look at him. It took a moment before recognition dawned. Alex smiled.

"I don't believe it. Roger Milken. How've you been, man?" Alex strode over to him and held out a hand, but dropped it again when he saw the blood streaking his fingers.

Roger lifted an eyebrow. "Better than you, apparently."

"He's got a gun!" the younger one shouted, and it took Alex a moment to realize the kid meant *him*. The gun he'd stuck in the back of his pants.

"Easy, Jeffries. He's a cop." Milken looked at Alex. "Well, used to be a cop, same difference. We roomed together at the academy. Still a P.I., Ramsey?"

"Yeah."

"Got a gun permit?"

"Yeah," Alex said, but for some reason, he didn't tell them that this gun wasn't his.

Milken gave his partner a bored shrug. "See, Jeffries. He's okay. So, what happened?"

Alex exhaled and shook his head. "I'm still not sure myself. I was eating lunch at that little place by the courthouse, with the red roof—"

"Polly's." Milken nodded. "Go on."

"—when I noticed a woman staring at me." He pointed at the ambulance. "*That* woman. Then she freaked out. I don't know what happened. She looked like she was going to have a stroke, then she flew out of there like a bat out of hell. I followed her, because I was a little worried. Then she—" Alex hesitated.

In that moment, he decided not to tell them about the gun, or his brother. Not yet. He didn't know Emily Jackson, or why she'd pulled a gun on him, but he felt responsible for her accident. Roger Milken was a good guy, but he was hard-nosed cop. Alex didn't want to cause this Jackson woman any more grief than he already had without giving her a chance to explain.

"She stumbled off the curb in front of a car," he finished.

"You don't know her? You're not working a case?"

Alex watched the ambulance pull away before replying, "I'm working a case, but nothing to do with her. Her license says her name is Emily Jackson, but I have no idea who that is."

Milken asked Alex several more questions, then nodded and snapped his notebook shut. "All right. Think that'll do it."

A mosquito landed on Alex's bare shoulder, and he swatted it with his ruined shirt.

Milken frowned. "Follow me."

Alex followed him to the squad car, and Milken popped the trunk. He extracted a powder blue bowling shirt and tossed it at Alex, who snagged it in mid-air. "It's semi-clean. Better than yours, anyway."

"Thanks."

"You got a card?"

Alex extracted one from his wallet and handed it to him.

"I'll call if I need you. Next time you're around, holler

at me. If I ain't working, I'll buy you a beer."

"Sounds good," Alex said, as he pulled the shirt over his head. He smiled and tugged at the loose material. "I see Shelia's still feeding you good."

Milken snorted. "Nah, man. She's barely feeding me at all. On some new diet kick. Protein and organic vegetables. Says if she's gonna diet, I'm gonna diet with her. Thank God for Dairy Queens and Pizza Huts."

Alex laughed, and waved as Milken got into his car and drove away. After checking the number on his hand to make sure he hadn't smeared it, Alex jogged back to the restaurant parking lot, where he unlocked his car and grabbed his cell phone out of the holder to call his office.

When his partner picked up, he said, "Hi, Rach. I need a favor."

"Lay it on me," she said breezily.

"Tennessee license 78065624. Emily Jackson."

"Emily ... ooh, wait. My pen died." He heard shuffling noises in the background and Rachel sighed.

"Come on, girl." Alex smiled as he laid his head back against the seat and closed his eyes. "What's the holdup?"

"I'm at your desk, that's the holdup. Geez, how do you find anything in this mess?"

"You just don't know my system."

She snorted. "Some system. Okay, Emily Johnson, 780 . . ."

"Jackson. 78065624. Get me anything you can find on her."

"Will do. Is she Bernie Wilson's honey?"

"What? Oh, no." Alex shook his head, remembering the case he was *supposed* to be working on. "This is something else."

"Please get me something soon," Rachel begged. "Mrs. Wilson's driving me nuts. We had a girl chat this morning. She asked my opinion and I told her I wouldn't have a man I couldn't trust."

"That's the thing, Rach. I've followed this guy for days. So far, that sack of Krystal burgers he sucks down every day at lunch seems to be his only vice. I think Mrs. Wilson is wasting her money and my time."

Rachel laughed. "Guess what she asked me to do?"

"Do I want to know?"

"Dress up in something snazzy, go to his office and proposition him. You know, to see if he bites."

Alex rubbed his eyes. He hated these kinds of cases. "Did you tell her we don't do entrapment? Besides, what chance would a poor slob like that stand against the likes of you?"

"That's what Mike said. He was sitting here when she called."

Alex rubbed the back of his neck. "See, that's what I'm talking about. He was some big, tough FBI guy when I introduced you, and now look at him. The man can't even work for mooning over you. Frankly, it's a little embarrassing to watch."

"So quit watching," she retorted. "I'll call you back in a minute."

Alex thought about going to the hospital, but then realized it would probably be awhile before he could talk to Emily. He gingerly removed the gun from his waistband, dropped it in a plastic bag, and stuffed it in his glove compartment. Remembering the company name on the pen, Alex stopped at a service station to get directions to Mid-Tennessee Realty. He didn't know what—if anything—he expected to find there, but it would give him something to do until Rachel called back.

He pulled into the real estate agency's parking lot a few minutes later. The building was small, but neatly tended. Lush red cannas splayed against the white building, their tall blooms rustling in the breeze as he strode up the sidewalk.

As serene as it looked on the outside, the building buzzed with activity inside. The phone rang as Alex approached the front desk. The harried-looking man behind it held up a finger and lifted the receiver. "Mid-Tennessee Realty, Joshua Reese speaking. How may I help you?"

Alex looked around the office while he waited. This first office was a waiting area, with chairs, a magazine rack, and the front desk. A hallway stretched behind the receptionist's desk, and he assumed the larger, glassed-in offices beyond belonged to the realtors.

He watched a slim brunette in the first office tap her keyboard as she spoke into a microphone.

Finally, the man at the front desk hung up and gave Alex an apologetic smile. "Sorry about that. How may I help you?"

Before Alex could respond, the phone buzzed.

"Emily, I need the Marsters file when you get a chance," a cool female voice said.

Alex sucked in a breath as the man replied, "Emily's not back from lunch yet, Pru, but I'll get the file as soon as I take care of this customer."

Glancing back at the brunette, Alex saw the startled expression cross her face when she looked up at him. She quickly turned away. He heard a click and the speaker went dead.

"Emily Jackson?" Alex asked.

"Yes," the man replied. "Do you know her?"

Alex frowned. "There was an accident. Emily was hit by a car. They took her to Lincoln Medical."

The man blinked. "Oh no! Is she okay? She's not . . ."

"I think she'll be okay," Alex said. "She's a little banged up, and it knocked her unconscious—"

"Wait a sec," he interrupted. "Let me get Pru."

The man barged into the brunette's office without knocking. Alex watched him deliver the news. Shock crossed Pru's face, and she covered her mouth with her hand. Then she shot Alex an accusing look through the glass and grabbed her purse.

While Alex was still trying to figure out what *that* was all about, Pru burst from her office. Instead of coming to him, she lowered her head and marched down the hall to her right. Alex hurried around the front desk and practically ran down the narrow hallway after her. He was more confused than ever.

"Wait, miss!" he called, but she acted like she didn't hear him as she pushed out a door and entered the parking lot.

Alex ran back the way he'd come and sprinted outside to his car. As he threw himself behind the wheel, a silver Camry roared through the parking lot, nearly cutting off another driver as it swung onto the main highway.

Alex raced after her.

Normally, he'd try to hang back, but he couldn't risk losing her at the intersection. She took a left onto a four-lane with heavier traffic and stayed in the fast lane. Alex switched to the far right lane, trying to hide his little black car behind a semi.

His cell phone rang and he jerked it up as he swerved around a slow moving U-Haul.

"Yeah," he barked.

"Hello to you too," Rachel said. "Guess what?"

"What?"

"The ID's a fake."

"Are you sure?" Alex demanded, playing cat and mouse with the Camry through traffic. This situation kept getting stranger. Who were these women and what was their connection to his twin?

Traffic thinned up ahead and Alex slowed to let Pru take a better lead. She took a sharp left and caught him off-guard. He zigzagged through three lanes of traffic and nearly got clipped by a Corvette when he took the ramp.

"The license is real, but when I started digging, I found

a short paper trail. Emily Jackson of 1217 Beaumont Street didn't exist five years ago. No prior credit history, no tax returns filed . . . you know what that means."

Alex knew. A fake birth certificate was used to obtain a fake social security card, which could then be used to obtain whatever else she needed. It was too easy.

"I need to get some prints run asap. You know anyone around here who can help me out?" he asked Rachel.

"Nobody in the immediate area, but I know a techie in Sparta who owes me a favor. Let me talk to him, and I'll get back with you."

"Thanks."

Pru led him through a series of turns designed to shake him from her tail, but fortunately, they'd entered a part of town Alex was familiar with. Up ahead, she hung a right. This time, Alex didn't follow. Anticipating the route she'd take, he took a shortcut, speeding the wrong way down a one-way street. He pulled back onto the two-lane and watched for the Camry in his rearview mirror. He hoped Pru would be so busy looking for him behind her that she'd never think he'd somehow gotten in *front* of her. He slowed to 60, then to 50.

Just when he thought he'd outsmarted himself, the silver car appeared in his rearview mirror. Immediately, he increased his speed. He passed a semi, then used the big truck as a shield between them. His ploy seemed to work. Pru slowed her breakneck pace. They continued on the road for nearly five minutes, until Pru took a left.

Alex turned around in a Kroger parking lot and

doubled back.

Up ahead, the Camry took another right and entered a residential area. Pru turned again and Alex started to follow suit when he saw the dead end street sign. He parked a block over and jumped from his car. He cut through someone's back yard, startling two young boys who shared a cigarette behind one of the brick houses.

By the time he caught up with her, Pru was out of her Camry and running up the driveway of a neat brick house. She twisted the front door knob. Finding it locked, she banged on the door with her fist. Alex slipped behind an oak tree and watched as a teenage girl opened the door and let her inside.

Intent on watching the front door, Alex ducked when Pru ran out into the carport a few moments later, clutching a blue tote bag in one hand.

"Joe, come on!" Pru yelled.

A little dark-haired boy raced out the door with a baseball glove tucked underneath his arm. Alex's heart gave a funny little spasm.

Oh, God.

Alex didn't need a DNA test to tell him who the kid's father was, and he was equally sure Cole had no idea the boy existed.

The ride to the hospital passed in a blur. Every time Jessica stared up at the overhead lights in the ambulance, she imagined she was somewhere else. Her kitchen, the office, even Joe's school. Disoriented, she'd mumble something to Joe or Pru, only to realize she was talking to the same EMT. He would pat her hand and reassure her that everything was going to be all right, and she'd be embarrassed for babbling, but moments later, she'd do it again. She caught him staring at the scar on her right wrist when he took her pulse, and was helpless to stop him when he gently turned her other wrist up. What must he think of her? He didn't understand. He didn't know Cole.

Where was Cole? Would he be waiting for her at the hospital? Had he really been there at all? Dear God, she didn't know what terrified her more, the thought that Cole was coming for her or that she'd just imagined he was. She couldn't let them put her in a horrible place like St. Anthony's again. She closed her eyes, remembering the terror and desolation she'd felt the day she'd been committed.

But things were different now. She had a son to think about. No matter what, she had to keep it together. She had to be strong. The police and doctors hadn't believed her then, and they wouldn't believe her now. She couldn't depend on anyone to help her escape Cole; she'd have to do it herself.

Jessica tried to look around when they wheeled her into the hospital, but she couldn't turn her head. She fought a wave of panic when they shone a light in her eyes and removed her contact lenses, though she didn't need them to see. She felt naked without them, stripped of one more layer of her disguise. She couldn't even reply when the nurse commented on how beautiful her eyes were. In fact, her nerves were so shot that she had to bite the inside of her mouth to keep from screaming whenever anyone spoke to her at all. She thought she heard one of the EMTs say "concussion" before she blacked out again.

She jolted awake when a smiling woman in Winnie the Pooh scrubs wheeled her down a hallway. "Shh." She patted Jessica's arm. "I'm taking you for some tests. You're pretty banged up. Do you remember what happened?"

Cole's face flashed in her mind again, but Jessica clamped her mouth shut. The less she said, the better. "Not really," she whispered.

"They said you stumbled in front of a car. Do you remember what you were doing before that?"

"Lunch. I was walking back from lunch." Jessica licked her dry lips. "Did someone come in with me? Is someone waiting for me?"

"Not that I know about, honey. Would you like me to call someone?"

"My boss. Pru Landry. She works at Mid-Tennessee Realty."

"What about family?" the woman asked as she opened a set of double doors with her hip.

"I don't have . . . anyone," Jessica said softly.

After the tests, the woman wheeled Jessica to a double room where a bored-looking policeman waited in one of the vinyl chairs.

Jessica struggled to act calm as he began questioning her. His first questions were easy, the same basic information the hospital staff asked, but her pulse speeded up when he said, "Ms. Jackson, a witness at the scene said you appeared agitated, distressed. Can you tell me what happened after you left Polly's Restaurant?"

Polly's. Had he spoken to Cole? If so, why hadn't Cole told him everything, about her faking her death, her alias ... that she was his nutcase wife? Jessica decided the best thing to do was to use her head injury to her advantage and act confused.

"I don't . . . I ate at Polly's? I remember leaving the office, but everything's a little . . . fuzzy after that."

He asked her a few more questions, and stood to leave. "I guess that will do it. I hope everything works out for you, Ms. Jackson."

Jessica forced a smile. "I do too."

Alex leaned against the oak tree and tried to swallow the sour taste in his mouth as he watched Pru with his nephew. The kid looked exactly like he and Cole had at that age. That explained Emily and Pru's reactions to seeing him, Alex supposed. But which one of them was Joe's mother, and why were they so desperate to hide the boy from Cole?

Emily, Alex guessed. Emily was Joe's mother. What had she said to him in the alley, when he'd said he wasn't going to hurt her?

Not this time.

What did that mean?

Alex slipped away while Pru buckled Joe in the front seat of the Camry. His thoughts flew in a thousand directions as he jogged back to his car. He couldn't let Pru disappear with that child.

He checked his phone and found a message from Rachel. He speed dialed the office while he waited for the Camry to reappear. After it turned the corner, he forced himself to wait a few seconds before he followed.

"Hey, I got the techie," Rachel said. "He said he can run them for you right away, but you have to be at the lab before four," Rachel said.

"It's nearly three now," Alex said, glancing at his watch.

"The lab's only twenty minutes away, on highway 50."

"I've moved since we talked. On the other end of town now." Alex winced in the late afternoon sun and pawed the dash for his sunglasses. "Hey, what's that kid's name, the one who helped us do surveillance on Sandy Freeman? Wasn't he from Woodbury?"

"Yep. Marcus Wrigley."

"You still have his number?"

Alex fished for a pen while Rachel looked it up. He jotted the number on a Burger King napkin.

"I hate to ask," Rachel said. "But what have you gotten yourself into?"

Alex sighed. "I wish I knew."

He hung up and called Marcus, the young P.I. in training. The kid answered his phone with a "Yo".

"Marcus, this is Alex Ramsey—"

"Yes, sir," Marcus interrupted, his voice eager. "What can I do for you?"

"You have time to do some tailing for me?"

"You bet I do. Where do you want me to go?"

"The gas station first. Fill up your tank, because I have no idea how far this woman is going."

Before the words were out of his mouth, Alex saw the silver Camry turn right up ahead. Good, at least maybe Pru wasn't leaving the state.

"Got a full tank," Marcus said. "Let's do this. Where are you?"

"I just passed the Quik Mart on highway 50. Heading past the old shirt factory."

"Gotcha. So who am I after?"

"Her name is Pru. She's about 5-5, 110 pounds, brunette. Driving a 2002 silver Camry. We just turned right again, heading down Mill Road."

"Straight toward me," Marcus said gleefully, and Alex smiled. He'd forgotten what it was like to be just starting out, to be thrilled by such mundane work as tailing.

"But she's not the important one," Alex added. "She's got a kid in the car with her, a little dark-haired boy who's about four or five. If she drops him somewhere, you stay with him."

"Got it."

Marcus launched into a story about the last case he'd worked, with Alex interrupting occasionally to update driving instructions.

"So I followed him into this—hey, you still in the black Accord?" Marcus asked.

"Yeah. What are you . . . " Alex broke off as the green Taurus barreled toward him in the opposite lane. A grinning Marcus waved wildly as he flashed by.

Alex watched in the rearview mirror as the kid pumped the breaks and did a U-turn in a lumber supply parking lot. Marcus was a little goofy, but he was going to make a good detective one of these days.

"Okay, I'm out of here," Alex said. "I'll call you soon. Don't lose that kid."

Alex made it to the lab with twenty minutes to spare. The techie shot a pointed glance at the clock as he chewed on a sandwich. "It's a little late," he said. "Might be tomorrow—"

"I need it now," Alex interrupted. "Please."

He sighed and took the baggie containing the gun from Alex. "Let me see what I can do."

A bottle of Rolaids sat on the guy's desk, and Alex helped himself to a handful while he waited. He chewed them like candy and read the cartoon on an out-of-date Farside calendar on the wall.

The tech returned in fifteen minutes. A blob of mustard hung on one corner of his mouth. He plopped into the chair across from Alex and shoved the plastic bag containing the gun across the desk.

"Got two prints off it. Alex Ramsey . . ." He peered at Alex. "Guess that's you."

Alex nodded.

"And a Jessica Ramsey. That your wife?"

Alex's jaw dropped. "What did you say?"

"Jessica Annette Ramsey."

Alex swallowed hard, then swallowed again. "Any priors?"

The guy stared at him with open curiosity. "No. Nothing like that. Prints registered by the State of California nursing board. You saying you don't know her or something?"

Alex stood and grabbed the baggie. "Thanks. Bill my office for whatever I owe you."

He hurried out the door before the guy could ask him any other questions.

Chapter 2

Jessica was alive. She had a son.

Alex thought that maybe if he kept repeating those two things in his mind, they would eventually make sense.

Had she had another breakdown? The swiftness of her mental collapse six years ago still rocked him. One day, she'd been laughing and talking on the phone like usual; the next, she'd been hysterical, crying and begging for his help and insisting that Cole had murdered her grandfather.

Not knowing *what* to think, Alex had caught the first plane to LA. He'd never forget the look on his brother's face when he finally tracked them to that little hospital.

Cole sat in the waiting room with his head in his hands. His shoulders shook with sobs, and that in itself stunned Alex. It had been drilled into both brothers early in life that Ramseys never, ever cried.

"What happened?" he asked, and his brother's head jerked up.

Cole gave an angry swipe at his eyes and demanded, "What are *you* doing here?"

Awkwardly, Alex slipped inside the waiting room and closed the door behind him. He sat beside Cole. "Jessica called me."

Cole shot him a disbelieving look. "She called—why would she call you? She doesn't even know you."

Alex hesitated, but then decided he had to be straight with his brother. "Jessica found the letters I'd written you, and she wanted to help. We've been talking on the phone for a couple of months . . . about you."

Cole jumped to his feet. "What about me?" he demanded. "Did you tell her—"

Panic flashed in his brother's eyes, and Alex knew how badly the past still seared him. Cole had nothing to be ashamed of, nothing to feel guilty about, but it was obvious that he did. Alex held up his hands. "Just that I wanted to see you, talk to you, maybe even act like brothers again."

Cole shook his head. "It's too late for that. You made your choice when you left with her."

"We were kids. She's our mother, and she was afraid Pop was going to kill her. I had to go."

Cole's jaw clenched, and he turned his head. He began to pace the room and Alex tried a new tact. "No matter what happened between our parents, we're grown men now. Can't we put it behind us and start over?"

"Start over?" Cole repeated, stopping to stare at him. "God, you sound just like her. Maybe you and Mother could start over, but there was no starting over for me. I live with what happened every single day of my life."

"It wasn't your fault," Alex said quietly.

Cole squeezed his eyes shut and shook his head. "Shut up. I don't want to talk about it. I don't want to think about it. If you care anything about me, you'll leave now. I've got enough to worry about."

"What happened to Jessica?" Alex asked again. "She was hysterical when she called me. She said—"

Cole laughed and pinched the bridge of his nose. "Oh, I can imagine what she said." He stared at Alex with distraught blue eyes. "Alex, she's lost it. Yes, her grandfather died a couple of days ago—that's what set this whole thing off—but I didn't kill him." Cole held his arms wide. "He was a feeble old man, eighty-five years old. Why would I kill him?"

"What happened to him?"

"He fell down the cellar stairs. The police investigated it. They didn't find anything suspicious. The doctors think Jessica's had some kind of mental breakdown. She's been ranting and raving, saying all sorts of crazy stuff, about me, about the doctors and police plotting against her. She's been under a lot of stress lately." Cole's shoulders slumped and he pushed a hand through his hair. "I don't know if she told you, but we've been trying to have a baby. It's tearing her up inside that she can't get pregnant, and this thing with her grandfather, it made her snap. She's not even talking now. She lies there crying, or mumbling to herself. Did they tell you what she did?"

"No," Alex said softly.

"I stayed home from work this morning to be with her." Cole sat back down and rubbed his eyes. "She was in the tub, but she was taking so long. I went in there . . ." Cole trailed off, staring into space over Alex's left shoulder. His eyes welled with tears. "The water was so . . . pink." He looked down at his hands. "The ambulance barely got here in time."

Another group entered the waiting room, and Cole motioned Alex outside. They walked down the hall to Jessica's room and stood over her bed. As Cole brushed a strand of blond hair out of her face, he whispered, "Oh God, I almost lost her. I don't know why this is happening to us, but I'll take care of it. I'll take care of her." He glanced at Alex. "Please . . . just leave us alone."

With Cole's permission, Alex spoke with Jessica's doctors and the police. They seemed to back everything Cole told him, so Alex flew home. Jessica called him the next week and apologized for her outburst. She recanted the whole story and cried when she said she didn't know what was the matter with her. She told him she was sorry that Cole didn't want to work things out with him, that she'd tried, but maybe it was best if he left them alone.

So Alex had. He didn't try to contact Cole for nearly a year, until he heard about Jessica's death.

Now, after parking his car, Alex stared through the windshield at another hospital in another town and felt the same sick feeling twist his stomach.

What was he supposed to do now?

―――――∞―――――

Jessica groaned as the nurse gently shook her awake. Her head throbbed, and she ached all over.

"Sorry, hon," the woman said. "I'm going to have to torment you all night. I have to wake you every hour to ask dumb questions, like what's your name?"

Jessica almost blurted out her real one, but caught herself in time. "Emily . . . Emily Jackson."

"Where do you live, Ms. Jackson?"

"1217 Beaumont Street."

"See, I told you they were dumb questions. Can I get you anything?"

"No, I—I'm okay."

Sleepily, Jessica watched the nurse leave the room. She rolled on her side and didn't see the dark-haired man in the corner until he leaned forward.

Cole.

With a screech, she tried to scramble off the bed, but he was quicker. A pair of strong arms caught her around the waist and pulled her back down in the bed. She twisted in his arms and clawed at his face. Jessica knew from experience that she was no match for him, but she wouldn't go down without a fight.

Never again.

"Easy, I'm not going to hurt you." Cole caught both of her hands in his. She took grim satisfaction in the long scratch she'd managed to administer to the side of his face. "You're hurt, and you're about to yank that IV out of your arm. Calm down before you bring on another asthma attack."

Jessica cursed him and, to her horror, started to cry. She knew Cole hated tears.

Shut up or I'll give you something to cry about.

Jessica had heard those words many times during their three-year marriage. She expected them now, expected him to hit her, expected anything but what he did.

Cole gently transferred both her wrists to one of his hands and brushed away her tears with the pad of his thumb. He touched her as tenderly as he had when they'd first become lovers. Before she knew what a monster she'd married.

Then he eased off her and climbed from the bed.

"Please don't cry, Jessica. I want to help, but first you need to tell me what's going on."

"What's going on?" she repeated, hating the shrill, hysterical edge in her voice. "Why can't you leave me alone? Why?"

Defeated, she slumped back in the bed. She could never get away from him now.

Cole didn't intend to kill her, or he would've done so already. What he had planned for her was worse than death. He was going to drag her back into that hellish life she'd escaped five years ago. Jessica buried her face in her bandaged hands and sobbed.

She jerked when Cole wrapped his arms around her, but he wouldn't let go. His hand smoothed her hair, his breath tickled her ear as he tried to soothe her.

What was he doing? What kind of game was this?

Maybe he was being nice to her until he could get her home. Jessica could just imagine what Cole had waiting for her back at their little house of horrors.

Being in his arms was unnerving. It brought back too many memories of the good days, days when she had thought she was in love with him. The way he'd courted her, the eyes that looked like quicksilver in the moonlight.

Before she had seen the evil within him.

"You have to be strong," he whispered as he stroked her back. "You have to think of Joe."

She stiffened when she heard her son's name.

He knew.

Suddenly, it was clear. He hadn't killed her because he didn't know where Joe was. Cole was going to use their son to destroy her.

A mindless fury kindled within her, then raged like a forest fire. She allowed Cole to hold her while she searched the shadowy room for a weapon. The slow, steady beat of his heart incensed her, because hers threatened to pound its way out of her chest.

She squinted at the tray beside her bed. Was that . . . yes! A roll of tape and small pair of scissors lay beside the water pitcher. Jessica lunged for the scissors and caught Cole off guard.

Pawing at the tray, her hands closed on them. Jessica whipped her arm in a wide, vicious arc, aiming for his throat. Cole jerked backward, and she missed him completely. She nearly tumbled off the bed from the force of her own momentum.

She scampered over the low rail and faced him.

They squared off like boxers in the small room. Jessica felt a tug from her IV and, with an impatient jerk, she ripped it from her arm. Blood streaked down her wrist to splatter on the white tile floor. She didn't care. Didn't care that the green hospital gown hung open in the back.

She focused on Cole.

Some part of her knew this was crazy. She was taking on the devil with a pair of manicure scissors, for God's sake, but her fear of Cole threw her into a frenzy. Jessica circled him, scissors held high, teeth bared. She may have even growled.

He was talking . . . talking . . . but she couldn't hear what he was saying. She didn't want to hear. Jessica screamed at him, barely realizing what she was saying.

"I should have killed you! I should've waited until you were asleep and driven a knife through your heart. Joe is not yours, he's *mine!*"

She was dimly aware of the doctor and nurses that burst into the room, of the hypodermic needle that stabbed into her arm. But in a moment, she was aware of nothing else.

Alex finally got away from the hospital staff.

No, he didn't know why she'd reacted like that. Probably confused and scared from her accident. No, he didn't want to press charges.

Alex wet a paper towel in the sink and gingerly cleaned the scratch on his face. His mother always told him that he had a knack for finding trouble and, apparently, she was right. He'd found a whole mess of it today.

Alex was just thankful Jessica hadn't been hurt worse than she had. He was also thankful for little old ladies who drove twenty miles an hour under the speed limit.

Jessica had taken a few stitches in her head and was pretty banged up, but she was going to be okay. Physically, at least.

Alex remembered all the telephone conversations they'd had, how funny and smart and sweet she'd seemed. They'd hit it off that first conversation, when she called to say she was Cole's wife and she wanted to help him heal his fractured relationship with his brother. She'd apologized for calling collect, but admitted she was afraid Cole would be upset if he saw the number on their phone bill. Alex, knowing exactly how his brother felt about him, had told her it wasn't a problem. They'd talked for hours, until it was time for Cole to get home. She gave him their number, asking him to give her time to work on Cole, and to call only when Cole was at the office.

Alex had called her back the next morning. At first, they'd only talked about Cole and his unwillingness to discuss his past, but soon they were talking about everything. He was surprised by how much they had in common. Alex had felt a little envious of his brother, who'd seemed to have found the ideal wife. He'd thought Jessica was the whole package, a perfect personality wrapped in a perfect package.

Now that golden beauty was gone, replaced by the crazed, pitiful woman in that hospital room.

Alex's hand shook. When he'd been a cop, he'd seen his share of mentally disturbed people, but he'd never been the target of such feral, insane rage before.

He shivered as he remembered all the things she'd shouted. What kind of life had his nephew led? The thought of that little boy twisted his gut.

Then he thought of Cole. Was his brother a part of this madness? Although Alex still didn't believe his brother was a murderer, he wondered if there was a reason behind Jessica's terror. After all, their father hadn't been one to hold back punches, not from his wife or his children, or anyone else who got in his way when he was drinking. But as far as Alex knew, Cole didn't drink. In all their prior conversations, Jessica had never hinted at any abuse, even when Alex told her about their father. Was her mind making him the villain because he was the person closest to her?

With a sigh, Alex went outside and called his office again. When the answering machine picked up on the third ring, he glanced at his watch and was shocked to see how late it was. Rachel was long gone. He thought about calling her at home, but decided against it, though he knew she wouldn't mind.

Jessica wouldn't be going anywhere tonight.

He checked in with Marcus, who told him that Pru and Joe seemed to have settled in for the night at a house on Breckenwood Street, not five miles from the real estate office. Marcus assured Alex that he could work all night, and even the next day if he needed him. Alex promised to send a replacement watch by noon. After he got that set up, Alex called his Aunt Gina. She was the only person on his father's side of the family that he still spoke with.

"Alex!" she said. "It's so good to hear your voice."

"You too, Aunt Gina. How have you been?"

They chatted for a few minutes, then Alex started probing about Cole.

"Have you heard from Cole lately?" he asked.

"No, but . . ." She hesitated. "He likes to keep himself busy. He's been like that ever since Jessica died. I worry about him."

"I do too." Alex frowned as he studied his fingernails. "Tell me, Aunt Gina. What did you think of her?"

"She seemed like a sweet girl, a little shy maybe. I doubt I ever heard her say more than five words at a time. She was the nurturing type. Reminded me quite a bit of your mother, actually. I always wondered if Cole saw that too, but I never dared to ask him. Maybe that helped heal him, to have someone like Kate love him and take care of him."

"Do you think they were happy? Did he love her?"

"He adored her. You should've seen the way he looked at her. It nearly killed him when she died. He blamed himself for not being there to help her, but I don't know what he thought he could've done. He had to work. There was no way to anticipate something like that. I knew Jessica's asthma gave her a lot of problems, but you don't think about things like that being fatal, you know?"

Alex leaned back in his seat. "Did you go to her funeral?"

"No. I was in the hospital with kidney stones. I wish I could've been there. I don't think your father showed up, and I would've liked to have been there for Cole."

"I didn't know anything about it until the funeral was already over. I flew to LA as soon as I heard, but Cole sent me packing." Alex shifted the phone to his other ear, remembering how haggard and grief-stricken his brother had looked. "I think I need to talk to Cole, or at least try. Do you think you could give me his number?"

Alex copied it down carefully and thanked his aunt. He stared at it as he clicked the phone shut and thought about calling Cole right then, but in the end, he decided to wait until morning. Just for his piece of mind, he would wait until he could run Cole's record. As much as he hated to admit it, his brother was a stranger to him.

Alex thought of their father and his drunken brawls. Earl Ramsey had a rap sheet a mile long. If Cole was like that, he would have to have something on his record, wouldn't he?

Reclining his seat, Alex settled in for an uneasy night of sleep.

The sun beat through the windshield, waking him early the next morning. Alex groaned as he rubbed a hand down his stubbled face. He staggered out of the car and made his way back to the fourth floor, where the nurse on duty assured him that Jessica was still resting peacefully. Even though Rachel was an early bird, he had some time to kill before she made it back to the office. He checked in with Marcus. When he heard Pru and Joe hadn't budged, Alex went to the cafeteria to grab a cup of coffee.

Alex sat at a chipped table and forced himself to eat half a pack of dry powdered donuts before he gave up and tossed the rest of them in the trash. He took his third cup of coffee outside and sat on an iron bench. The chirp of his cell phone startled him.

He dug the phone out of his pocket and smiled when he saw the office number. He gulped the last of coffee before answering. "What are you doing in so early?" he asked Rachel.

"I was worried about you and couldn't sleep. You never did tell me what was going on yesterday. Is something wrong?"

Alex sighed. "Something. Everything. So much has gone wrong since yesterday, I don't know where to begin telling you about it. But I'm glad you're there. Do you think you could run a name for me? I'm looking for a police record."

"Sure. Let me get booted up here. Okay, what's the name?"

"Cole Justin Ramsey."

"Your brother?" Rachel paused. "Alex, what's happening?"

Alex shook his head. "You wouldn't believe me if I told you."

"Try me."

Alex briefed her on all the crazy events of yesterday. He had to back up and fill her in on some of the details of his childhood, because even though Rachel was a good friend, there were things he'd never told her. Things he'd never told anyone. She didn't say a word until he was finished.

"Oh, Alex!" she gasped. "What do you think?"

"I don't know what to think," he admitted.

"Cole doesn't have anything on record," she said. "Not even a parking ticket."

Alex wiped his face with his hand. "Compare that to my father's. You've seen his arrest record. Every indication I have is that Cole is a successful businessman, that he loved his wife. I was there, Rachel. I was there when he was crying over her at that hospital."

"Could've been remorse. That bastard my friend Sarah was married to would cry like a baby and apologize when he hit her."

"This is my brother, Rachel. My twin. I simply can't believe he would do that. What if she *is* crazy? There's a little boy out there who's never known his father. Jessica threatened to kill me twice yesterday. He's going to need someone to take care of him. I don't think that poor unstable woman in that room can do it any more."

"Sounds like your mind is made up."

Alex rubbed his eyes. "Maybe it is. Do you think

I'm wrong?"

"I don't know, Alex. I don't know Cole, and I don't know Jessica. You do, so it will have to be your decision."

Ignoring the thought that flashed through his mind that he didn't know them, either, Alex stood.

"What are you going to do?" she asked.

"I'm going to call him."

Don't answer it!" the blonde commanded. Cole ignored her and snatched up the ringing phone on the nightstand.

"Yeah?" He fumbled for his cigarettes, then shook one out and lit it.

"Cole? This is Alex."

His brother's voice gave Cole a jolt.

"What do you want?" he demanded. He sat up in the bed and tried to untangle himself from the black satin sheets. "How did you get this number?"

The blonde—Teri, Kerri, whatever her name was—reached around him to run her nails across his chest. Cole impatiently pushed her hand away.

"I know you don't want to talk to me, but I have something important to tell you."

"Nothing you could say would mean a thing to me, dear brother. Unless you're calling to tell me that old hag you call Mother is finally dead."

Alex fell silent on the other end, and Cole smiled. He'd struck a nerve.

"Why do you have to talk about her like that?"

Exhaling a cloud of smoke, Cole said, "Hey, she's the one who left me, and you did too. I don't owe either of you anything. A real mother doesn't walk out on her twelve-year-old son."

"You could've come too."

Cole snorted, and Alex continued, "She always wanted to be part of your life, but you wouldn't let her. You wouldn't let me."

"Yeah, well, I don't need her and I don't need you." Cole took a long drag on the cigarette and said, "Why are you bothering me? If it's just this same old crap, I've got to go. I've got better things to do."

The blonde giggled behind him and took that as an invitation to tell him all the things she was going to do to him once he hung up the phone.

"It's about Jessica," Alex said.

The blonde was still talking, so Cole jerked the phone away from his ear and pressed it to his chest.

"Shut up!" he hissed.

She fell silent and tugged the sheet up around her chest, pouting.

"What about Jessica?" he snapped.

"Cole . . . she's alive. She's in the hospital here."

Cole gripped the phone a little tighter.

What was this?

Cole frowned and flicked a long gray ash into the marble ashtray on the nightstand. "Jessica is dead. I identified the body myself, down at the county morgue.

Whatever game—"

"It's no game. Jessica's alive, and she needs you, Cole. I think she's having mental problems again—"

"You're the one with mental problems, brother, if you think she's alive. I'm telling you, I saw her myself. Touched her, even. She's deader than Kennedy. Besides, you barely knew her."

"It's her, Cole. She thinks I'm you, and she's out of her mind."

"I'm out of my mind, for not hanging up on you before now—" Cole grumbled and stretched to hang up the receiver. Alex's voice grew louder, and Cole could still hear him as he lowered the phone.

"She has a son, Cole. A little boy named Joe. Your son."

Cole stared dumbly at the receiver he'd just hung up.

Had Alex said what he thought he had?

The blonde was crawling up his back again. Furious, Cole jumped to his feet and spun around. He swung with all his might, but the blow was a little askew. His fist glanced off her jaw and knocked her across the bed. Her head bounced off the brass headboard, and she sat there, stunned, her mouth a perfect red O.

Cole watched a thin trickle of blood snake down her chin.

"Get out!" he shouted, and she nearly tumbled off the bed in her haste to get to her clothes.

She started to cry, a wet, blubbering sound that made Cole grit his teeth.

How he hated that sound!

It grated on his nerves like fingernails on chalkboard, and Cole turned his back to her. He started mentally ticking off the seconds in his head. If she wasn't out of here by the time he hit ten, he was going to give her something to cry about and enjoy doing it. A surge of anticipation was beginning to build by the time he hit nine, and Cole started to turn when he heard the door slam shut behind her.

A little disappointed, Cole tried to force his mind back to his conversation with his brother. Alex had to be crazy, or maybe just mistaken. Cole didn't really think Alex was running a game on him—not his goody-two-shoes brother. He wanted to dismiss the idea, but the name kept reverberating in his head . . . Joe . . . Joe.

If Jessica had a son, she would've named him that, after that grandfather of hers.

A bitter smile twisted his features when he thought of the old goat, the palsied old man who'd put a shotgun to his chest and threatened to kill him if he ever laid hands on Jessica again.

Well, nobody threatened Cole Ramsey—much less told him how to deal with his own damn wife—and lived to tell about it.

He'd made sure she'd known. He wanted Jessica to know what would happen to anyone who tried to help her leave him. She'd scared the hell out of him with that suicide attempt, but things had settled down after that. She was his wife, and she wasn't going anywhere. She knew that and accepted it.

That's what made this so ridiculous. His timid little mouse of a wife would never have the guts to pull something like that on him.

Would she?

Cole jerked on his robe and reached for the pack of cigarettes. He walked out on the balcony and stood staring down at the emerald green ocean, lost in his thoughts as a salty breeze blew against his face.

If Jessica had managed to fake her death, she could never have pulled it off without help. A lot of help, someone on the inside.

Bennett. That was the name of the morgue worker who had stood beside him when he'd identified Jessica's body after her presumably fatal asthma attack. Cole had a knack for names and faces, and he was sure he was right.

Had Bennett been nervous that day? Cole couldn't recall.

If this guy *had* helped her, he had put a lot on the line for her. Jessica had friends at the hospital—had worked there before they were married, had volunteered there afterward—but had she had friends who would go to such lengths for her?

Cole snuffed out his cigarette on the brick terrace. He was going to find Bennett and get some answers. If he couldn't find him, then he'd pay Jessica's sister Laura a visit. If Jessica was alive, Laura would know.

And if Jessica had fooled him—if she had hidden a son from him—he was going to deal that bitch a hand she'd never forget.

Chapter 3

Alex paused outside the door, hating to go back in and hating not to. Cole hadn't believed him, but he hadn't really expected him to. They had shared the same womb, but his brother was a stranger to him.

He wanted to walk away, but he couldn't stand the thought of that little boy being left to fend for himself.

Alex thought Jessica would still be asleep, but her eyes flew open when he entered the room. She tried to scoot up the bed and gave a terrified yelp when she realized her hands were restrained. The blood drained from her already pale face. She looked so ghostly Alex half-expected her to vanish before his eyes.

"Get out," she pleaded, her voice groggy. "Please, just go away."

"Jessica, I want to help you." He kept his voice soft as he approached the bed. "I want to help Joe."

"Cole, do what you want to me, but please don't hurt him."

"I tried to tell you before, I'm not Cole." He extracted his billfold and flipped it open to show her his driver's license. "I'm Alex, Cole's brother."

"What?" She looked dazed, and he wondered if she was too doped up to understand. "Alex?"

"Do you remember talking to me?"

She laughed, and then flinched as he sat on the edge of the bed. "Twins?" she said, and laughed again. She started talking fast, more to herself than to him. Alex feared she was slipping into another manic episode. "I didn't know you were twins. That's so funny. Why didn't Cole mention it? Why didn't *you* mention it?"

Suddenly, her eyes hardened, and she said, "Take off your shirt."

Alex blinked. "What?"

She glared at him. "Take off your shirt."

A little weary of the whole situation, Alex stood and moved away from the bed. He tugged the shirt Roger had loaned him over his head and watched her take a deep breath.

"Oh, thank God," she whispered. Relief smoothed the sharp edges from her features, and Alex saw a ghost of the beauty she'd been. "Cole doesn't know about me."

Before Alex could say anything, she squeezed her eyes shut and launched into a breathless explanation. "You can put it back on now. Cole has this tattoo . . . a panther."

He slipped the shirt back on and resumed his seat on the edge of the bed. Her beautiful green eyes flew open. "Please, you can't tell him about me. If Cole finds out, he'll kill me."

"No one's going to hurt you," Alex soothed.

"You don't know him!" Jessica cried.

She reached to touch his hand—she could reach it, despite the restraints—but then dropped her hand as if she couldn't bear to do so. "I can't go back to that. Oh God, I can't let him hurt my son!"

"Why do you think he'll hurt you?" Alex felt sorry for her. However far removed from reality her fears were, they were real enough to her. She blinked and looked away. He tried again. "Please, I want to help you."

She sniffed, and her eyes glittered with tears. "Like you did before?" she said softly. "I thought we were friends. I finally got the nerve to tell you . . ." A tear slipped down her cheek as she turned her gaze back on him. "I *begged* you to help me, but you never came."

Alex took her hand. Her fingers were cold. "Jess, I did come. I caught the first flight I could to LA." He took a deep breath. "I found you at St. Anthony's. I talked to Cole and talked to your doctors . . . I even talked to the police."

He glimpsed the pain in her eyes before she looked away. "But you didn't talk to me."

"No," Alex admitted.

"Cole told you I was crazy, so you just hopped back on that plane . . ."

"They said you tried to kill yourself."

"It was my only way out," she whispered. "The only way I could protect my family. I told you the truth about my grandfather. Cole murdered him, because he tried to help me."

"But you called me, remember?" Alex said gently. "You told me it was a mistake, that you were confused—"

"Yeah," she mocked. "I'd tell you a lot of things to save myself from one of Cole's beatings. You don't get it, do you? Cole *made* me call you. He was sitting right beside me when we talked."

She sounded so clear, so sane . . . could she be telling the truth?

"Cole told me he'd killed my grandfather. He taunted me with it. That last conversation you and I had, the last real one, before St. Anthony's . . ." She frowned, and looked over his shoulder. "I was putting away laundry. I hung up the phone and turned around and there he was. I screamed because he startled me. He wasn't supposed to be home that early. He demanded to know who I was talking with, if it was some man. I laughed and told him not to be silly, that it was just my sister. He slapped me. Knocked me across the bed and told me not to lie to him. I didn't want to tell him about you, but I didn't have a choice. I thought it would be better if he knew I was talking to his brother and not some . . . lover."

"What did he do?" Alex asked, not wanting to believe her, but finding himself drawn by the look in her eyes and the helplessness in her voice.

She shut her eyes again, but tears spilled from beneath her lashes. "I thought he was going to kill me," she whispered. "I'd never seen him like that before, not in three years of marriage. He went ballistic. He held a pillow over my face until I blacked out. I really thought I was going to die. I-I left that night. Waited until he was asleep and slipped out of the house. I'd never done that before, and I think it surprised him. It surprised me."

"You went to your grandfather's?" Alex asked, and she nodded.

"I was so stupid, but I wasn't thinking. I was so scared. Cole knew exactly where to look for me. He came by the next day to bring me home, and my grandfather threatened him. Pulled a shotgun on him. The next day he was dead."

"I saw the police reports," Alex said cautiously. "They said it was an accidental fall."

She ignored him. "Cole grabbed me outside the hospital. He showed me a picture he'd taken." Jessica glanced at him. "It was my sister, Laura, and her newborn. He'd broken into her house and stood over them as they slept. He said—he said he wouldn't bring his camera next time. He told me if I left again, he'd scatter them from Tucson to Tampa. The police wouldn't find enough of them to put in a shoebox. They were all the family I had left. I couldn't risk them."

"From Tucson to Tampa," Alex repeated dully. His mind flashed back to a different time, a different man who'd made that same threat.

If you leave with my boys, Kate, I'll scatter your body

from Tucson to Tampa. Won't be enough of you left to fill a shoebox to send back to your mama.

"Oh God," Alex whispered.

Cole waited until nearly four o'clock before he drove to University Hospital. He scanned the lobby, searching for familiar faces. When he saw none, he headed toward the elevator. A pretty blond nurse gave him a shy smile as they passed in the corridor. Cole smiled back and was struck by a sense of déjà vu as he remembered the first time he'd ever seen Jessica.

He'd had to have an emergency appendectomy. She had been there when he'd awakened the next morning and was surrounded by the golden glow of sunlight streaming through the window. Still groggy from the anesthesia, he'd asked her if she was an angel.

She hadn't laughed. Instead, she had smiled. A smile that lit her green eyes and made her more than merely beautiful. Ethereal, almost. Cole might've mistaken her for an angel even if he wasn't drugged. She had chatted gaily with him as she changed the bandage on his abdomen, and Cole had wanted more than anything to free her hair from the clasp that held it, to see the golden mass fall around her face. At that moment, as her hands gently tended his wound and he breathed in the sweet, floral scent of her perfume, Cole had known he would marry her.

Only four weeks later, after a whirlwind courtship, she was his wife. He had thought Jessica was special, his own angel, a woman who would never betray him or never leave him. If Alex were right, she was just another lying bitch like his mother.

His father had told him not to trust any of them, but he had argued that Jessica was different. Yeah, he had smacked her around a little, but he'd never meant to hurt her. She'd brought it on herself. None of that would've ever happened if she'd just followed the rules. He'd given her a fine home, she didn't have to work, and he'd never cheated on her. A lot of women had it worse.

With a sigh, Cole got in the elevator and pressed the button to take him to the basement. He was trying to keep an open mind and not taint his memory of her until he knew for sure.

For Jessica's sake, he really hoped she was dead.

Alex listened in horror as Jessica told him about the day she had finally seen a way out.

"I thought maybe if I were dead, he'd leave them alone, you know? I didn't know how I could live like that, and I didn't know how to get away from him."

There was such misery in her eyes, such sincerity, that he couldn't help but believe her, even though it was horrifying to believe that someone who shared his genes could be capable of the things she described.

Dear God, no wonder she'd acted so crazy.

He knew Cole was bitter, but he thought his brother's anger was directed at him and their mother. Alex hadn't been around his brother since they were eleven, but he'd always imagined Cole was like him. Alex had even traveled to California a few times and had watched his twin from a distance, wishing that they could be close again. Every time he'd tried to contact Cole, however, his brother had made it painfully clear that he wanted nothing to do with either Alex or their mother.

"But then I found out I was pregnant. I had to figure out something. I had to get out of there. I couldn't let my child grow up in that, can you understand? I had to leave to keep my child safe."

"How did you do it? How did you fake your death?" Alex asked.

"I had the help of a wonderful friend who risked everything for me." She smiled at him then, a soft smile that lit her face, making her beautiful and stealing his breath away.

"And if Cole were to find out that you were alive..." Alex felt sick as he grasped the mistake he'd made.

"He would hunt me down and kill me." Her voice was somber, full of quiet conviction, and Alex's stomach knotted. She squeezed his hand and said, "I'm so glad you didn't tell him."

He closed his eyes. "I did, Jessica. I did tell him."

She snatched her fingers away, and he heard her breath leave her body in a hiss, like air going out of a tire. He opened his eyes and said pleadingly, "I didn't know. I thought you were mentally unsound. I was worried about Joe."

"Cole knows about him?" she choked. Alex hated himself for the despair in her eyes.

"I don't think he believed me. He hung up on me," he tried to reassure her, but she shook her head.

"Cole won't let it rest until he knows for sure. He'll be coming for me. And for Joe." She shuddered. "Let me up."

When Alex didn't move, she said, "Please."

Reluctantly, he unfastened her arms. Jessica pulled the needle from the IV out of her arm. He reached for her, but she was already climbing out of the bed.

"When did you call him?" She cried out as she tried to wiggle her bruised hip into her ruined slacks.

"About half an hour ago. You can't leave here, Jessica. You're hurt."

She glanced up at him, and Alex knew he would never forget the look on her face. There was such sadness, such resignation.

"If I don't leave, I'm dead," she said simply, and started down the hall in her bare feet.

"Yoo hoo!" Cole called, recognizing the back of Bennett's head immediately. Flame red hair. Such an unfortunate color. Made him almost unforgettable.

Bennett jerked upright, startled, and banged his head on the open drawer, as Cole had known he would. Cole gave him a small, tight smile as Bennett rubbed the sore spot. He turned to Cole, saying, "Hey, this is a restricted—" His words died on his lips as he stared up at Cole.

"Mr. Ramsey," he said a little breathlessly. "Wh . . . what can I do for you?"

Uh oh, bad sign.

He'd only met Bennett once, nearly five years ago. There was no reason the man should know his name.

"You remember me!" Cole said, and Bennett went a shade paler.

"Well, I'm good with names, and Jessica worked here."

Cole watched with a kind of flat curiosity as the man's eye began to tic.

"I didn't know she knew any of you morgue guys. Hey, doesn't it creep you out, being down here with all these dead people?" Cole asked, knowing full well it wasn't the dead creeping Bennett out at the moment.

"You get used to it. What can I do for you, Mr. Ramsey?" he asked, and Cole smiled again.

Very well, let's get to it.

"I got the most curious phone call this morning. Seems that someone saw my wife today, looking pretty frisky for a woman five years in the grave. Since I don't believe in ghosts and I know such an esteemed gentleman as yourself would surely know a corpse when he saw one, I thought you might help me figure out what was going on."

"The person was mistaken," Bennett wheezed, sounding almost like Jessica when she had one of those asthma attacks. "Your wife is dead, Mr. Ramsey. You saw her yourself."

"Yeah. I did, didn't I?" Cole said mildly. "Probably just a case of mistaken identity. What's that they say, we all have a twin somewhere?"

Bennett nodded, and Cole slapped him on the back. "Good to see you again, Bennett. Just had to set my mind at rest."

Cole gave him a friendly wave and pushed open the doors. Whistling, he caught the elevator back to the first floor and wandered to the parking lot. He wondered if Bennett had any idea of how badly he had screwed that up.

Maybe he would ask him later.

One of the many things he and Mr. Bennett were going to talk over tonight. Cole got behind the wheel of his black Jaguar and settled in for the wait.

"I'm going with you," Alex said, and Jessica almost laughed.

"No offense . . . but I think you've done enough."

"If what you say is true, you can't face him alone," he persisted.

"I can't ask you to help me. He's your brother."

"And Joe is my nephew. Besides, you're not asking, I'm volunteering. I can get you out of here and take you someplace safe. I got you into this mess."

He looked so remorseful she couldn't tell him that there was no place on earth where she'd be safe if Cole Ramsey decided to hunt her down.

No place at all.

She wanted to be angry at him, but he had done what he thought was the right thing at the time and tried to protect her son.

"You seem like a good man, Alex. Do yourself a favor and steer clear of Cole." Without waiting on his reply, she pushed past him and hobbled down the hall.

She had to get Joe and get out of Tennessee.

Jessica climbed out of the cab, handed the driver her money and limped up the lawn. She was angry. Angry that the peaceful existence she'd created for her and her son was over, angry that her life once again depended upon Cole Ramsey's whims. As she rubbed her eyes, she glanced at her reflection in her front window pane. Jessica uttered a dry, humorless laugh.

No wonder Alex had thought she was crazy.

She looked like an escapee from the mental ward. Her brown hair stuck up wildly on one side of her head, and the other side was matted down with dried blood. Her clothes were torn and dirty, and she was pale as a ghost.

Hey, it's a perfect Halloween costume. Too bad it's only August. If Cole could see me now, he'd think I really was dead. He'd—

Jessica screamed when his reflection appeared behind hers in the glass like a conjured demon.

Jessica jerked forward and nearly tumbled into her forsythia bush before he caught her by the waist and hauled her back up.

"Alex!" he shouted as she flailed against him. "It's Alex."

"Let go of me." She slapped at his hands. Furious, she spun to face him. "Don't ever do that to me again."

"I'm sorry. I didn't mean to scare you—"

"What are you doing here?" she screeched. "Just leave me alone!"

"Jess, I can't do that. If Cole comes after you, you're going to need all the help you can get. Look at yourself. You can barely walk. How can you protect your son?"

"I'll manage." She pushed past him and staggered up the steps.

"Let me get you out of here, to another city, to somewhere safe, and I'll go. You'll never have to see me again."

Jessica groaned, but she left the door open behind her. Alex took that as an invitation and wandered into her house.

The colors struck him at once. Walls as bright as a child's painting. The living room was a sunshiny yellow, the curtains and carpet a light purple. The sofa and loveseat matched the deep purple color of the African violets scattered about the room. The kitchen was visible from the entryway, and it was a brilliant orange that seemed oddly compatible with the oak cabinets. The hallway beyond glowed apple green.

It was a little too bright, but somehow Alex liked it. It felt homey, alive.

"I guess you're rethinking the crazy thing," Jessica said from behind him and laughed. Alex turned to look at her, surprised by her laugh. She looked surprised too.

"I know, it looks like clowns live here." Jessica glanced around with a pained smile that said she was afraid she'd never see the place again, and Alex's heart tugged.

"Cole's house is all white, except for the master bedroom, which is black. Everything else is white and gold and glass. He thought white was clean, but to me, white is like death—the absence of color, the absence of life." Seeming embarrassed by her philosophy, she looked at Alex and said, "Cole has OCD."

"OCD?"

"Obsessive Compulsive Disorder. He has a real thing for neatness. Do you?"

"Hardly," he said with a wry grin. "Mom calls my place the bachelor pad from hell. Nothing matches, and my cleaning is kind of hit and miss."

Jessica nodded as if this were a fine thing. "Well, with Cole, everything had a place, and he'd go nuts if he found fingerprints on the glass or a stain on the carpet. Sometimes when he beat me, I'd find myself lying there, hoping it would be over soon, not because he was hurting me, but because it was so much easier to get blood out of the carpet before it dried."

She laughed again, a dry, wretched sound that might have been a sob, and Alex fought the urge to take her in his arms. He had seen enough battered women in his time that he had no doubt she was telling the truth. Rachel volunteered at a shelter for abused women, and they all had the same haunted look in their eyes. Jessica looked so fragile, so small, that he didn't know how anyone could lift a hand to harm her. Especially a man twice her size.

"I worked at the hospital. We met there. Sometimes I wonder if what turned Cole on was the white uniform and the smell of rubbing alcohol." She laughed again, a laugh devoid of humor, and announced, "I'm going to take a shower. I hate to waste time, but I can't let Joe see me like this."

She started down the hall, then turned back to him. "Look, if you want to do me any favors, be gone when I come out. You don't know Cole like I do. He'll kill you if you try to help me, and I don't want to be responsible for your death."

She hurried off, not waiting for his reply.

"I don't want to be responsible for yours, either, Jess," he told the empty hallway.

His hands.

Cole had zoned out again, but the sight of his red-slicked hands snapped him out of his daze.

Without warning, the memory assailed him, springing out of some dark corner of his mind where he had hoped he'd buried it forever.

The sneaker. He saw the sneaker first, the cartoon character emblazoned on its side. He held his bloody hands in front of his face, but they were no longer a man's hands. They were small, a boy's hands. And he knew if he looked down, he would see her face ...

"11 times 11 is 121. 11 times 12 is 132. 11 times 13 is—oh, God," Cole gasped.

He staggered to the sink and twisted the knob labeled hot. The memory threatened to push through a door in his mind he could barely hold shut. He didn't want to see her face. "11 times 13 is 143!" Cole shouted and thrust his hands under the steaming water.

He had no idea how long he'd stood there, reciting multiplication tables and washing his hands in Bennett's sink, but finally he was able to shut the faucet off. His reddened fingers were stinging and swollen, and he was scared.

It couldn't be starting again. He couldn't let it happen. He'd worked so many years to control it, to keep it from controlling him.

"Damn you, Jessica," he choked. Glancing behind him, he frowned at the corpse slumped on the kitchen floor. He still had work to do.

Luck was with him. Bennett's apartment was the top half of a duplex, and the bottom half was vacant. Surveying the scene with a critical eye, Cole tried to picture what the investigating officers would see and made adjustments accordingly. Then he rummaged through the closet until he found some oversized sweats that would fit him and headed for Bennett's shower.

He didn't bother to turn on the cold water, just turned the lever to hot and methodically cleaned himself in Matt Bennett's shower, using the dead man's toothbrush to scrub underneath his nails.

Where was she?

Bennett, after a somewhat slow start, had been very helpful toward the end, but he hadn't known where she was. Cole was sure he hadn't lied. By the time they'd gotten to that question, the little rabbit would've given up his own mother if Cole had asked.

Ah, well. That's what Alex was for. Alex would help him find Jessica and his son.

Jessica.

Her name burned in his mind and played an endless repetition in his brain. She had tricked him. She had made a fool of him.

"Fool me once, shame on you. Fool me twice, shame on me," he said, repeating one of his father's favorite sayings.

The fog in the bathroom was so thick it was almost solid. Cole opened the door and used a hand towel to rub away the steam on the mirror. He scarcely recognized the flat blue gaze staring back at him.

Who fooled Cole Ramsey twice?

"Nobody, bitch. Nobody fools me twice," he muttered.

The next time his sweet little wife died, he'd make sure it was done right.

And his son . . .

He was actually a father.

The thought caused an anxious feeling to tighten his chest. At times, he dreamed of having a son, but now that it was a reality, it was a little unnerving.

What if Jessica had poisoned his son's mind against him? What if his son hated him?

Cole tried to push the thought from his mind. He would find his son, and he would explain. After he took care of Joe's lying mother, he would make everything right. Joe wouldn't be like Jessica. He would learn the rules, and they'd be just fine.

Rule number one, you never trust a woman, even your mother.

Hell, especially your mother.

He went outside and took the gasoline container out of his trunk. Upstairs, he doused Bennett and the surrounding area and lit it, then took his own discarded clothes with him to be destroyed later. There was no chance of making it look like an accidental death, but at least this would take care of most of the evidence. Cole hoped it would look like a botched robbery, but even if it didn't, there was no way the police could connect him and Bennett. No motive that they could see. Once he'd found out where Bennett lived, he'd even rented a car. The nondescript sedan sat boldly in the driveway. Its midnight blue color was hard to discern in the night shadows. Bennett could've used an outdoor light.

When Cole pulled out of the drive, the orange flames were a faint glow through Bennett's windows.

Jessica shut her bedroom door behind her and moved toward the closet. She yanked the black duffle bag from its hiding place in the back of her closet and did a quick inventory of its contents. Extra cash, maps, a new set of identification for both her and Joe. How she'd hoped she'd never have to use it.

Jessica hurried into the adjoining bathroom and

turned on the shower. As steam filled the room, she exited again, making sure to lock the bathroom door behind her. That should buy her a little time. Moving toward the bedroom window, she eased it open and popped out the screen, letting it fall to the bushes below. She tossed the bag out and winced as she swung her legs over the window sill.

The short drop to the ground made her sore muscles scream and jarred her senses. She grabbed the side of the house for support until a wave of dizziness passed. Then she fled.

Jessica paused at the edge of the yard. A helpless rage ripped through her when she glanced back at her house. She hated Cole Ramsey. Hated the fact that once again she was being forced to run with little more than the clothes on her back. He had stolen so much from her—her life, her family, her friends—but he couldn't have her son. She'd die before she let him have Joe.

Alex sat on the sofa, still feeling a little punched by the events of the day. In a matter of hours, he had wrecked the safe life that it had taken Jessica five years to build. He'd disposed of evidence, lied to the police and was harboring a woman who'd faked her own death. Now, if everything Jessica had said was true—and he had the gut feeling that it was—a homicidal maniac was coming for her and his nephew. A homicidal maniac who happened to be his twin brother.

"Ain't life grand," he said dryly.

The memories of his father and mother fighting were

shadowy, dreamlike at best. He knew they should be clearer—he was eleven years old, for Pete's sake—but they were like the hazy remnants of a bad dream, the kind that vanished after you woke up.

There was one night he'd never forget, though. The night they left. He and Cole had been sitting in the living room watching *The Dukes of Hazzard*, neither of them having a clue that anything was going on, when suddenly their mother had *flown* through the kitchen entryway into the living room. Alex had tried to defend her, even Cole had tried, but their father had swatted them off like pesky flies. He'd never forget the memory of his mother lying there, curled up in a ball as his father cursed her. Finally, Earl Ramsey had administered a swift kick to her ribs and stalked out the door. That night, Alex had seen something new in her eyes, a look of grim determination.

"Come on, boys," she said as she struggled to her feet. "We're leaving."

Cole had stunned them by refusing to go. His mother had begged and pleaded, but had finally gone without him. Alex knew it ripped her heart out to leave Cole sitting in their threadbare living room, but he had seen the unspoken thought in her eyes.

If I don't leave now, I'll never have another chance.

Instinctively, he knew that had been true. There was a difference in their father that evening, and something inside Alex had known his mother would die if they weren't gone before Earl came back. He wondered if the same type of premonition had caused Jessica to leave Cole.

Caught up in his thoughts, he let more than thirty minutes pass before he realized Jessica was taking an awfully long shower. Concerned that maybe she'd passed out, he ran down the hall to her bedroom. The bathroom door beyond it was locked. Alex pressed his ear to the door and heard the soft patter of water.

"Jess?" He rapped on the door. "You okay in there?"

A cool breeze blew, billowing the white curtains in the window. Alex froze when he noticed it was wide open. He rammed the bathroom door with his shoulder and the flimsy lock gave way without protest.

He yanked back the blue shower curtain, confirming what he already knew.

Jessica was gone.

Chapter 9

After catching a cab to the realty parking lot to retrieve her car, Jessica drove to Pru's mother's house to get Joe. She was guessing, really, but knew that Pru would've known better than to take him to her home if she felt he was in danger.

She lifted a hand to knock, but the door flew open before she had a chance.

"Oh, thank God!" Pru exclaimed. "I called the hospital, but they said you were gone. I was afraid he'd taken you—"

"I'm okay." Jessica hugged the cousin who happened to be her boss. "But I have to leave before Cole finds us."

"He was at the office. I didn't talk to him, but I knew who he was as soon as I saw him. Joe's just like him." Pru flushed. "I mean, Joe looks like him."

"That was Alex, Cole's twin brother." Pru gaped at her, and Jessica rolled her eyes. "I know, I know. I thought it was Cole too. I was running from him when I fell in front of that car. He thought I was crazy, and called Cole. He didn't think Cole believed him, but I know Cole. He won't rest until he knows for sure. Where's Joe?" Jessica knew she was talking fast and was probably not very coherent, but she was having a hard time keeping her panic tamped down.

"He's upstairs playing Nintendo. I rushed to get him as soon as I heard. We've been here ever since."

"I appreciate everything you've done for me, Pru." Jessica hugged her again, sudden tears stinging her eyes. "Maybe one day we'll be able to come back." She started up the steps, and Pru grabbed her arm.

"Jess . . . where are you going?"

"I don't know yet," she admitted.

"My brother-in-law has a rental house in Indiana he's trying to sell. It's not much, but it's vacant. Let me call him."

"I can't put you in danger like that. If Cole finds out we're related ..."

"If Cole finds out we're related, I won't be safe anyhow," Pru said matter-of-factly. "I'm going to call him." She hurried down the hall without waiting for Jessica's response. With a frown, Jessica went upstairs to get her son.

"Mama!" Joe bounded across the room to throw his arms around her. Jessica bit back the cry that rose in her throat when he slammed into her bruised hip. Looking down at his little face, she had to fight a wave of despair. How was she going to keep him safe?

It was disconcerting sometimes to look at her own child. With his dark hair, pale blue eyes and tan skin, he did indeed look like Cole. But, dammit, that was all. He was her son, and she could never let Cole get his hands on him.

"Mama, you're squeezing me." Joe struggled out of her embrace.

"I'm sorry, honey." Jessica released him and plastered on what she hoped was an enthusiastic smile. "Guess what? You and I are going to take a trip. Won't that be great?"

"Where are we going?" he asked. She could tell the idea excited him. Joe always liked to travel.

"Well, it's a surprise, but we have to go right now." She glanced at her watch, knowing she had precious little time before Alex realized she'd tricked him and started searching for them. She hustled Joe down the stairs. Pru met her at the bottom and held out an envelope.

"Take this." She thrust it at Jessica. "It's a little cash to get you started and the address to that rental house."

"Pru, I can't . . ."

"You can, and you will," she insisted. "Now get out of here. The utilities are still connected, and I left Randall's phone number. Give him a call when you get into town. I know you can't call me, but figure out some way to let me know that you're okay, will you?"

Jessica nodded through the tears that threatened to blind her, and headed to the driveway where her little blue Pontiac waited.

The sight of that empty bedroom made Alex panic. He reentered the bathroom and shut off the shower, spraying himself with water for his trouble. He didn't want anything to look out of the ordinary, in case Cole managed to track her this far.

He retrieved a dry T-shirt from Jessica's closet and yanked it over his head. The cell phone in his pocket began to ring.

"Hey, Alex," Marcus said. "Some woman in a blue Pontiac just picked up the kid. They're heading west on 108."

Thank God, Alex thought. He'd forgotten about Marcus.

"Don't let them out of your sight," he said. "I'm on my way."

Before he made it back to his car, his phone chirped again. He flipped it open as he climbed behind the wheel. "Yeah."

"Hey, bro," Cole said casually.

"Cole . . . I was just about to call you," Alex lied.

"Find out something else about Jessica?" he asked. "Look, Alex. I'm sorry I hung up on you. You caught me off guard. I loved Jessica, and it took me a long time to accept her death. And then you call and tell me she's alive—"

"About that," Alex said. He tried to put the right inflection on his words. It was crucial that he did this right. "Cole, I was mistaken. The woman I met looks a lot like Jessica, but it wasn't her. I'm sorry I called you before I got the facts straight."

That part, at least, was true.

"Really? Tell me what happened, from the start."

"I met this woman in a restaurant. I kept staring at her, thinking I knew her face. Then it hit me. I saw your wedding pictures. She looked a lot like Jessica—her face, her build, even those brown eyes—"

"Jessica doesn't have brown eyes," Cole interrupted, sounding a little irritated. Alex managed an uneasy laugh.

"I guess I was further off than I thought. Well, I started talking to her, and the poor thing was talking crazy, ranting about her ex-husband and how he was trying to get custody of her son Joe."

"You said she was in the hospital, that she thought you were me."

"It was the damnedest thing. She started cussing me and accusing me of working for her ex, then she stumbled out in front of a car. I followed her to the hospital. She took a pretty good hit and must've been delirious. That's all I can figure. That's when I called you. A little while ago, I talked to the local cops here, and they knew her. A local girl. I'm sorry I got your hopes up, but I really thought it was her until her ex showed up to claim her."

"Yeah, well, that's what I figured, but I thought

maybe—just maybe—you were right and thought I ought to listen to you. Look, Alex. Maybe I've been a little hard on you. You were a kid back then too. I was thinking that maybe we could get together soon, do a little catching up."

He had caught Alex off guard again. "Sure," Alex replied with an enthusiasm he didn't feel. "I've got a couple of cases going right now, then maybe I could fly out—"

"Or I could come there," Cole offered. "I have some time on my hands lately. Give me a call, bro." He hung up before Alex could reply. The whole conversation left him shaken. Had he pulled it off? Had Cole believed him?

Before he could set his phone down, it rang again.

"Yeah," he said.

"She just left Coffee County and entered into Cannon. Mike's keeping the trace open for me, but last position was heading north on highway 41."

"You're a lifesaver, Marcus," Alex said, and gunned the engine. Jessica had a good forty-five minute head start on him, but with Marcus's help, he could catch her.

"Mama, I gotta go to the bathroom," Joe said. "And I'm hungry."

Jessica glanced at him through the rearview mirror, then down at her gas gauge. She'd have to stop soon to fuel up, anyway. "What are you in the mood for?"

"McDonalds?" Joe laughed when Jessica made a face. "Or KFC," he added.

"KFC it is," she said with exaggerated relief. "I think

there's one a few miles up ahead. I need to get some gas. We're riding on fumes here, pal. Can you make it?"

"Yeah, I'll live."

As she stood at the pumps, Jessica caught Joe watching her through his window a couple of times. She'd tried to act cheery, but Joe was a smart kid. He knew something was wrong. She'd never told him anything at all about his father. Thankfully, he hadn't asked yet, but she knew it was coming.

The bright light over the pumps made her squint when she glanced at her watch. She felt a little jolt at the time: six fifteen.

Cole could be in Tennessee even now.

The wind picked up, blowing her hair in her face, and she smelled the approaching rain. A California girl since birth, she'd never expected to love this place. She'd never expected to think of it as home, but she did. It hurt just as much to leave Woodbury as it had to leave Los Angeles.

Jessica heard the click that indicated the tank was full and replaced the nozzle. Joe blew her a kiss through the window. She caught it and smiled at him. Tennessee was the only home Joe had ever known. He talked like a Tennessee kid, a slow, drawling dialect she thought was charming. She'd been too upset to notice it at the time, but Alex talked like that too.

Alex.

She'd won a bet at work this morning, having guessed the closest to Mary Jane Melton's due date and remembered thinking that today was her lucky day.

Yeah, real lucky.

Hit by a car, forced to run away and pursued by twin brothers, one who wanted to kill her, and one who might just get her killed.

Jessica had to stifle the nervous laughter that bubbled in her chest, lest the poor checkout girl think she was nuts. She didn't want to believe in luck, because if there was good, there was bad, but how else could you explain she and Alex running into each other in that restaurant today?

When she hurried back outside, Jessica thought of a line from her favorite movie. "Of all the gin joints in all the cities in all the world, he had to walk into mine," she muttered, then started giggling, a habit of hers when she was tired and stressed. A man glanced at her, then averted his eyes when he walked by, and Jessica laughed again.

God, she was going crazy.

As she got into the car and pulled back onto the highway, her thoughts drifted again to Alex. How could identical twins be so different? Warm eyes instead of icy ones. Arms that had held her and tried to comfort her even when she was trying to hurt him. The warmth of his breath as he whispered in her ear.

Jessica gave a startled yelp when she realized that she was thinking of the chiseled chest she'd seen twice today, the hard slabs of his pectorals and what it had felt like to rest her head on that chest.

"Get a grip, girl," she whispered, then realized that

talking to herself probably wasn't a good sign, either.

"Mom, are you okay?" Joe asked.

"I'm fine, honey. We're almost there."

Yes, she was definitely going crazy and traveling at the speed of sound. Alex Ramsey was the last man on earth about whom she should be daydreaming. She'd vowed that if Prince Charming himself rode up on a white horse to carry her away, she'd run screaming. Because that's what she'd thought Cole was.

She'd been so young when she'd met him. Cole dazzled her with his good looks and charm, made her feel flattered that such a man would chase her—poor little unsophisticated Jessica Shanahan—when he could've had any woman he wanted. She'd admired his confidence and decisiveness before she'd recognized the domineering personality it stemmed from.

Orphaned when they were not much older than Joe, Jessica and her sister Laura were shuffled between aunts and uncles before ending up with their maternal grandparents. Her grandparents had loved them, but they were old and pretty much let them do as they liked. When she met Cole, it was nice for awhile to have someone take care of her, to pamper her and make decisions for her.

She should've run when he told her on their first date that he was going to marry her, but at the time it had seemed incredibly romantic. Cole had taken her to one of the fanciest restaurants in LA, had bought her a lovely white gown to wear and hadn't even made it feel awkward. No way could she afford something like that on her LPN salary from the hospital. When he'd taken her hand across that table, while the soft glow of candlelight had played off his handsome features, she'd truly felt like Cinderella.

But that's all it had been, a fairy tale, one that started to turn sour on their honeymoon when he'd accused her of flirting with the captain of the cruise ship they were on, and had knocked her across their luxurious cabin. She'd spent the remainder of the trip concealed behind dark shades and hiding in their room at night, because not even make-up could disguise the ugly purple bruise and the bloodshot eye.

Cole had apologized and cried in her arms. He begged her to forgive him, but there weren't many more beatings before he quit apologizing, and the only one left begging was her. It was her fault, all her fault, because she hadn't followed . . .

"The rules," she whispered. She wondered what hid behind Alex's handsome face and realized she didn't want to know. She couldn't afford to find out and no longer trusted her own judgment. And even if Alex was exactly what he seemed, Jessica couldn't get involved with Cole's twin brother, estranged or not.

There you go again, she thought, swinging into the KFC parking lot. *Fantasizing about this man. Besides, he isn't attracted to you. He feels sorry for you. Big difference, girl. He thinks you're off your rocker.*

Still, it was all too easy to picture him leaning over her as he'd mopped the blood from her face. She remembered the concerned look in his eyes when he'd followed her home. With a concentrated effort, Jessica pushed him from her mind. She couldn't afford to trust him even in her dreams.

Jessica ate on automatic pilot, barely tasting the food in her mouth. She knew she had to keep up her strength if she hoped to protect her son. With a smile, she brushed back a lock of his hair. He was so beautiful and innocent. Was she ruining his life? It seemed horrible to think so, when he was the one who had saved hers.

Incredibly, Cole had started talking about having children on the very night he'd beaten her because she'd let him run out of his favorite chips. She'd been on her hands and knees, toilet paper stuffed up her nose to stop the bleeding, scrubbing the crimson stains from the living room carpet when he'd announced it was time they had a baby.

Jessica had barely been able to choke back the derisive laugh that would've probably earned her an express ticket to the emergency room. As Cole rambled on about what beautiful children they would have, she remembered thinking, no way. No way in hell.

Cole had thrown her birth control pills away that night, but she had gone to CVS as soon as he left the next morning and gotten a refill. She kept them hidden in the lining of an old coat that hung in her closet and never missed a dose.

After a year went by with no baby, Cole started to suspect her, and his random searches began. He even called the drugstores. Fortunately, that wasn't a problem because a friend who worked at the walk-in clinic kept her supplied with pills. Jessica had learned a lot during her time with him and she could lie to him without blinking an eye, even managing a tear or two when she professed her desire for a baby. Eventually, Cole began to believe her. But then it happened.

Even though she'd never missed a dose and took her pills at the same time every morning (at eight forty-five, fifteen minutes after Cole left for work), Jessica got pregnant. She had sat on the white tiled floor of the bathroom that smelled of Clorox and was more immaculate than any surgery room, and sobbed when she saw that little pink line appear. She remembered thinking that this just proved she'd been born to lose. It was the cruelest stroke of luck yet.

The next day she had stood outside of an abortion clinic. It had been a scorching day, but Jessica felt cold inside as the tears pouring down her face mingled with the sweat trickling off her brow. It was then she realized what she'd become; a woman who was contemplating killing her unborn child to spare it from the same wretched existence that was her life. It was then that she had a bona fide James Joyce epiphany, a realization sparked by a little pink line on a ten dollar home pregnancy test.

She had to leave Cole.

It might have seemed obvious to a woman who had never been in her shoes, but to Jessica, the idea was as startling as it was simple.

She would never have left him if it had only been her life at stake. She probably would've stayed there until he got too wound up one night and killed her. But the thought of that innocent little baby, a child whose very life depended on what she decided right then, shoved the cowardly, simpering Jessica into a closet.

How could she kill a baby, *her* baby, just because she was too afraid to leave Cole?

For the first time in years, she felt a lightness in her heart, a feeling that took her a minute to identify.

It was hope.

She was going to leave Cole. Although she hadn't known how, she knew it had to be soon.

"Mom? Are you okay?"

Joe's voice startled Jessica from her thoughts.

"I was talking to you, and you weren't listening," he complained and took a sip of his iced tea.

"I'm sorry. Mommy's just really tired right now. What were you saying?"

"I said, there's a man out there, sitting on our car."

With the sluggishness of a woman caught in a nightmare, Jessica turned to stare out the window. Cole leaned against her front fender. When his eyes met hers, he reached to take something out of his pocket.

It hadn't been as hard to find her as he'd expected. She had changed a little over the years, but he would've recognized her anywhere. Cole grabbed his cigarettes out of his pocket, shook one out and lit it up. As he watched the mother and child through the window, he took a greedy drag on it and exhaled slowly, watching the perfect smoke rings evaporate into the dark sky.

His wait was almost over.

Chapter 5

Paralyzed, Jessica watched him flip open his cell phone, say a few words and click it shut again. Then he gave her a sheepish grin and waved.

Alex.

Jessica released the breath she hadn't known she was holding and didn't know whether to laugh or cry. The number one reason not to get involved with Alex Ramsey: she'd known him less than twenty-four hours, and the man had already given her more scares than a carnival funhouse. A woman wanted a man who made her heart race, not one who stopped it altogether.

Alex pushed away from her car and swaggered toward the entrance. As he opened the door and headed toward their table, Jessica squinted at him and frowned.

His shirt stretched too tight across those broad shoulders and thick biceps, revealing the shape of the roughly hewn muscles beneath. She took in the UT Vols logo and the little tear at the bottom hem—

"That's my shirt!" she said indignantly.

Alex flushed and glanced around to see if anyone was listening. A couple of teenagers in the next booth snickered.

"Shhh," he said, and slid into the booth beside her without asking permission. Jessica was too conscious of the blue jean encased thigh that pressed against hers, of the spicy scent of his cologne. She gave him a shove, but he never budged, sitting there like a rock.

"Joe, is your mom always this rude?" Alex asked the wide-eyed boy across from him. Joe shook his head.

"What are you doing in my shirt?" Jessica hissed.

"Remember, you used mine for a big band-aid this afternoon, then I got the one I borrowed all wet when I was cutting off your shower." He had the nerve to grin.

"How did you find us?"

"I'm a detective. That's what I do."

Jessica groaned and slapped her head, immediately regretting it when she realized how sore it was. A detective. She was rethinking the born-to-lose thing.

"Wow! A real detective! Are you a good one?" Joe asked, his eyes lighting up.

"Oh, yeah. I'm the best."

"Modest too," Jessica muttered.

Alex waggled his eyebrows, and she snapped, "Do you detect that I don't want you here?"

"Yeah, I kind of got that impression," he admitted. "But lucky for you, I'm also stubborn."

"Lucky for me," she echoed and rubbed her temple.

"Are you okay, Jess?" Alex took her hand.

Maybe it was the concern in his voice. Maybe it was just the simple human kindness that she no longer expected from men, but a lump rose in her throat and Jessica had to blink back tears. She quickly turned her head to stare out the window to keep Joe from seeing her cry.

"Hey, Joe. Do me a favor, would you?" Alex dug his wallet out of his back pocket. "I'm starving. Go give this money to the lady behind the counter. Tell her I want a two piece, extra crispy dinner to go. And there should be enough change to get you one of those tattoos from that machine up there."

"Okay, thanks!" Joe exclaimed.

As soon as he was out of earshot, Alex said, "Come here." He put his arm around her and pulled her to him. "It's going to be okay, Jess. I won't let him hurt you or Joe, I swear it."

Jessica knew she should pull away, knew she should distance herself from this man, but it felt so good to be held.

Instead of doing what she should've done, she laid her head on his chest. His heartbeat was steady and hypnotic. She felt lethargic, almost drugged. She didn't know how long she stayed like that before Joe's voice jolted her out of her trance.

"Look what I got." He shoved the tattoo across the

table to her. Jessica's stomach lurched when she stared into the yellow eyes of the panther. It had to be a bad omen. It had to be—

"A dragon," Alex said. "Cool."

Startled, she glanced at it again.

A dragon. Not a panther. Now she was seeing things.

"Where were you going?" Alex asked.

"I _am_ going to Indiana. A friend has a place where I can stay."

"Pru Landry?"

"How . . . how did you know that?" she stammered, and Alex frowned.

"I've had someone watching her since yesterday. Well, we'd better get going _somewhere_. It's getting late."

"You're not going with us," Jessica said, shaking her head. She blinked at the dots that flashed behind her eyes with the sudden movement.

"Sorry, Jess, but you're not losing me again that easily. Once I get you settled and safe, I'll leave, but not before then."

As she stared into his blue, unwavering gaze, Jessica decided she was too tired and out of sorts to argue with him. She'd figure out how to get rid of him later, maybe ditch him on the interstate. With a sigh of resignation, she slid out of the booth after him.

As she watched Alex and Joe dump the trays, Jessica felt lightheaded and grabbed a chair for support. She closed her eyes for a moment, and was startled when

Alex's hand brushed her back.

"Easy, there. Are you okay?"

Jessica nodded, but she didn't feel okay. Alex was looking at her oddly and when he put his arm around her waist, she didn't try to resist him. Instead, she leaned into the strength and warmth of his body. Alex was opening the passenger door before she realized what he was doing.

"Here, you can sleep while I drive," he said.

"No, I . . . your car . . . what about your car?"

"I have someone coming to pick it up. Get in."

Maybe it was a good idea to let him drive until she got her head together. She didn't want to risk wrecking and injuring Joe. Compliantly, she slid into the passenger seat and buckled her belt.

Jessica closed her eyes. She was still a little afraid of him. What if this was all a trap? What if he was taking her to Cole? Her instincts told her to trust him, but her instincts had been proven wrong before.

But she was so tired, so sleepy. She just wanted to shut her eyes for a little while. Her eyes flew open when Alex leaned across her, his chest brushing against hers as he pulled the handle to recline her seat. He gave her another worried look and said, "Get some rest, okay?"

Rest. That sounded good. She was so sleepy.

Alex frowned. Jessica was scaring him. She had dropped off so suddenly, and her complexion was chalky. He took her wrist, almost afraid he wouldn't find a pulse, but there it was. She'd been through a lot today and was probably just exhausted, but he was keeping an eye on her.

"Is Mama okay?" Joe asked. His voice sounded small and scared from the backseat.

"Yeah, she's okay. She just needs to take a nap." Alex looked up in the rearview mirror and said, "Hey, I hear you like baseball."

Joe was a regular chatterbox once he got going, and Alex had to laugh at some of his observations. The kid was sharp. In fact, his intellect was sharper than most of the adults Alex was used to dealing with.

Still going strong two hours later, Joe was discussing NASCAR drivers when Alex pulled into a gas station to take a bathroom break. He shook his head. The boy had a real thing for numbers. He could rattle off more car drivers and their numbers than Alex knew.

"Need a bathroom break, Joe? I need to stretch a minute."

"Sure."

Alex thought about waking Jessica up, but she was resting so peacefully he hated to disturb her. He smoothed an errant lock of hair from her face and frowned. He pressed his palm to her forehead.

Was she running a fever? It was hard to say, but he thought she might be. Taking one of her hands, he was startled by how icy it was. Jessica never stirred, and Alex was uneasy.

"C'mon, Alex. I gotta go," Joe said from the sidewalk,

shifting from foot to foot. Sparing another glance at his sleeping passenger, Alex climbed out of the car.

The floor beneath Jessica rocked and swayed as she stumbled toward the light up ahead, but the harder she ran, the further the light seemed in the distance. Taking a deep, gulping breath, Jessica tried to calm herself before she launched into another asthma attack. Cautiously, she began edging toward the tunnel again. The floor pitched violently, and she lost her balance and tumbled to her knees. Not trusting herself to stand, she started to crawl.

"Mama!" she heard a voice cry, and her heart lurched.

Joe. She had to get to Joe.

Finally, she reached the entrance to the tunnel and looked at it in despair as she slowly rose to her feet. It was a spinning cylinder of orange and green.

One step inside and she was disoriented. The bright colors swirled around her and made her dizzy. There was a minute of vertigo where Jessica was exactly nowhere, then she heard Joe call to her again. It finally came to her. She was in a funhouse. She had no idea how she'd gotten there, and it didn't even matter.

All that mattered was Joe.

Squeezing her eyes shut, Jessica pressed onward with grim determination, one hand raised above her head to brush the top of the cylinder. When her fingers touched only air, she opened her eyes.

And nearly tumbled backwards.

A house of mirrors, and in all the mirrors she saw Cole's face. Jessica tried to scream, but all she heard was a whistle. The eerie whistle of the asthma that had plagued her all her life. She searched for her inhaler, but her pocket was empty. Panic seized her, and she began to wheeze.

When Alex rounded the corner, he saw Jessica flailing in the front seat and realized she was in trouble. He ran to the car and jerked the passenger door open.

Jessica fought for breath, clawed at her throat. Alex grabbed her duffle bag and dumped the contents onto the floorboard. Two inhalers tumbled out, and Alex snatched them up.

"Which one, Joe? Which inhaler, do you know?"

"That one." Joe pointed to the inhaler in Alex's left hand. He sounded positive and Alex didn't question it. He fumbled the lid off and forced Jessica's mouth open. Ignoring the frenzied hands that slapped at him, he administered a dose.

"One, two, three, four, five, six, seven," Joe said. "Give her another one."

Alex did as instructed, but still Jessica gasped for breath.

"Breathe, dammit. Breathe, Jess," he said.

"Breathe, Jess," she heard Alex say, and she realized that not all the faces in the mirrors belonged to Cole. Some were Alex. Jessica entered the room of mirrors because she knew intuitively that she'd have to pass through here to find Joe. Somehow, it didn't surprise her that she had no reflection at all.

"Calm down and breathe, Jess. You're going to be okay," Alex soothed. She thought she'd found him, reached to touch his face, but her fingertips slid on smooth glass. Encountering a dead end, she spun and found herself face-to-face with Cole's scowling reflection.

"You're dead," he rasped. "You're dead, and Joe is all mine. He's not stupid like you. He's going to learn the rules."

"No!" she sobbed and backed into another glass. "No, Cole, leave him alone."

"Don't listen to him, Jess. Listen to me. Follow my voice," Alex said, and Jessica tried to do as he said. Her heart raced and threatened to beat its way out of her chest. Death waited around one of these corners.

Cole taunted and threatened, but Jessica didn't respond to him. She focused all her efforts on following Alex's voice.

Then she saw him just in front of her and grasped for his shirt. Alex grabbed her hand.

"Jessica!" He gave her a relieved grin. "You made it. But we have to get out of here. He's not far behind."

He let go of her hand and moved toward a blackened doorway. Jessica wanted to scream at him, to tell him not to go in there, but he vanished inside it and left her no choice but to follow.

Jessica stepped into total blackness.

Blindly, she thrust her hands out in front of her, but touched nothing. Then she found a small rail. It was too low to be comfortable, but she clung to it, grateful for anything to hold onto in the terrifying darkness.

"Alex!" she screamed. "Where are you?"

"I'm here, Jess," she heard him say, but he sounded so far away. The rail beneath her hand was twisted, and she had to crouch to follow it. She had the sudden terrifying thought that the next step she took would give way to nothing and she would fall into some black hole below. What if the rail gave way?

Somewhere behind her—at least she thought it was behind her—she heard Cole laugh.

"Ollie ollie oxen free. Come out, come out wherever you are. You can't beat me, Jessica. I always win."

With a strangled cry, Jessica ran headlong through the darkness with her fingers skimming the rail. She no longer cared if she fell to her death. Cole was catching up.

Then she felt strong arms around her and knew instinctively that it was Alex.

"Don't leave me, Alex," she sobbed and clung to his neck. "Please don't leave me."

"I'm right here, Jess. I'm not going anywhere. Look up ahead."

And she saw it, a faint light. Clutching Alex's hand in a death grip, she hurried toward the light. They emerged in a long, dimly lit corridor lined with doors.

"What is this place, Alex?" she asked, confused.

"This is my home." He smiled and squeezed her hand.

"It will be your home too."

As he opened the door, Jessica heard Cole's laughter again and looked back at the dark hole they'd just escaped. Alex tugged her hand, pulled her through the doorway, and the door closed behind her.

When Jessica turned to look, she had to shield her eyes from the brilliance of the room. Everything was white, blindingly white.

"Welcome to my home, Jess," Alex said with a smile. "I can't wait to show you around, but first I have to tell you the rules."

Alex whipped the car around a semi, traveling as fast as he dared down the interstate. To hell with Indiana and to hell with Cole too. Jessica needed help. Her screams had turned to whimpers, and she was still now. Thankfully, Joe had even gone to sleep.

What nightmare world was she trapped in? He'd tried to talk to her, tried to reach her in that place, but he wasn't sure if he'd done more harm than good. Her pitiful cries had ripped out his heart. Even in her dreams, she ran from Cole. Then she had called out his name, begging him to help her. Alex was still trying to shake the chills he'd gotten and the feeling of utter helplessness that had fallen over him as he watched her battle her imaginary demons.

He pressed his hand to her forehead again and found it cool. Maybe he'd been wrong about the fever. It must be a concussion.

As he crossed into Monteagle city limits, he picked up his cell phone and punched in the numbers without looking.

"Hey, it's Alex. I need your help."

Alex's voice cut through the fog that surrounded her and Jessica tried to shut it out. His soft voice with its beguiling innocence scared her as much as Cole's now. Her head ached, and she knew this was real. She could feel herself moving and realized she was still in the car. Alex was talking to someone, and it wasn't her. She risked a peek through her eyelids and saw that he was on the phone.

"No, she doesn't know where I'm taking her. The boy's asleep. She scared the hell out of me at the gas station with an asthma attack, and she's been delirious. I don't know what else to do."

He paused, and Jessica quickly shut her eyes, feigning sleep.

"Yeah, I can't wait for you to meet him, either. He's asleep now, but we got to talk a lot earlier. He's great kid. Of course he'll like you. He's only four. You'll be able to make up for lost time."

A single tear slid down Jessica's cheek.

Her dream had been prophetic. Alex was betraying her.

Her mind raced, trying to find a way out. Maybe he'd have to stop again. But she knew she was too weak to fight, much less escape with a sleeping four-year-old.

Alex was taking her to Cole, and there wasn't a damn thing she could do about it.

The first drops of rain splattered the windshield as Alex pulled in the driveway. His mother was standing on the porch waiting for them, as Alex had known she'd be. By the time he cut off the switch, she was running across the yard to meet him.

"Mom, do you think you can carry Joe? I'll get Jessica."

"Yes, of course," she said, already opening the door. Alex knew it had broken her heart to hear about the man Cole had become, but the news of a grandson had thrilled her. She lifted the sleeping boy and exclaimed, "Oh, Alex, he's beautiful! He looks exactly like you did at this age." She cast a worried glance at Jessica and asked, "His mother, how is she?"

"She's been pretty quiet for the last half hour, but I'll be glad when Mason can check her out. Where is he?"

"He's in the shower. He was still at work when you called."

Alex nodded and opened Jessica's door. She stirred as he scooped her into his arms and nudged the car door shut with his knee. The light rain misted her face, and those beautiful green eyes opened, widening when she focused on him.

He hated the way she looked at him, although he knew she couldn't help it. He hated the look of fear that flashed in those eyes, because he knew his face was what inspired it.

"Where are we?" she mumbled, trying to lift her head.

"We're home, Jess. Welcome to my home."

A look of horror crossed her face, and she whispered, "No. Please, no."

Cole watched the woman wave goodbye to her daughter and step back onto the sidewalk. The minivan backed out into the street, and she stared after it before she dug a set of keys out of her pocket. Unlocking the trunk of the little red car, she grabbed an armload of shopping bags and started back toward the house. Cole chose that moment to move out of the darkness and bound up the steps after her.

"Here, let me get that for you," he said.

She gave a yelp and dropped one of the bags. When she whirled to face him, her shocked expression turned to a scowl.

"What are you doing here?" she demanded.

"Is that any way to greet your brother-in-law? You don't write, you don't call—I'm beginning to think you don't like me." Cole flashed her a brilliant smile.

"I never liked you," she replied, as she twisted the doorknob and walked inside. Cole started to enter behind her, but she turned to block him. "And you're not my brother-in-law anymore. Jessica's dead, and you are *nothing* to me."

"Well, that's just what I wanted to talk to you about." Cole shoved her through the open doorway. She slammed into an end table and sent a vase of flowers crashing to the floor. He shut the door behind him and twisted the lock. "We've got a lot of catching up to do, Laura."

"What are you doing?" Laura asked, her voice betraying an edge of panic. "What do you want from me?"

"For starters, I want to know where my wife is."

"You're crazy! You know as well as I do that Jessica's dead."

"Now, Laura," Cole chided. "Didn't your mother ever tell you it's a sin to lie?" He snapped his fingers and said, "No, that's right. She didn't. You never really knew her, did you?"

Fury sparked in Laura's green eyes. She opened her mouth, then shut it again, maybe sensing that angering him wasn't the best thing to do.

Too late, bitch, Cole thought. *I'm way past angry now.*

"Cole, I don't want you to get in trouble. My husband will be home any minute. He went to the store to get cigarettes."

Cole laughed. "Two years ago? C'mon, girl, haven't you figured it out yet?"

He'd been delighted to find out Laura was divorced, but not exactly surprised. As Earl Ramsey might say, the woman had a terminal case of diarrhea of the mouth. Who could stand to live with her?

"You know what, I don't think anyone's coming. I really don't think anyone can help you at all."

Chapter 6

"Is she all right?" Alex jumped from the couch when his stepfather eased the door to the guestroom shut.

"I think she's going to be fine," Mason assured him. "But she most definitely has a concussion."

"Do we need to get her to the hospital?"

"Let's just keep a watch on her tonight, see how it goes. I'm sure a little bed rest will do the trick."

"Thanks, Mason," Alex said.

His mother's footsteps echoed down the hall. She smiled as she came around the corner, and Alex asked, "Joe. Is he okay?"

"He never stirred. I put him in the room next to ours, because I wanted to be able to hear him when he wakes." A pained look crossed her face. "Tell me the whole story. I need to know."

Alex nodded and told her everything, starting with all the trouble he'd caused by smiling at a pretty woman in a restaurant. By the time he finished, his mother was in tears. Alex wrapped her in his arms.

"I should never have left him with that man," she sobbed. "He was only a boy, and I knew what kind of man Earl was."

"You didn't have any choice. Cole wanted to stay with him. Told the judge he did."

"That's my fault too. He thought I didn't love him."

"Don't do yourself this way," Alex interrupted, and kissed the top of her head. "Cole made his own decisions. You couldn't have changed a thing."

She pulled back and gave him a hopeful look. "You're sure Jessica is telling the truth? She could be lying, could be running some sort of scam . . ."

"No, Mom," he shook his head, hating the defeated look in her eyes. "She's scared to death of him. Nobody could fake that."

She gave him a sad nod and brushed a kiss across his cheek. "Go get some rest, honey. You look beat."

"Yeah." Alex glanced at the door to Jessica's room and said, "I'm going to sleep in there tonight, keep an eye on her. If she has another asthma attack in this condition . . ."

"I'll sit up with her."

"No, go to bed and listen for Joe. He might be scared if he wakes up in the middle of the night in a strange place."

"Are you sure?"

"Come on, Kate. Let's go to bed," Mason said gently. He pushed a hand through his gray hair and took her elbow. "The same thing applies to Jessica. She might be frightened if she wakes up and sees an unfamiliar face."

Kate nodded and glanced at Alex. "Do you know where the extra pillows and blankets are?"

"I know." Alex smiled. "But do I still have any clothes here? I want to grab a shower."

Kate disappeared down the hall and brought back a laundry basket full of neatly folded clothes. "Your laundry. I felt sorry for you when I picked up those rental tapes and brought the overflowing hamper home with me."

"Thanks, Mom. You're the best." Alex brushed another kiss on her cheek and padded down the hall.

He felt guilty relaxing under the hot spray when he knew how grungy poor Jessica must feel. He hurried, afraid she'd have another attack while he was gone.

"What a day," he murmured, and pulled on a pair of faded gray sweatpants. Using his towel to wipe away the fog on the mirror, Alex stared at his reflection and thought about what Mason had said.

"Familiar face. Right. Too familiar."

For the first time he could recall, he wished he could change his face. Change it into something that wouldn't scare Jessica every time she looked at him.

When he opened the door to her room, he heard her mumble to herself. Her brow was furrowed, and she was tangled in the sheets. Carefully, Alex straightened the linens and used the washcloth on the nightstand to wipe a fine sheen of perspiration from her forehead.

"Alex, where are you?" she asked in a pitiful voice, and his gut clenched. It hurt to think that, although she wouldn't admit she needed him when she was conscious, Jessica needed him in her dreams. The one place he couldn't help her. He wished he could crawl inside her nightmares and pull her to safety. But all he could do was crawl in the bed beside her and take her in his arms.

"I'm right here, Jess," he whispered in her ear.

Why did he feel such a strong connection to her? Why did she feel so right in his arms?

Still whispering to her, Alex breathed a sigh of relief when she quit mumbling and settled against his chest. The frown on her face smoothed, and she was peaceful.

Alex drifted off to a hazy dream of her, golden and beautiful in her white beaded gown. But this time, Cole didn't hold her as they danced across the floor.

He did.

Jessica's head throbbed, and she opened her eyes. Confused, she stared at the unfamiliar beige wall and the clock on the nightstand.

Where was she?

In a moment of utter disorientation, she tried to shake off the remnants of the nightmare she'd just escaped. Then she heard it.

Breathing. Right beside her.

She rolled over and found herself staring into Cole's

sleeping face.

With a startled whoop, she gave him a hard shove that sent him tumbling off the bed.

"Ow!" he exclaimed as his head bounced off the other nightstand, and she recognized his voice.

Alex. She was here with Alex.

"Jessica, are you okay?" He peeked over the edge of the bed and rubbed the back of his head.

"Where is he—where is my son?" she demanded.

"It's me, Alex."

"I know who you are. Just tell me where my son is, dammit."

"He's asleep down the hall, and you're going to wake him up if you don't be quiet."

"Where are we? What is this place?"

"This is my mom's house."

"You were supposed to drive me to Indiana. You said—"

"You were sick. Talking out of your head, and you had another asthma attack. I didn't know what to do, so I brought you home to my stepfather. He's a doctor."

"You're not taking me to Cole?"

He shot her a hurt look. "Are you ever going to believe that you can trust me?"

Alex rose to his feet and flipped on the lamp. Sitting on the edge of the bed, he said, "I'm not going to turn you over to Cole."

"Alex . . . I'm sorry," she said. "You don't understand what it's been like for me. Always looking over my shoulder, afraid to trust anyone."

"I know, and I'm trying, believe me. I just hate the way you look at me sometimes, like you're expecting me to sprout horns and a tail." He gave her a crooked smile and she returned it.

Then he lifted his hand to touch her face.

Jessica couldn't help it; she flinched.

Alex dropped his hand and said, "See? That's what I mean. I've never hit a woman. I'd never hurt you."

"I guess what I don't understand is why. Why are you helping me? Why are you going against your own brother for me?"

She watched Alex lie back in the bed, lace his hands behind his head and stare up at the ceiling.

"Lots of reasons," he said. "First of all, it's wrong. No one should be treated like Cole treated you. No one should have to live in fear. Second, I'm the one who got you into this mess. If not for me, you and Joe would still be living a peaceful life in Woodbury, and Cole wouldn't know about you. Third, I used to be a cop. I've seen a lot of women in your situation, some that made it out and some that didn't. I don't want my nephew's mother to be one that didn't."

Jessica lay back on the bed and propped up on an elbow to stare at him.

"A cop too. Why did you quit?"

Alex rolled over to face her, and Jessica's breath

caught in her throat. Less than a foot separated them, and the faint, clean scent of Irish Spring soap hung in the air. She found herself staring at his mouth and at the five o'clock shadow that he hadn't bothered to shave. Somehow, she liked it. It made him look rugged and sexy—and not like Cole.

In all the time that she'd known him, Cole had never had stubble. He'd always been obsessive about his personal grooming.

"The bureaucracy. Everything is all screwed up. I got sick of arresting the same people for the same thing over and over. It's like trying to carry water in a bucket with a hole in the bottom. All you accomplish is wearing yourself out."

"And here I thought you were some kind of adrenaline junkie." God, was that her? Her voice was light and teasing and . . . flirting.

Alex laughed. "In Tennessee? I don't think so. Maybe the New York guys are adrenaline junkies, but we don't see much around here. Drunks and crackheads mostly. Definitely no one like you before. I could get into this rescuing beautiful women thing."

Jessica laughed, even though her nerves were jumping.

He was flirting too.

"Why did you join the force in the first place?"

"Can you keep a secret?" He lowered his voice to a conspiratorial level. Jessica nodded and found herself fascinated by that crooked smile. He glanced swiftly at the door, then back at her. "I like donuts."

He said it earnestly, straight-faced, and Jessica cracked up. "You're nuts," she said, giggling.

"Oh, hey, all that stuff you see on TV, it's true. You patrol Tastee Donuts, they give you free donuts and coffee. Lots of places did. Um, raspberry filled—no, make that chocolate covered crème filled . . ." He smacked his lips.

"Keep that up, buster, and I'll have you hustling me up a midnight snack."

"You want something?" He sat up in the bed. "I'll go find us something."

"That's okay." Jessica made a face as she touched her sweaty, lank hair. "What I'd really like is a shower."

"Down the hall, first door on the left. You'll find towels in the closet in there. You think you can walk?"

"Yeah, thanks." When Jessica stood, she did have a moment of vertigo, but it passed as she concentrated on the cool wood floor beneath her. Pausing at the door, she turned to look at Alex. "I just wanted to say . . . thanks."

Her heart fluttered when he gave her another one of those crooked smiles. Cole's smile was nothing like that.

"You're welcome."

Embarrassed and more than a little unnerved by her reaction to him, she hurried to the bathroom.

Not trusting the legs that were still a little rubbery, Jessica decided to take a bubble bath instead of a shower. The hot water felt wonderful, seeping into her aching muscles. She hurt all over, especially her hip. And her head felt as big as a basketball. Tilting her head back

Cain and Abel 103

and closing her eyes, she lay there for several minutes and let her mind drift. Behind her eyes, she kept seeing Alex's smile.

A soft knock on the door startled her. The water around her had grown cool and she realized she'd been asleep.

"You okay in there?" Alex stuck his head in the door. In a gesture Jessica found adorable, he had his eyes covered with his hand.

"I'm okay," she assured him. "Just getting out."

He entered the room and tossed a bundle of clothing onto the floor by the sink. "Here's something for you to put on. Hope you don't mind, but I opened your suitcase." He sounded almost apologetic, and Jessica lifted her eyebrows.

"Thanks, Alex."

He nodded and left, his hand still clamped over his eyes.

When he shut the door behind him, Jessica spotted the cause of his embarrassment. On top of the pile was a lacy pair of black underwear. Grinning at this shy side of him, Jessica climbed out of the tub.

What was wrong with him?

He hadn't seen her, hadn't even peeked, but Alex thought he might have to take another shower. A cold one. Prowling around through Jessica's underwear had gotten him as excited as a schoolboy. Shaking his head, he tried to push his thoughts aside as he carried the tray back to the guestroom. He knew without her having to say it that he was the last man on earth she wanted to be involved with. Next to the last, anyway.

Still, Alex couldn't help the way his heart lurched when she entered the room. She looked like a waif in his oversized Marion County PD T-shirt. Alex had found a gown in her suitcase, but he had wanted to see her in something of his.

"You didn't have to do that." She gestured at the tray and gave him a genuine, breathtaking smile.

"Who said it was for you?" he asked with a wink. "I'm a growing boy. But if you get over here, I might share."

Jessica sat on the bed beside him and took the ham sandwich he proffered. While sneaking a glance at her long legs, Alex saw the bruise.

"Ow." He lifted the hem of the T-shirt and peered at the bruise that extended halfway down her thigh. "That looks terrible."

"Feels terrible too," she said, and tugged the hem back down modestly. She needn't have worried. The sight of that bruise and the knowledge he was responsible for it squelched any romantic feelings he'd been having. Instead, Alex felt a little queasy. He laid his sandwich back on the tray untouched.

"Why did you quit nursing?" he asked.

Jessica stared at him while she munched on the sandwich, then swallowed and averted her gaze. "I just couldn't do it anymore. I used to be able to handle anything, but I freak in situations like that now. Joe got his nose bloodied this summer playing T-ball, and I was almost hysterical." She smiled and added, "You sure know a lot about me."

He shrugged and offered her a lopsided grin. "Well, we did talk a lot. I *was* paying attention, you know."

Jessica fingered the pattern on the bedspread. "You did, didn't you? I had so much fun talking to you. You were so nice and funny. I know this sounds pathetic, but you were pretty much the only human contact I had besides Cole. I used to wake up in the mornings and think, 'maybe Alex will call today'." She laughed and covered her face with her hand. "Oh God, I can't believe I just said that. Most definitely pathetic."

Alex caught her hand and pulled it down. "Not pathetic. I felt like we connected, and I looked forward to our conversations too. I kept thinking about how lucky Cole was to have found someone like you, someone so smart and beautiful. I was jealous of him."

Jessica coughed, and blushed even brighter. "I used to wonder how on earth you could be his brother. It gave whole new credence to the nature versus nurture debate, then to find out you're twins …"

This time it was Alex who looked away. "Cole didn't have an easy life. There are things in his past that you don't know, things I wasn't sure if I should tell you-"

"Can we maybe . . ." Jessica shook her head. ". . . not talk about him right now? What's this?" She pointed at the bowl in the center of the fruit tray.

"This is Mom's secret recipe. Fruit dip." Alex studied her from a moment, then grabbed a strawberry. He dipped it in the white fluff and held it out to her. Shooting him a wary look, she took a bite.

"Oh, this is great!" she said. "What is it?"

"She won't tell me. I said it was a secret." He chuckled. His face flushed when she took the rest of the strawberry in her mouth.

So much for neutrality.

He wasn't a bad guy, but he was no saint. It was hard to sit with Jessica while he fed her strawberries, and not let his thoughts wander.

"Good with grapes too," he said, hoping she didn't see his hand shake when he skimmed a green grape in the dip. He held it up to her, and she took it in her mouth, looking at him with the smoky eyes of a lover. Alex swallowed hard and his groin tightened when his finger brushed her bottom lip. More than anything, he wanted to kiss her, to taste her fruit sweetened mouth, to wind his fingers in that wild tangle of brown curls.

Instead, he ran his thumb gently across her cheekbone, then cupped the side of her face. Her green eyes widened and he expected her to pull away, but she didn't. She nestled her face against his palm and closed her eyes. Alex froze for a long moment, not knowing what to do, then noticed the sudden heaviness of her face against his hand.

With a soft laugh, he pushed the tray aside and eased Jessica's sleeping form back in the bed.

"Some hot date you are, Ramsey," he said with amusement. "Knocked her out cold."

After putting away the tray, he flipped off the lamp

and crawled back in bed beside her, pulling her to him. He kissed her damp hair and wondered what he'd gotten himself into.

"Wakie, wakie, you insufferable bitch." Cole straddled the sleeping woman in her bed and briskly patted her cheeks. "Time to try Jessica again."

Laura groaned and pulled at her restraints. "Can't you get it through your thick head that she's gone?"

Holding up the gleaming butcher knife he'd found in the kitchen drawer, Cole said, "If I were you, I'd watch my mouth. A tongue like that's begging to be cut out."

"You're a big man, aren't you?" Laura spat. "I told Jessica from the start that something was wrong with you, that—"

"Shut up!" he said. "I loved her."

"Loved her," Laura snorted. "Cole, you beat her up one time for buying green soap."

It took all his restraint not to cut her throat right there. Jessica had told her about him. They had probably laughed . . . the thought incensed him.

But he still needed Laura.

In an effort to control the rage swelling within him, he left the room. As he walked down the hall, he began reciting his multiplication tables, starting as always with 11 x 11, keeping his voice low so the witch in the next room couldn't hear him. If she laughed one more time, he'd lose it. And maybe lose his best chance at finding Jessica.

Cole surveyed Laura's living room with contempt. The place was a pigsty. He walked around the Oriental rug and straightened the fringe to make it all face outward. Then he moved on to the messy computer desk. As he was tidying the stack of papers, his eyes fell on a brown envelope in the stack of mail. Although there was no return address, Cole recognized the graceful handwriting at once. Snatching it up, he used the butcher knife as a letter opener and shook the contents out.

The picture made Cole's heart clench, his vision blur. He would've known the boy anywhere.

Joe was beautiful, perfect, and so big. Jessica had deprived him of that. He didn't know what his son liked, what he ate, who his friends were. He knew nothing about Joe at all. It wasn't fair.

The next picture was a snapshot of Jessica with the boy. Cole looked long and hard at the photo, memorizing her. She'd changed her hair, was a brunette now. It wasn't very flattering. Her face, even though she was smiling, had the tight look of a woman who was accustomed to looking over her shoulder.

"You'd better look, Jessica," he said. "You'd better watch for me, because I'm coming."

Cole raised his arms over his head and brought the knife down as hard as he could, stabbing it through Jessica's smiling face and into the cheap wooden desk.

When he tried to get the knife out, he discovered it was buried more deeply than he thought. After wrestling with it for several minutes, Cole pulled the picture out from around the blade, ripping Jessica's face. He shoved the photo back into the envelope, and replaced the one of Joe as well. After another fruitless tug at the knife, he paused to wipe off its handle with his shirttail. Evidence. He had to be careful not to leave any evidence.

Now he needed another knife. Cole walked back to Laura's kitchen. He stood in the doorway, loath to reenter. Her kitchen was cluttered. A pile of dishes sat in the drainer, waiting to be put away. Cookbooks were scattered across the counter, along with two empty ice trays.

Laura had so much junk on the counters, porcelain pigs and cows, that it jarred his senses. How did she stand it? Cole's kitchen never looked like this. He'd burn his house if it got in this shape. No wonder Jessica had been such a slob. Reluctantly, he walked inside.

Laura's kitchen floor was tiled in green and yellow squares. He really hated floors like this. The squares made him uneasy, although he wasn't sure why.

Feeling foolish and unable to stop himself, Cole made his way to the sink, careful to step only on the yellow tiles. Laura would get a big kick out of this. Stupid bitch. He tried to remind himself that he'd get the last laugh, but the thought that she and Jessica had discussed him, had discussed his eccentricities, made him furious. Was nothing sacred between a husband and wife?

Then he thought of Alex. What part did he play in all this? Was he with Jessica, or had she fooled him too? He sincerely hoped his brother wasn't helping her.

At times, Cole wanted to contact Alex, to get to know his brother. They had been so close at one time, but Alex had chosen Kate over him. And Kate hated him.

It hurt to think his own mother hated him, but it was true. He hated her too. The thought of her name made him feel dirty, so he started his multiplication tables again.

Taking another knife out of the peg, Cole washed it in the antibacterial dishwashing liquid on the counter. It was nearly thirty minutes before he felt that the knife and his hands were clean. Grimacing, he walked carefully through the tiles and headed back to Laura's bedroom.

"I'm out of patience, sister-in-law. We're going to call Jessica's cell phone again and if we can't find her, we're going to find someone who can."

He hated to touch her phone, but he couldn't show weakness in front of her, no matter how much it pained him. Cole punched in the number and waited, but Jessica's cell phone rang on and on.

"Who would know where she is? Who?"

A horn blared in the driveway, startling Cole. He hurried to the window and peered through the blinds.

"Uh-oh," he said with a smile. "Your kid's home. I somehow think you're going to be a little more helpful now."

"Noooo!" Laura moaned, and Cole chuckled. Deftly undoing the knots that held her to the bedposts, he forced Laura to her feet.

"Listen up, sister-in-law. You're going to go to the door, wave at your ex and let the little girl in the house. If you make one wrong move, I'll gut you like a fish in front of her. You'll be dead before your body hits the floor."

He shoved her toward the living room, hauling her up by the back of her shirt when she stumbled and nearly fell. She reached to open the door, and Cole pulled her back.

"Not yet," he hissed, watching the little blond girl skip up the sidewalk. "Before you get any stupid idea about being heroic and sacrificing yourself to spare her, let me warn you: I can kill you and be on her in a second, before that pasty-faced ex of yours even knows what's happening. All I want is what's mine, and I won't hurt her if you cooperate. Do you understand?"

Tearfully, Laura nodded. As the little girl started up the steps, Laura opened the door and waved to her ex-husband. With another beep of the horn and a cheerful wave, he backed out of the driveway.

Chapter 7

Outside, Joe was screaming.

Bolting out of the bed, Jessica stumbled to the window. She saw him dart past, and a wave of relief washed over her.

He wasn't screaming. He was squealing, trying to take a football from a panting Alex. Jessica pressed her fingertips to her mouth and laughed at the fierce look on Joe's face. Alex feinted left, then right, but Joe managed to throw him off balance with a well-time attack at his ankles. Joe howled with laughter and did a triumphant victory dance when Alex tripped and fell. Alex tossed the football to the side, grabbed Joe, and rolled him on the ground.

Jessica watched them with mixed emotions. A million times, she'd wished that Joe had a male role model, someone he could play with and learn from, but it made her nervous to see him with Alex. Not that she didn't think Alex was a good man—she was convinced now that he was—but there were too many reasons that Alex could never be a part of their lives, and she didn't want Joe to get attached.

"He's a wonderful boy. You've done a terrific job with him."

The voice startled Jessica, and she whirled around. She hadn't even noticed the woman sitting in the corner.

"I'm sorry. I didn't mean to frighten you." She stood and offered Jessica her hand. "I'm Kate Watson."

"Cole's . . . mother," Jessica said.

She was taken aback by her first glimpse of her son's grandmother. Kate was nothing like she'd expected, nothing like the sons who'd inherited Earl Ramsey's coloring. The woman before her was cool and blond and petite. What stole her breath was how much Kate resembled *her*. Cole's mother looked more like her than her own mother had.

"So, you see it too?" The woman smiled, and Jessica finally remembered to take her hand. Instead of shaking her hand, the woman squeezed it briefly and released it. Fingering Jessica's hair, she said, "Alex said you used to be blond. I bet the resemblance was really remarkable then."

Cole hated his mother. It seemed inconceivable that he'd married a woman who looked so much like her. Then Jessica thought that maybe through her, Cole had found a way to take out some of the anger he'd felt toward Kate, the mother he hadn't been able to mention by name.

"I know," Kate nodded, as if she'd read her thoughts. "I was surprised too. Alex never mentioned it. I'm not sure he even noticed. Men don't seem to notice that type of thing." Kate glanced out the window and a soft smile touched her face as she watched Joe play. "I'm glad Alex brought you here. I was thrilled to learn I had a grandson."

"Have you told him . . . ?"

"No. I figured it was your decision. But I would love to be part of his life." Kate looked sad and hopeful at the same time, but Jessica didn't know what to say. She didn't want to make any promises she couldn't keep, especially one that could compromise Joe's safety.

"I'm sorry." Kate gave Jessica another pained smile. "I realize you have other things to worry about right now. Alex brought your suitcase in. If you want to, you can get dressed and come with me. The boys have already eaten, but I saved you some lunch. Or I can bring you a tray."

"Lunch?" Jessica asked. She cast a quick glance at the clock and was stunned to see it was nearly two. "I *have* been out of it," she said with a nervous laugh.

"Alex has been worried to death. He peeks in that window every ten minutes, but Mason says there's nothing to worry about. He's my husband," she explained. "And he's a doctor. He says the first twenty-four hours of a concussion are the worst and predicts that you'll start feeling much better today. Would you rather I bring your tray in here?"

"No, that's okay. I need to move around a little."

Kate nodded and gave her another smile before she shut the door behind her.

Jessica dressed quickly in a pair of faded blue jeans and a green, sleeveless pullover. Without the benefit of a comb, she ran her fingers through her hair and tried to tame the unruly mess as best she could. Having guaranteed herself an epic bad hair day by going to bed with it damp, she made a face at her pale reflection and limped down the hall in her bare feet.

It was a beautiful old house, simply but tastefully decorated. Even though she knew Cole had never set foot in this place, the hair prickled on the back of her neck when she glanced at the photos hanging in the hallway. Pictures of Cole and Alex as boys. It was disconcerting to see Cole as a smiling, gapped-tooth first grader.

He looked too much like Joe.

She shivered. It was too easy to believe Cole had been born a monster, that evil had always been present within him. She didn't want to believe that he had once been as innocent as Joe, that he had ever been simply a normal little boy.

Although she didn't want to admit it, Joe scared her sometimes. He had an uncanny ability with numbers, could memorize sports' stats and telephone numbers with ease. She didn't know any other four-year-olds who could do that; she'd asked. Sometimes, she watched him play with his little cars or his dinosaurs. He would sit on the floor, carefully turning and correcting them until they were perfectly aligned. It was hard to keep from storming into the room and messing them all up. She never scolded Joe if his bedroom was messy. She was relieved.

A picture of a younger Kate with her sons caused another chill to race down her spine. She didn't know what unnerved her more: the thought that Cole had purposely sought a wife who looked like his estranged mother, or the thought that he had done it subconsciously.

The next picture made her frown. It was a posed setting with a Christmas backdrop. In between Cole and Alex sat a little blond girl. A girl who looked like Kate.

"Who are *you*?" she whispered.

Caught up in her thoughts, Jessica didn't hear Kate approach. She jumped at the sound of her voice.

"She's the reason Cole hates me," Kate replied. "It's time you heard about her. I think it will explain a lot."

Alex burst through the door with Joe on his heels, startling the two women who sat at the kitchen table.

"Mama, I beat him," Joe crowed.

"Cheater," Alex gasped. He opened the refrigerator and grabbed a container of iced tea.

"Sore loser," Joe taunted.

It was then that Alex noticed the tightness of his mother's face and the pallor of Jessica's.

"Something wrong?" he asked quietly, then turned his gaze to Jessica. "Are you okay?"

"I was about to tell her about Kaitlyn," his mother said.

"Oh," was all he could say.

Joe tugged on his wrist, wanting him to go back outside, but Alex talked him into watching TV.

"I'll be right back," he said, and hustled Joe off to the den, armed with a snack of chocolate chip cookies and milk. His mother would need him if she was going to talk about Kaitlyn.

"Okay," he said. "He's found the cartoon channel."

His mother nodded, and he could almost see her bracing herself. Eighteen years later, it still hurt her to talk about that day. Alex squeezed her hand.

"Kaitlyn was my daughter. The boys were seven when she was born, and they doted on her, especially Cole. He would do anything she wanted—play baby dolls, take her for endless rides in his wagon—anything." She paused to brush a tear from the corner of her eye. "It was almost Kaitlyn's birthday. Earl had lost another job and was down at the local pub. He didn't allow me to work, and I was desperate to earn a little money to buy her a dollhouse she wanted. I decided to have a yard sale. The boys knew what I was trying to do, and they went through their things, looking for anything they could contribute. Cole stunned me when he came outside toting his marble case. He was always collecting things, but his marble collection was his prized possession. He wanted me to sell it to buy something for Kaitlyn."

A shuddering sob escaped her, and Alex said, "Mom—"

"No, Alex. She needs to know, and I need to tell her."

Alex glanced at Jessica, who was being very still and

very quiet.

"I tried to tell him no, that I didn't want him to do that, but he insisted. We lived a miserable existence back then and even at ten, my boys tried to shield their sister from that. The yard sale was going pretty well, and I was beginning to think we were going to make enough to buy that dollhouse. I'd even managed to deflect a couple of buyers for the marble collection when Cole wasn't looking. But Kaitlyn, as any four-year-old would, soon grew tired of having to stay around in front with me. Poor Alex was upstairs in bed with the chicken pox. I kept running in and out between customers, checking on him and fetching snacks for Kaitlyn and Cole. Kaitlyn started crying to go around back, to their swing set. I was pretty busy at the time and told her no, that I couldn't watch her back there. Cole took her hand and said he'd watch her. He was always doing that. I let her go with him. A few times, I'd walk around the side of the house to check on them, but they seemed to be doing fine."

She was crying in earnest now, and Alex tried to comfort her, but she waved him off. "I was putting things away when I heard the brakes squeal. It was the most terrifying sound I'd ever heard. Somehow, I think I knew, even before I ran around to the backyard. Our yard had a fence, but it was in poor repair, and there were a couple of big holes in it. From what I could piece together after that, Kaitlyn was chasing a cat, some little stray that had wandered up. Cole had found a bird's nest in the lily bush and didn't notice when she slipped out. When I ran around the corner of the house, I saw that tractor trailer sitting crossways in the road. The driver was still sitting behind the wheel. He *knew*. He knew."

"Cole was running down the road, and I was thinking, 'Where is he going?' but he was running to her. It had knocked her that far. Knocked her out of her shoes. I started to run too, and when I saw that little yellow sneaker—oh, God," she gasped.

As Alex watched helplessly, his mother started talking faster and faster, her voice going higher and higher. Jessica looked like she was going to faint.

"God forgive me for what I did. If I could take back anything I ever said, it would be the words I said to Cole that day. He was holding her when I got to them. She looked like a broken doll lying there, and there was so much blood. I screamed at him. God forgive me, I screamed at him, 'You were supposed to be watching her.' I'll never forget the look on his face. Then he looked down at his hands, and they were covered with blood too, and he started screaming. People were gathering by then, and someone pulled him away from her. I tried to get him, but he was kicking at me and still screaming. I can still hear his screams in my sleep. He ran back into the house and started washing his hands. It took two grown men to pull him out of that bathroom an hour later. He kept begging and telling them that he couldn't get the blood off his hands. Any time anyone mentioned her name, he'd clamp his hands over his ears and start shouting his multiplication tables. He didn't let me touch him, didn't want anything to do with me. I lost two of my children that day."

"Oh, God," Jessica murmured.

"It's my fault Cole is the way he is," Kate choked. "It's my fault he hurt you."

Intent on comforting his mother, Alex didn't notice when Jessica walked around the table. She laid a hand on his shoulder, and he saw the unspoken message in her eyes. He retreated, and she wrapped her arms around Kate. His admiration for Jessica, already high, skyrocketed as she held his mother.

"I'm so sorry," Jessica whispered. "It wasn't your fault. It wasn't anyone's fault. It was just a terrible, terrible accident."

"If I hadn't said that to him—I shattered him."

"Shh, don't do that to yourself. Horrible things happen that aren't anyone's fault."

As Jessica continued to talk to her in that calm, soothing voice, Alex marveled at her compassion. Her own life was coming apart at the seams, and she was comforting the mother of her greatest enemy. He felt a moment of deep sadness for his brother. If anyone had been capable of saving Cole from himself, it would've been Jessica.

Mason chose that moment to walk in. He shot Alex a questioning look and Alex mouthed "Kaitlyn."

With a grim nod, Mason walked over and touched Kate's hair. Jessica stepped back, and he wrapped Kate in his arms. Alex swallowed over the lump in his throat, grateful that his mother had found someone who loved her. A man who was so many things Earl Ramsey could never be.

"Kate, honey, why don't we go lie down a little while?"

Mason asked, and she nodded. Mason gave Alex's shoulder a reassuring squeeze as they passed. Jessica sighed and walked out the backdoor. Alex trailed along behind her.

Even though the afternoon was warm, Alex watched her hug herself and wished he knew what she was thinking. But somehow he was afraid to ask.

Following the cobblestone path to the gazebo, Jessica wandered inside and sat in the swing. Alex sat beside her without waiting for an invitation. They sat close together, shoulders brushing, but neither said anything for awhile.

"Your poor mother," Jessica said. "All that guilt . . ."

"I know." Alex sighed. He leaned back and threw his arm across the back of the swing. To his surprise, Jessica laid her head against his shoulder.

"Cole never said anything about her. I never knew."

"I'm not surprised. He never mentioned her name again. Then the next year, Mom left. She begged Cole to go too, but he had distanced himself from her by then."

"That's terrible. Even though Cole put me through hell, I can't help but feel sorry for him."

Alex stroked the side of her bare arm, wishing he knew what to say. He was thinking of the first few weeks after they'd left, when his mother had lived in fear of Earl hunting her down and killing her.

"How did you do it, Jess? How did you fake your death? Cole said he touched you."

"God, it seems so amazing now, that we really pulled it off." Jessica shook her head. "I've never been more scared in my life. It had to be timed perfectly."

She glanced at Alex. "I had friends at the hospital who knew what my situation was. Then I got pregnant. I was hysterical and knew that Cole would never let me leave. And if there was a baby involved, he would have no trouble gaining custody. Cole is a powerful man. I was nothing, a lowly little LPN when we met. I figured things out fast the one time I called the police on him. He talked to them—I don't know if he paid them off or what—but he knocked me across the living room and threatened, *in front of them*, to kill me if I ever did that again. They just tipped their hats and said, 'Sorry to trouble you, Mr. Ramsey'. That was it." She shrugged.

Alex gritted his teeth. It was hard to believe there were actually cops like that, but he knew there were.

"Well, my friend Matt was trying to cheer me up that day. We were talking about the plot of some movie, where the woman jumps off a boat and the husband thinks she drowned. Then he said, 'Well, we could shoot you up with curare and drag him into the morgue. He'd think you were dead for sure.'"

"Curare?"

"Sorry. It's a paralytic used in delicate surgeries when the patient has to be completely immobilized. The patient has no noticeable pulse or reflex, but it doesn't affect the heart. He was just joking, but then I got to thinking..."

She shot Alex a quick glance. "You have no idea how desperate I was by that point. I asked him if it crossed the placenta, and he started trying to talk me out of it. It wouldn't cross the placenta, but he was afraid it would kill me, especially with my history of asthma. Plus, the time frame was really tight. He would have to get Cole in and out of there very quickly, because it shuts down your system, and after three to five minutes, you would need a machine to breathe for you."

"So, if Cole had dawdled too long, you would've really died."

"Yes. It was crazy. I actually laid in one of those drawers for awhile before he called Cole, so my skin would be really chilled. Then someone called Cole, summoning him to the hospital. Once he got there another friend, a nurse, broke the news to him that I'd died of a severe asthma attack. She stalled him, and Matt gave me the dose while Cole was standing *right outside the door.* I could never tell you how horrible it felt. I was aware of everything and couldn't even lift a finger as my body shut down. Poor Matt had to hustle Cole in there and hustle him out within minutes. Then he had to hook me to oxygen for another eight minutes until I could breathe on my own again. He was scared to give me a stronger dose, afraid he couldn't resuscitate me on his own. If anyone would've come into that morgue . . ." she shuddered.

"That sounds so crazy," Alex said. "How did you guys do that in the hospital with no one finding out?"

"I don't know. Matt broke more laws than I could count in less than ten minutes. His whole life would've been destroyed if anyone had caught us. And he wasn't the only one. I had left instructions that I wanted to be cremated upon my death. If Cole had balked at that, the whole thing would've blown up in our faces, but he didn't. My sister Laura handled that part of it. She would never tell me how much it cost, but she found a man who made a death certificate. That man also handled my phony cremation. I honestly don't know how she got all of it done—I was long gone by then—but Cole received a silver urn filled with stove ashes."

"And the fake ID isn't much of a problem these days," Alex mused.

"No, it wasn't. I had a new name, a new driver's license, and social security card before I slipped out of the hospital."

She smiled gamely at him and said, "What are you thinking, that I'm nuts?"

"I don't think that," he said, staring into her green eyes. "I was thinking you're the bravest woman I've ever met."

Too close. He was too close to her.

Alex saw her leaning toward him, maybe to kiss his cheek, and he turned his head. His mouth brushed against hers. He wanted to know how she kissed, how she tasted. Jessica's mouth was warm and inviting beneath his, and Alex tilted his head, deepening the kiss. He felt her hand in his hair, pulling him closer, as his tongue teased hers.

Then he traced the hollow of her throat with his mouth, his stubble rasping across her skin. She smelled clean, like soap and green apples, and Alex found the scent headier than perfume. He felt, rather than heard, the moan rise in her throat.

The next thing he felt was her hand at his chest, pushing him away.

"Alex." Her voice was breathless, soft. "Alex, I can't do this."

"Why not?" he murmured, running his lips across her jaw line.

"Please." Her voice was stronger this time, almost desperate. Alex pulled away and stared at her. He was stunned to see her eyes well with tears.

"Jessica?"

"I can't do this. I can't give you what you need."

"And what do I need?" Alex frowned as she untangled herself from him and stood.

"You need to find someone with a heart more stable. My life is a wreck, and I can't get involved with anyone right now, especially—"

She froze, unwilling to finish what was on her mind, but he could see it in her eyes.

"Especially me." Alex finished. It hurt, dammit. Without another word, he turned and walked back into the house.

Jessica followed him in a few minutes later, and he cursed himself for her red eyes.

"Can I borrow your cell phone? I really need to let Pru know I'm okay," she said, swiping at the tear that streaked down her cheek. Alex wanted to say something, anything, but instead he just handed her his phone.

Jessica turned her back to Alex and fought her tears. Couldn't he see that this was an impossible situation? She hated the hurt look on his face, but what else could she do?

"Pru?" she said when her cousin picked up the phone.

"Jess, thank God! Where are you? Randall said you never made it."

"I'm with Alex."

Pru gasped. She was silent for a moment, then she asked, "Can you trust him?"

Jessica glanced at Alex over her shoulder. He was staring out the window with an enigmatic expression. "Yes," she said.

"Jess, you need to call Laura." Pru sounded hesitant.

Jessica's stomach dropped. There was something in Pru's voice . . .

"What is it? What's happened?"

"She wants you to call her."

Jessica could tell by the tone of Pru's voice that she would say nothing further. "Okay, I'll call her."

"Take care, Jess," Pru said, and the phone clicked in her ear.

"What's wrong?" Alex asked.

"I don't know." Jessica punched in the numbers, and Laura answered on the second ring.

"Laura, it's me. What's happened?"

"Jessica. Jessica, where are you?"

"It's complicated, Laura. I'm with Cole's brother. And we're at his mother's house."

"What?" Laura gasped. She didn't say anything for a long time.

Jessica rubbed the back of her neck. "Alex is helping me."

"Cole was here. Jessica, he knows where you are, and he's coming for you. You have to get out of there."

"Cole was at your house?" Jessica's knees buckled and Alex grabbed her. He eased her into a chair. "Laura, are you okay?"

Her sister was crying, and the sound of her sobs scared Jessica more than anything. Laura was the strong one. She never cried.

"What did he do to you? What about Kacie?"

"We're fine. He tied me up, threatened me. Kacie had just come back from Daniel's. She didn't see much."

"And he just left?"

Silence.

When she spoke, Laura's voice was bitter. "A friend of mine dropped by and scared him off. Bastard jumped out my bedroom window."

"I'm so sorry," Jessica choked.

"I love you, Jess. I'm sorry too," Laura sobbed.

When she spoke again, her voice was frantic. "You have to get out of there. You have to go somewhere else. Call me when you get there."

"Okay," Jessica whispered.

"Call me."

"I will."

Jessica hung up the phone and buried her face in her hands.

―――――――∞―――――――

"Oh, God, what have I done?" Laura cried.

"You did something right for once," Cole said, grinning at her.

He tore the page out of the notebook he'd been scribbling in. He hadn't given Laura a chance to warn her. "My kid in exchange for your kid."

Laura seemed to crumple before his eyes, and Cole took satisfaction in seeing the haughty witch brought down to size. He jerked his head toward the living room where Laura's daughter watched cartoons, blissfully unaware.

"See, she doesn't even know anything's going on."

He could've gone to his mother's house to get them, but he didn't want to see Kate.

Much better to get them alone. Once he picked off Alex, Jessica and the boy would be easy to control.

"Now what?" Laura asked.

She was still crying, and Cole shot her an irritated look. If she didn't stop that, he was going to cut her throat.

"Now, we wait."

Chapter 8

"Jessica?"

"Cole knows where we are. He's coming for me." Jessica pushed a hand through her hair and tried to figure out her next move.

"What? How?"

"I don't know, but he told my sister he was headed here. He threatened her. We have to get out of here, not only for my safety, but for your mother's." She shot Alex a wary look and said, "That is, if you still want to help me."

"You think I won't help you anymore because you don't want to kiss me?" Alex's pained expression tore at her. "Jessica, would it kill you to have just a little faith in me?"

"I do."

"No, you don't." He shoved his hands in his pockets. "But we don't have time to argue about it. How long since Cole left her place?"

"I don't know," she admitted. "I didn't ask her."

"Call her back and find out. I know a place where we can go, but we need to know if Cole might already be outside, waiting for us."

Jessica nodded and dialed Laura's number again.

"It's me. How long has it been since Cole left your place?"

"Uh, a couple of hours."

Jessica breathed a sigh of relief. "Good, then he hasn't had time to get here."

"Do, uh, do you know where you're going?" Laura's voice sounded funny, tight, and Jessica felt sick. What had Cole done that she wasn't telling?

"Did he hit you?"

"No."

Cupping her hand over the receiver, she asked Alex if he had a number for the place they'd be staying.

"It's 555-2359," he told her, and she repeated it to Laura.

"J.J., I'm sorry I couldn't protect you from him."

Laura's reverting to her childhood nickname shook her. Jessica swallowed hard and said, "I'll make it somehow. I have to, for Joe."

Jessica hung up the phone and turned to Alex. "What now?"

"Now we leave. How long has Cole been gone?"

"A couple of hours."

"It takes nearly five to fly, so we have a little time left." He pinched the bridge of his nose and said, "I need to ask you something. What do you think about letting Mom and Mason take Joe with them? Then, even if Cole catches up with us, he won't get Joe."

"No," she said automatically. "I'm not leaving my son. What if Cole catches up with them and not us?"

"Everything you've told me indicates that Cole is coming after you first. He wants revenge. If Joe is safe, then all I have to concentrate on is keeping you safe."

"You can't guarantee he'll be safe," she insisted, and Alex met her gaze.

"I can't guarantee that anyhow, but I can tell you what I think. He'll be in less danger if he's not with us."

It felt wrong, and the thought of leaving Joe terrified her, but she knew Alex was suggesting what he thought was best for her son. She squeezed her eyes shut.

"Okay."

"Okay?" he repeated, sounding surprised.

"Yes. If you think it's best for Joe, okay."

"What's going on?" Kate walked into the room, ruffling Joe's hair as he rocketed past her and out the back door.

"We have to leave. Cole's on his way," Alex said. "Mom, can you and Mason take Joe somewhere, keep him safe? I thought it might be better if we split up."

Kate's eyes widened. "Yes. Yes, of course. When do we need to leave?"

"Now."

Jessica tried to listen while he gave Kate instructions, but her thoughts kept turning to Joe.

For the first time ever, she was going to leave him.

She had always been overprotective—she knew that—but it wasn't something she could help. He'd never even spent the night away from her before and here she was, trusting his care to a complete stranger.

Not a stranger, she realized. His grandmother.

She didn't know whether to be reassured by that, or terrified.

What if this was all a trick, a ploy to take her son away from her? Kate could run with him and never look back. She might never see Joe again. Dozens of paranoid ideas raced through her mind. Blood was thicker than water, after all, and what if things had changed between Cole and his mother in the last five years? What if . . .

Jessica glanced up to see Alex staring at her, a concerned look on his face.

No, she thought. *It's not a trick.*

Taking a deep breath, she willed herself to calm down. In every scenario she'd just pictured, Alex would have to be an accomplice to pull it off.

And he wasn't.

Jessica knew that as surely as she knew anything. The mere sight of his smile eased her nerves. For no reason she could explain, Jessica knew she trusted him with her life.

"Are you going to tell Joe?" he asked, taking her hand. Grateful for his touch, Jessica squeezed his hand and nodded. When Alex called for Joe to come inside, she struggled to control her emotions.

"Hey!" she said brightly. "I have to go somewhere with Alex. What do you think about going on a little trip with your grandmother?"

"I have a grandmother?" Joe asked, and Jessica realized she'd never told him. She glanced at Kate over his shoulder and smiled. Kate was blinking back tears, and her hands were steepled in front of her.

"Yeah, you have a grandmother. Grandmother Kate."

"Cool," Joe said. He looked back at Kate and said, "I like you."

"I like you too," she said softly.

Whatever objections she had expected from Joe weren't forthcoming. He was excited to be going on another trip. Jessica's heart broke a little that he didn't seem to mind going without her, but she knew that's how kids were.

Then her heart fell apart completely when he wrapped his little arms around her and kissed her goodbye.

"Alex, I think the keys to the four-wheel drive are on top of the bookcase." Mason patted his pockets. "If they're not on the bookcase, I probably left them on my dresser."

Kate rolled her eyes and smiled. "Actually, you left them in the laundry hamper in the pocket of those old jeans, but I found them and hung them on the peg in the kitchen, where they belong."

"Ah." Mason kissed the top of her head. "What would I do without you?" Briefly, Mason hugged Alex. "Be careful, son," he whispered, and nodded at Jessica. "We'll take good care of Joe."

Jessica nodded back and even managed to smile and wave as they climbed into Kate's Lincoln and backed out of the drive. As soon as Joe was out of sight, however, she lost it.

"Hey!" Alex took her in his arms. "Don't cry. He's in good hands, and we'll be able to call." Giving her a little squeeze, Alex promised, "You'll be back with him soon."

"I know," Jessica said, swiping at her eyes. "But it's always been just the two of us. The longest I've ever left him at one time was when I was at work. I feel lost without him."

"We need to talk about things, figure out where we're going from here."

For one insane moment, Jessica thought he was talking about their relationship and opened her mouth to tell him there was no 'we' when he said, "I think we both know Cole will never let this rest. He's hunting you, Jess, and I don't think he'll give up easily." Alex sighed. "You'll have to start over again, a new life, a new name. But this time, he'll know you're out there."

The impact of his words left her breathless. For the rest of her life, Cole would hunt her. She would never be able to set foot outside her home without looking for his face. She would never be able to shut her eyes at night without wondering if he was waiting outside her window. He would search and search until he found her, then one day he would kill her.

Unless she killed him first.

"We'd better get going," he said, releasing her and grabbing up her suitcase.

"Where are we going?" Jessica heard herself ask, even though she didn't really care. She had the feeling that anywhere they went wouldn't be far enough.

"I have a cabin on some land Mason's uncle left him. My name isn't on the records, and I can't see how Cole could trace it to me. In fact, not even a handful of people know it's there. We just built it last year."

"But it has a phone?"

"Yeah. Mason uses it some during squirrel season. Cell phone reception there is hit and miss—all those trees, I guess—and even when he's not on call, he likes for the hospital to have a way to contact him."

He opened the garage door and gestured at the old brown Chevrolet pickup inside.

"Your chariot awaits, Madame." He opened passenger-side door for her, and Jessica climbed inside. As they rumbled onto the highway, she daydreamed about killing Cole. She could do it; she knew that without having to think about it.

But could she get to Cole before he got to her?

The ride up the mountain was made mostly in silence. Alex tried a couple of times, but she didn't feel like talking. There was nothing left to say. In an effort to deflect further attempts at conversation, Jessica closed her eyes and pretended to doze.

Half an hour later, Alex gave her a gentle shake. "Hey, we'll stop at this little market and get something to eat. I don't know if there's anything at the cabin."

"I'm not hungry," Jessica replied.

"Too bad. You have to eat something." Alex parked the car and went around to open her door. Reluctantly, she tagged along behind him.

"I'll get a few things, and we'll check out what we've got at the cabin. I can come back tomorrow with a list."

The store reminded Jessica of one of the old time general stores she'd seen on television, complete with the grizzled old shopkeeper behind the counter. The shelves were dusty and she wondered if some of the items might be older than she was. But the aroma of fried chicken coming from the deli smelled good. Jessica was surprised by the hunger pang that clenched her stomach.

"You like chicken?" Alex asked as he set an armload of groceries on the counter and dug out his wallet.

Jessica nodded, and Alex ordered two fried chicken specials. Afraid that he'd want to sit inside at one of the dingy looking booths, Jessica grabbed a couple of the bags and headed back to the truck.

Alex followed her out a few minutes later and announced, "There's a state park a few miles down the road. Do you want to eat there? They have a picnic area."

Jessica shrugged and twisted around to stare out the

window. The area was beautiful, and it was a perfect summer afternoon, but Jessica found it hard to care. It was hard to feel much of anything at the moment.

They had the park to themselves except for a family of four hauling a grill out of the back of a camper. Alex returned their friendly waves and selected the table furthest from the road.

As she opened the foam container that held her food, Jessica felt her stomach roll. The food that had smelled appetizing in the store now looked greasy and unappealing. She looked up at Alex. He was watching her with those cop eyes—eyes that missed nothing. Jessica sighed and reluctantly took a bite of potato salad. The family with the camper had broken out a Frisbee, and the little boy sent a wild toss that landed near their table.

Although he looked nothing like Joe, he was about the same age and when he grinned at her, Jessica nearly choked on the bite of chicken she'd just taken. The longer she chewed, the tougher it seemed. Finally, she managed to wash it down with a swig of her cola.

Joe was gone and she had the sickening feeling that she would never see him again.

Alex watched her face and knew Jessica was thinking about Joe. He was too.

"You know, identical twins have the same DNA. I couldn't have a child of my own that was more closely linked to me genetically than Joe is. They couldn't even prove in a court of law that I'm not his father."

Jessica gave him a funny look, and Alex was afraid she was going to ask him what the hell he meant by that, when he had no idea himself, but she merely nodded. Taking another sip of her cola, she surprised him by saying, "That's a nice thought."

"Look, Jessica, I want to apologize to you. I shouldn't have kissed you. I know that you don't want me in your life—"

"What life?" she interrupted, her voice trembling. "I don't have a life. Just this." She made a sweeping motion with her hand. "Running and hiding. That's my life."

"Jess—"

With a hollow laugh, she said, "Think of all the torture Cole will deprive himself of if he kills me."

Her voice trailed off to a whisper as she said, "Nothing could be worse than this."

The desolation in her eyes broke Alex's heart. He wanted to be her hero, to promise her a normal life and happiness, but he couldn't make her a promise he might not be able to keep.

"Sometimes it makes me angry, but mostly it just hurts." She traced the lip of her soda can with her finger and met his gaze. "You want to know how I feel? I'll tell you. I wish I'd met you first, in another time and place. I wish you were Joe's father. I wish I were someone else. Anyone else."

She paused, her green eyes sparkling with tears. "That's what hurts the most, to meet someone like you and know that everything I ever wanted is right here, but I can't have it. Can't you see that any relationship between us would be doomed from the start? It's like freaking Romeo and Juliet."

Jessica shoved away from the table and scooped up her carryout plate. Tossing it in the garbage can, she started walking to the pickup.

Her words had stunned him, and for a moment he couldn't think, couldn't move. She had feelings for him.

"Jessica!" he managed. "Jessica, don't run away."

Slowly she turned to face him. The wind whipped her hair around her face.

"That's all I know to do," she said, and walked away.

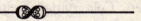

Something was wrong.

Cole pressed the heels of his palms into his eyes and willed himself to concentrate. He couldn't lose it. Not now.

"What did you say?" Laura gasped.

The uneasiness that gripped him grew more profound, and Cole teetered on the edge of panic. His heart threatened to beat its way out of his chest, but he struggled to keep his voice calm as he said, "You heard me. Pack a bag for her. She's going with me."

"You can't take her, Cole. I won't call anyone, not the police, not Jessica."

Cole glanced toward the living room, where the little blond girl sat with her back to them, watching TV. Quietly, he shut the door to keep her from seeing what was going on with him and her mother.

Yeah, right, Cole's inner voice mocked. You did that so *you* wouldn't have to see *her*. She's a little older, but doesn't she remind you of someone? All that blond hair. Even her name—

"Shut up!" Cole whispered and clamped his hands over his ears. It was hard to breathe, hard to think. He was sweating. Suddenly, he realized his shirt was clinging to him, even though he was cold inside. "She is not like Kaitlyn. She is not—"

Oh, God, he'd said her name.

It hung in the air like a curse, echoed in his brain.

Terrified, Cole started reciting his multiplication tables. A pain ripped across his chest, staggering him and leaving him nauseous.

A heart attack. I'm having a heart attack.

But it wasn't. He knew exactly what this was. The door was open and the monster was out. It was coming for him, teeth bared and ready to devour him.

Kaitlyn, it hissed.

"No!" he whimpered, and was shocked by the voice that came from inside him. It was in a voice that could never come from his adult throat.

"Oh, God," Laura said, her eyes widening. In his peripheral vision he could still see her, but she sounded like she was in a tunnel. "You really are crazy, aren't you? You really are."

"Shut up," he choked. "I'm not crazy, don't say that."

Kaitlyn, the voice said, more insistent this time.

His vision distorted, speckling like static on a TV. He knew the black hole was there. It was going to suck him in.

"No," he groaned. "No!"

Cole snapped his head back, and slammed it into the door behind him. Stars exploded behind his eyes, but the blow brought him back in focus, back to the present. Laura was still talking, but he could make no sense of her words. They were garbled, idiotic, and he had the sudden intuition that she was doing it on purpose, speaking gibberish to confuse him. The thought enraged him.

"Mama," another voice intruded, and Cole nearly screamed. It came from the other side of the door, and he had the sudden, terrible knowledge that if he threw open that door, Kaitlyn would be standing there. Kaitlyn with her long blond hair stained that strange, crimson color. Kaitlyn with one shoe off and tiny pebbles embedded in one pale cheek.

Kaitlyn staring at him with accusing blue eyes.

"Mama," she said again, and some part of Cole realized that it wasn't Kaitlyn. It wasn't Kaitlyn. Laura stared at him with a kind of horrified fascination.

"Tell her you're okay. Tell her to go outside and play," he hissed. When Laura didn't say anything, he seized her arm. "Do it. Don't make me kill her."

Haltingly, Laura did as she was told while Cole struggled against his thoughts, against the nausea that gripped him.

Disoriented, he willed himself to concentrate on the present, to fight the fear that threatened to paralyze him.

He stank. He did. Cole could smell himself, the thick, acrid scent of perspiration, the faint smell of urine—

Mortified, he glanced down at the stain darkening the crotch of his black jeans. He had wet himself.

Dear God, he had wet himself.

Shame burned his face as he glanced at Laura. She was staring at him with eyes huge as half dollars.

And then she laughed.

A nervous giggle like Jessica's. Helplessly, Cole was sucked into the vortex, sucked into the past.

And the monster stood before him.

It had first appeared to him the night of Kaitlyn's death, so deceptive in its appearance. It looked like her. And as always, Cole felt a tremendous rush of relief. She was alive. She was okay. But when he rushed to take her in his arms, it laughed and bared its teeth.

Cole recoiled in horror. No human, no animal had teeth like that. They were demon teeth, belonging to the creature that guarded the gates of hell.

It's your fault, Cole. You were supposed to be watching her.

"No, I didn't mean it! It was an accident." Cole dropped his head and sobbed. The years vanished. He was no longer a man. Just a boy, and the monster had come for him.

Your fault! The voice insisted. *Look at me, Cole.*

Look at what you've done! it screeched.

"No, I . . . I won't. I can't . . ." but his head jerked up just the same.

The Kaitlyn creature had changed, looking startlingly innocent. She held out her hands to him, and they were covered in blood.

"Cole, help me," she said tearfully. As she reached for him, Cole staggered backward.

"No, don't touch me," he pleaded. "I'm sorry, Katie."

"Sorry?" she said bitterly. "Sorry? You were supposed to be watching me."

As he watched, its face began to morph into another face, a face that caused tight bands of anxiety to tighten around his chest.

"Mama," he whispered.

Her eyes flashed at him with a mixture of horror and outrage. "You were supposed to be watching her!"

Cole knew he was going to die. He hadn't seen the monster since he was thirteen; he had found ways to fight it off. But now it was back, and it was going to drag him into hell.

Terror fueled him. He grabbed the monster by the throat, the monster that wore his mother's face, and was amazed by how human it felt. Its eyes flew wide, startled, and Cole felt a stab of hope within him. It feared him.

A ten-year-old boy hadn't stood a chance, but maybe a man did.

With a cry of outrage, Cole lifted it by the throat and

slammed it into the wall. He took grim satisfaction in the crunching sound he heard as its skull thumped against the drywall. The monster's face went slack, its eyes glassy and unfocused. Releasing his grip on its throat, Cole watched it slide down the wall, leaving a bloody streak down the pale blue paint.

He watched it for any movement, any sign of life, but Laura was still.

Laura.

Bewildered, Cole stared at the crumpled body of his sister-in-law.

Chapter 9

"Squirrelly Creek Road?" Jessica laughed and glanced at Alex. "Squirrelly Creek Road. Who names the roads around here?"

"Why, shucks, ma'am," he said with a grin. "You ain't seen nothin' yet. Squirrelly Creek Road cuts off onto Possum Holler Road, and that leads to—hey, you know a sure sign that you're a hillbilly?"

"No." Jessica gave him a wary look.

"You think of possum as the other white meat."

"Ew!" she exclaimed, wrinkling her nose.

Her reaction must've encouraged him, because he gave her a delighted look and said, "Directions to your home begin with, turn off the paved road."

Jessica groaned and covered her face with her hands.

"Your home has more miles on it than your car."

"Stop," she said, laughing.

"You think loading the dishwasher means getting your wife drunk."

"Stop," she said, trying to sound stern. "You're—ow! What was that?" Jessica rubbed the back of her head gingerly where it had struck the window.

Alex flashed her a brilliant white grin. "We turned off the paved road."

The gravel road before them was narrow and twisted like a snake. Tree branches scraped against the side of Alex's pickup as he negotiated the turns. Then the gravel tapered away, and they were on a little dirt road that would've more accurately been called a path.

"Alex, look out!" Jessica pointed out the windshield at the huge mud hole in front of them. It was longer than the pickup and twice as wide.

"What?" he said, lifting an eyebrow. "That little old thing?" Alex shook his head and made a tsk-tsk sound. "You really are a city girl, huh? I keep forgetting that."

"Four-wheel drive," he explained, and plowed straight ahead. Jessica screamed when they dropped into the hole. Alex just laughed as the tires tried to find purchase. Mud struck the windshield with a thud-thud-thud that sounded like muted gunfire. Then they were safely on the other side.

"Whew, that was a close one," he said. "Imagine how stupid I would've felt if we'd gotten stuck in that. I can just see you, having to climb out the window and wade through the mud to get to dry land."

"Not hardly," Jessica snorted. "I would've waited right here until you got it out."

"What if the muddy water started coming in?" he teased.

"Then you would've had to carry me out on your shoulders, I guess. I warned you not to drive into the thing. It's not my fault you have no common sense."

They traded insults all the way to the cabin, and Jessica was surprised to find herself in a light mood. Alex had a way of taking her mind off of even the most horrible things, even when she didn't want to be cheered up. When they'd passed through the small town of Pelham, Alex had drawn her out of her silence with his inane banter after they'd seen the name "Jessie" spray-painted on a water tower. She still felt a little tired, though, and the jarring ride had given her a headache.

"Here we are," he announced.

"How can you even see it through this windshield?" Jessica grumbled, straining to peer through the mud-caked glass.

Sticking out his tongue at her like a three-year-old, Alex hopped down from the truck and came around to help her out.

Jessica had to admit it; the place was beautiful. The red cedar was complemented by a green tin roof, and a hand-carved cedar swing on the front porch that spanned the length of the cabin. And all around, the lush greenness of the Cumberland Plateau.

The place was quiet, peaceful, and she envied its

tranquility.

"How did you get telephone lines back here?" she asked.

"It's not as secluded as you might think. Over that ridge . . ." he paused, pointing toward the east. " . . . is a farming community. Tobacco and corn. So they didn't have to run the lines that far. Come on, I want to show you something." He seized her hand, dragging her up the front steps.

Jessica braced herself as he unlocked the door, a little nervous about her first glimpse of a place where Alex often stayed. She had the sudden fear that he would throw open the door to reveal white carpet, white walls, antiseptic housekeeping. Instead, she found herself staring at gleaming hardwood floors, rugged cedar walls, and the look of absentminded clutter that people associated with bachelor pads. It was clean, but a newspaper lay open on the coffee table, a stack of outdoor magazines on the kitchen table. The sofa and chairs in the living room were forest green and a beautiful but worn rug with woven strands of green, mauve and tan took up much of the area in the center of the room. It looked masculine and homey, and Jessica almost wished it was cold outside, just for an excuse to build a fire in the big iron fireplace.

"This way." Alex pulled her hand. He led her to a pair of sliding patio doors, and when he threw them open, the view took Jessica's breath away.

The back deck was built on the rocky edge of the bluff. Jessica allowed Alex to lead her to the railing, and they stared down at the valley below.

"This is beautiful," she gasped. "Those little specks—"

"Houses in the Pelham Valley. That little blue thing over there is the water tower that I was teasing you about."

"Really?" It was terrible to have no sense of direction. If she'd been pressed, she would've thought Pelham Valley was back behind them.

"This evening, we can watch the sunset out here. It's truly something to behold."

"I bet," she said, rubbing her temple.

"You okay?" he said, staring at her with worried blue eyes.

"Your driving rattled my brain. I've got a headache."

"There's a bottle of pain reliever in the bathroom medicine cabinet. Why don't you take a couple and lie down for awhile?"

Jessica nodded and fumbled with the patio door. Alex let her struggle with it for a moment before he reached around her and slid the door open with ease.

Following her back inside, he quipped, "I forget that you're a blond California girl in disguise. You know what they say about blond California girl—"

"Shut up." Jessica cast him a warning glance.

"Hey, I like blond California girls. Dated one once. She thought the capital of California was C."

"You're hilarious." She rolled her eyes. "Might I remind you that your own mother is a blond California girl?"

"Jess, Jess," he clucked. "If we're going to engage

in a battle of wits, you're going to have to get with the program, learn a little slang. You could've said all that with two simple words and got the point across . . . yo mama."

She snorted. "If we're going to engage in a battle of wits, you're going to have to arm yourself," she replied and walked down the hall.

"Ouch!" she heard him say, and grinned to herself.

She found the bottle of pain reliever and went in search of a bed. Jessica peered in one of the doors. A small twin bed was its sole furnishing and it didn't look all that comfortable. Making a face, she tried the door at the end of the hall.

Alex's bedroom. Had to be.

More hardwood floors with cedar walls. The thick comforter and curtains were navy blue. A picture of a grizzly fishing in a mountain stream hung above the king-sized bed.

Realizing it was a little mean to take over his bedroom, Jessica felt a pang of sympathy for Alex, but it passed quickly when she remembered the blonde joke.

"Too bad," she muttered, and grinned at her reflection in his dresser mirror.

Jessica stretched out on top of the comforter, grateful the bed was as soft as it looked. With a contented sigh, she pulled his pillow to her face and rolled over on her stomach, burying her face in it.

It smelled like Alex. Like his cologne and his hair. It was nice.

Alex with his corny jokes and crooked smiles.

She could get used to them both.

When she awoke, Jessica was surprised by the darkness of the room. A glance at the clock on the nightstand made her bolt upright. Four hours. She'd slept all afternoon. Her first thought was Joe. She didn't even know where he was right now.

Yawning and raking a hand through her hair, she opened the bedroom door. The aroma hit her immediately and made her mouth water.

"What *is* that smell?" she asked in delight as she wandered into the living room. Alex stood by the stove in the adjoining kitchen, and he looked up with a grin.

"Sleeping Beauty, glad you could join me." He gestured at the pots on the stove. "Sorry. Thought I was better stocked than I actually was. Looks like spaghetti tonight."

"I like spaghetti." Jessica strolled into the kitchen. She watched Alex stir the sauce and check the bread in the oven.

"Here." He took the wooden spoon out of the sauce and cupped his other hand under it. "Enough garlic? Careful. It's hot." He held the spoon to her lips as Jessica leaned toward him.

Tentatively, she tasted it and rolled her eyes. "Alex, it's perfect."

"Good." He looked pleased. "Maybe you'll eat something today."

"I've eaten today."

"Three bites; I counted."

Jessica surveyed the counter and looked at Alex in surprise. "You made this? Not a jar, not a can?"

"Of course I made this," he said, offended. "Does it taste like something that came out of a jar or a can?"

"Wow. I'm impressed," she said, ignoring him. "Where did you learn to cook?"

He gestured at the open cookbook on the counter. "A confirmed bachelor either learns to cook or learns to like TV dinners. I hate TV dinners."

"Why?" she asked curiously.

"Why?" He quirked an eyebrow. "Well, they taste like—"

"No. Why haven't you gotten married?"

"The right one's never asked me," he said with a wink.

"I figured it was your jokes."

"Ha ha. By the way, I talked to Mom. Joe's conked out. Seems he's a sleepyhead like his mom."

"He's okay?" Jessica's heart speeded up. "He's not scared?"

"He's fine. Talked Mom's ear off, and she thinks he's the smartest kid since Solomon."

"He is," Jessica said with a grin. She glanced out the patio doors, and her smile disappeared. "I missed the sunset."

"There's always tomorrow," Alex said, squeezing her hand. "I hated to wake you."

"Always tomorrow," Jessica repeated, and glanced around. "What can I do to help?"

"You can cut up the stuff for the salad if you want." Alex handed her a knife and the bag of produce he'd purchased earlier.

As Jessica washed and started cutting the lettuce, she felt Alex's hand on her waist.

"Let me reach around you here."

Suddenly, he was right there, his hard body pressed against her back, his stubbled cheek brushing against hers.

"Potholder," he said. His warm breath stirred the hair by her ear, making her shiver. In his low voice, the word sounded like a seduction. He surrounded her, his big body dwarfing hers, and Jessica fought the urge to lean back, to snuggle against his warmth. She felt the hand on her waist tighten, and time seemed to slow as he reached for the green-checked piece of cloth. Her nerve endings were shooting off little sparks like static electricity where his body touched hers, and she wondered if Alex felt them too.

Then he was gone. He'd pulled away from her and turned back to the stove. Jessica's chest hurt, and she realized she was holding her breath. Slowly, she released it, but Jessica took her time on the lettuce and tomatoes. She couldn't turn around yet; she didn't dare.

She was afraid of what Alex might see written on her face, and of what she might not see on his.

"We could eat on the deck," he said when she finally

handed him the bowl. "But mosquitoes are pretty rough this time of year. They might eat us before we can eat our food. And I hate these kitchen chairs. Some sadist made them. They make my back hurt just looking at them."

"Well, where do you usually eat?" she asked, smiling.

He looked abashed, like Joe when he got in trouble. "Living room floor."

"Fine with me," she said.

"Really?" he asked happily.

"Alex, I have a four-year-old son. Do you think we never sit at the coffee table to eat supper?"

"Great!" He fixed their salad plates, carried them to the coffee table, and pushed the old newspaper onto the floor. "You like wine?"

"Never really drank much," she admitted.

"You have to try this. It's good stuff, 1997 red Zinfandel."

"Red wine?" Jessica made a face.

"It won't give you that pucker face like most red wines. You know, like that face you're making right now. It's actually pretty sweet. Like me."

Jessica made a harrumph sound in the back of her throat as she slid her feet under the coffee table and watched Alex pour the wine. Carefully setting the glasses on the table, he sat beside her. It was a small coffee table, and Jessica found herself distracted by the shoulder that brushed hers, and the long leg stretched alongside hers. For just a moment, she let herself pretend that Alex was hers.

"C'mon, chicken, try the wine." Alex held his glass under her nose, swirling the ruby-colored liquid. "Doesn't that smell good?"

Sniffing, Jessica gave him a skeptical look. "Okay." She sighed and raised her glass to her lips. Taking a hesitant sip, she said, "Kind of smoky tasting. Not too bad."

Alex grinned as she took another sip. "You like it, admit it."

"I like it," she said, spearing her last piece of lettuce.

"Here, let me get that," Alex said, struggling to his feet. He grabbed their salad plates. "On to the main course."

"Oh, I could get used to this being waited on thing." Jessica wrinkled her nose at him.

Alex tried to think of something witty to say, but her smile robbed him of his thoughts. He was beginning to think the cabin was a bad idea.

In the kitchen earlier, an errant curl had nearly been his downfall. As he'd leaned around her for the potholder, the curl had tickled the side of his face, and it had taken all his restraint not to tuck it behind her ear. And if he'd touched her hair, he might've wanted to touch her neck, and maybe kiss her. Then he would've been lost for sure.

After sitting back down beside Jessica, it wasn't long before Alex regretted the heaping plate of spaghetti he'd fixed himself. It was hard to think about anything other than the beautiful woman beside him. Alex tried to tell himself he was being foolish, that Jessica had told him more than once she didn't want a relationship with him, but he couldn't keep from stealing glances at her.

He had to stifle a laugh. Jessica obviously wasn't as love-struck as he was. She was eating with marked enthusiasm, and here he was, barely able to choke down a few bites. With a sigh, he took another sip of wine.

As she finished up, she gave him a wary glance. "Should I be worried? It's a bad sign when the chef won't eat his own cooking." She pointed at his nearly untouched plate.

"Too much bread." Alex patted his stomach, even though he'd only eaten one piece.

"I'll be nice, since that was so good," she said, picking up their plates and heading to the kitchen. "I'll do dishes."

"We'll get them later. Come back and sit down for awhile. Let your food digest. We did dishes as we went, so there aren't many anyhow."

"Okay," she said, and poured herself another glass of wine. "You talked me into it."

When Jessica sat back down, her elbow bumped the table, spilling her wine on the rug.

The transformation on her face shocked him. Her easygoing expression turned to one of horror.

"Oh, God. Alex, I'm sorry!"

She jumped to her feet and dragged the coffee table away from the spill. Blotting the liquid with a napkin, Jessica was almost frantic as she said, "Salt! Where's the salt? Salt will absorb the stain."

"Jess—" Alex said, the panic on her face alarming him.

Ignoring him, she ran into the kitchen and grabbed the salt shaker. As she furiously sprinkled it over the spot, Alex tried again. "Jess—"

"I'll get it up. I'll . . ."

She was falling apart in front of him

"Jessica!" he almost shouted. "Stop it."

He grabbed her wrists, hating the way she flinched, hating the way she stared at him with huge, terrified eyes.

"I'm not him," he said, almost pleading with her. "I'm not the one who hurt you. Don't be afraid of me."

Her breath came in ragged gasps, and she looked like she might cry.

Not knowing what else to do, Alex kissed her.

As he slid his hand through her hair, resting it on the back of her neck, he felt her stiffen. Then, to his amazement, she started kissing him back.

Her mouth was warm and tasted like the sweet raspberry wine. Alex had never been so acutely aware of another person. Every breath she took, the smell of vanilla in her hair, the soft skin at the nape of her neck. He felt her begin to pull away.

Reluctantly, Alex let her break the kiss, but he didn't remove his hand from her neck. Resting his forehead against hers, he said, "I don't give a damn about the wine ... or the dishes. But I do care about you, Jess."

When she said nothing, Alex let go of her and leaned

back against the sofa, trying to judge what he needed to say. Finally, he decided it was too late for diplomacy.

"You asked me earlier why I've never married. You'll probably think this is silly, but I used to think that when I met the right woman, I'd know it immediately. Love at first sight, I guess."

Her voice was barely a whisper when she said, "You don't think that anymore?"

"No." He raked a hand over his new beard. "I don't think that anymore. I know it."

Alex watched her freeze, but he blundered on, his stupidity exceeded only by his optimism. Even if she shot him down, he had to tell her how he felt.

"What I'm trying to say is—I'm in love with you, Jess. That maybe I fell in love with you over a telephone line, but now that you're here, I can't walk away."

It'll never work. It's crazy. We can't do this.

Jessica thought all these things, but said none of them. Instead, she pressed her hand to his jaw, enjoying the feel of his beard against her palm.

"I'm scared."

"Of me?" Alex covered her hand with his.

Jessica shook her head. "Of this. Of us. I don't know how much I have to give, Alex."

"I'll take whatever you've got," he replied. "You don't have to say anything right now. I just want you to know how I feel."

Jessica nodded and decided to take him up on that. Rising to her feet, she thought about the dishes in the sink. Then she glanced back at Alex.

As he watched her with that unnerving stillness of his, Jessica realized how crazy she was. Realized how much Cole still controlled her life. This wonderful man—the kind of man she'd dreamed of meeting her whole life—had just said he was in love with her, and she was walking away from him because of Cole.

Her heart pounded as she fumbled with the radio on the counter, tuning it to a classical station. With a tremulous smile, she turned to Alex and held out her hand. "Dance with me?"

Surprise touched his eyes, then a slow smile lit his face as he crossed the room to her. Her stomach was flip-flopping when Alex took her hand and pulled her into his arms.

Turning her face into his neck, Jessica rested her cheek on his soft flannel shirt and fought the urge to pull away from him, the urge to run. She hadn't dated, hadn't allowed any man to get close to her since escaping Cole. The past five years had been more flight than fight, but this time she'd found someone worth fighting for. She trembled as she inhaled the heated scent of his body.

"I've wanted to hold you like this since the first time I saw you," Alex said.

She shivered, and he tightened his arms around her waist. Jessica found she could say nothing at all, so she pressed her lips against the throbbing pulse in his neck. Alex groaned deep in his throat when she began to touch him, then taste him. She undid the first two buttons of his shirt and slid her hand inside to caress the smooth, warm skin that covered hard muscle.

"Make love to me, Alex," she murmured against his throat as one of his hands stole beneath her shirt, tracing her spine.

"Jessica," he rasped. "Are you sure?" He groaned again when she pushed his shirt aside and exposed his neck. She gently nipped at the tendon in the curve of his shoulder. He shuddered, and Jessica felt heady, intoxicated by the power she instinctively knew she had over him.

"I'm sure." She unbuttoned his shirt and pushed the unwanted obstacle off his shoulders. She splayed her hands across his chest, aroused by the feel of him and the heat that radiated from his bare skin.

His hands tugged at the hem of her T-shirt. She moved back and allowed him to pull it over her head. Alex made quick work of her bra, unsnapping the front hook and sliding it down her arms. He made her gasp when he rubbed his calloused hands over her nipples. As he cupped her breasts in his palms, Jessica found even the sight of his rough, tan fingers against her pale skin erotic.

Alex unfastened her jeans and carefully slid them over her bruised hip, kissing and caressing as he went. Jessica held her breath when he hooked his fingers in the elastic of her bikini panties and tugged them down around her ankles. Wordlessly, she stepped out of them.

She stood before him, feeling as naked emotionally as she was physically, as if Alex had also stripped away the thin veneer that protected her soul. There was another moment of pure panic, but then he scooped her up in his arms. At his touch, her fear vanished. He carried her to his bedroom and laid her on crisp white sheets.

Alex's languid kisses and caresses were driving her insane. Heat built inside her, along with a tension that made her body hum. In another minute, she'd be begging.

His hand was between her legs now, torturing her with his slow strokes.

"Faster," she pleaded, and he obliged, stoking the fire inside her until she thought her nerve endings couldn't endure any more. Her hoarse cries sounded like a stranger's as the waves of her climax slammed inside her.

Alex chose that moment to thrust himself inside her, and she lifted her hips to meet him.

"Jessica," he growled. The low sound of his voice made her skin tingle. She wrapped her legs around him, urging him deeper, faster, until they were both panting.

Alex came, his big body rocking, pressing her into the mattress.

Afterwards, Jessica lay in his arms, comforted by the steady beat of his heart, and for the first time in years, she felt safe.

Taking the girl had been a mistake.

Cole didn't risk a glance at his passenger, but he could feel her eyes on him. It was like riding with a ghost, and it was all he could do to stay focused on the road ahead of him.

Fleeing Laura's house, he'd almost left her there, playing on her swing set. But he watched her, her blond hair fluttering behind her like a ribbon, and knew he couldn't let her go back inside that house. The house where her mother lay dying.

He'd made up some story, he couldn't even remember what he'd said now, but Cole had talked her into coming with him.

"What's your name?" she asked, and Cole's nerves jumped at the sound of her voice. He was having trouble shaking off his strange hallucination, and he felt antsy, paranoid. He had to be very careful. Any mistake from this point on could hang him.

"My name is Jose. I'm your mom's new boyfriend." He kept his sunglasses on, hoping she wouldn't remember his blue eyes when the police questioned her. The easiest thing to do would be to kill her, but Cole already knew he couldn't bring himself to do that.

"No way, Jose," she said, giggling, and Cole frowned, unable to connect her words to anything meaningful. Then he realized he'd just told her that was his name. His head was still fuzzy, and that tight feeling was starting again in his chest.

"I'm Kacie," she said, and merely the sound of her name made his panic spike. It was too close. She was too close. His multiplication tables weren't working anymore, so Cole started reading the license plates of passing cars, reciting each letter and numeral in his head.

A battered station wagon came off the entrance ramp ahead of him and Cole was forced to slow as he caught up to it. Reading the license plate, he happened to glance at the bumper sticker.

I'm not as think as you drunk I am.

A finger of ice slid down his spine. They had once owned a car with a bumper sticker exactly like that, an Earl Ramsey witticism. The coincidence felt like an omen, and Cole broke out in a sweat.

He glanced back at it.

I brake for no apparent reason.

Blinking, he read it again. The fact that he'd hallucinated scared him more than if it'd been real.

God, what was wrong with him?

An eighteen-wheeler roared by in the left lane, making the car shimmy, and Cole realized he was holding his breath. He hated those trucks, hated to see them looming in his rearview mirror. His heart rapped in his chest like a fist on a door.

Grasping the fact that he was on the verge of another panic attack, Cole jerked his car onto the next exit ramp. By the time he found himself in a department store parking lot, he was shaking.

"Come on, Kaitlyn." He jerked open his car door and shoved a baseball cap on his head. "Let's go in here and find your mom a present."

Cole glanced down at his jeans, thankful the dark stain wasn't that noticeable on the black denim. It wouldn't have mattered, though. He had to get away from her.

"My name is Kacie, not Kaitlyn," the little girl said, shocking him when she took his hand. Her fingers were warm in his, and Cole made a mistake. He stared down at her—and fell through the looking glass.

"C'mon, Cole," Kaitlyn begged, tugging on his hand. "Let's go play."

The asphalt of the parking lot disappeared, replaced by the seedy backyard of the rental house he'd grown up in.

People stood around, poking through the things displayed on a picnic table, through the clothes stacked on the blankets on the grass. His mother was talking to old lady Henderson from next door, and she smiled at him when she caught him looking.

"Katie, come here," she said. "Quit pestering Cole."

"It's okay, Mom," Cole heard himself say. "I'll watch her."

Kaitlyn tripped, and Cole bent to tie her shoe. Her shoes were always coming untied. Alex got tired of tying laces, saying she was old enough to tie her own shoes, but Cole didn't mind. Kaitlyn was impressed by his knot tying.

She clamored up on the swing and commanded Cole to push her higher and higher, squealing when he did. Her hair glimmered in the sun, as shiny and pale as an angel's, and he wished he had blond hair like that. His belly itched, and he hoped he wasn't getting the chicken pox like Alex.

"Kitty!" Kaitlyn yelled. "Stop the swing."

Cole frowned at the cat. He had a niggling feeling something was wrong. It was a scruffy ball of fur and bones that his father had been threatening to shoot for getting into the garbage. He knew he shouldn't let her play with it, but Kaitlyn was already down, running towards it.

"Don't grab its tail, or it'll scratch you," Cole warned. He felt a little sorry for the kitten. It was probably hungry, and maybe thirsty too. He was searching for something to put some water in when he saw it.

A bird's nest.

Walking toward it, Cole heard the cheep-cheep of the baby birds.

Don't go over there.

Cole frowned again. The voice in his head was loud and clear, and he jerked his head around. Kaitlyn was climbing out the hole in the fence, chasing that cat.

"Katie!" he shouted, but she paid him no heed. Cole sprinted after her.

He wriggled through the hole in the fence, tearing his shirt. Kaitlyn stumbled, then righted herself and resumed the chase.

Cole could hear the eighteen-wheeler coming. Its air brake whooshed when it hit the hill below their house.

"Katie!" he shouted again. He felt his heart stutter as she neared the road.

He could almost reach her, almost touch her. His hands skimmed the back of her jacket.

Then he had her.

Cole yanked her jacket, sending her skidding backward onto the asphalt as he felt the wind off the passing vehicle hit his face.

Asphalt.

Shaken, he glanced down at the girl on the asphalt. Kacie stared at him with huge eyes.

"Mister!" a woman's voice cried. "Is she okay?"

Dazed, Cole glanced up at the woman rushing over to them.

"Thank God you caught her. That maniac didn't even slow down. He would've run right over her."

"I'm okay." Kacie stood and dusted off her jeans.

Feeling suddenly weak, Cole squatted down beside her and leaned against a parked car. His heart leapt in his throat when she threw her arms around his neck. Awkwardly, he started to pat her hair, but she was already pulling away by then.

"Let's go," she said. "Find Mom a present."

The woman laughed and nodded at Cole. "I think he's already given your mom a present today." Then she turned and walked away.

Cole left Kacie in the toy section, surprising himself by kissing the top of her head. "Be right back," he said.

As he headed past the registers, he told the elderly greeter at the door, "There's a little blond girl in the toy section. I think she's lost."

He knew he'd been captured on their surveillance tapes, but he also knew they were generally poor quality. He'd kept his head down, and now all he could hope was that no one would recognize him. He had never met Laura's second husband, so maybe no one could connect him.

Even though it was out of his way, Cole drove home to shower and shave. It gave him such a sense of peace to step inside his own door that he briefly considered staying here. But he had come too far now. He had to find Jessica.

Thumbing through the yellow pages, he punched in the number for Blake Airlines. "Yeah," he said. "When's your next flight to Nashville?"

A few hours later, he was on a plane. The flight was long and, even though he was desperately tired, Cole was wired, unable to sleep for the first half of the trip. Then he finally *did* go to sleep, and what a mistake that turned out to be.

Even his dreams were haunted. Visions of Jessica, Alex, and his son played in his head. Images of bloody hands in a dead man's kitchen. Images of a tiny shoe in the middle of the highway.

Cole didn't mean to hurt the flight attendant, but she shouldn't have touched him while he was asleep. By the time he realized what he was doing, she was on her knees beside him, and another attendant was trying to pry his fingers loose from his death grip on her wrist.

Cole was tired and irritable when he exited the plane; his brief nap only succeeded in making him feel worse.

He managed a smile and another apology to the flight attendant, who smiled back but watched him with wary eyes.

It was embarrassing. He hated calling attention to himself, and he could only imagine what he looked like. His eyes were grainy, and his perspiration-soaked clothing clung to him.

Hazy remnants of his dream nagged at Cole and, as he stood outside the rental car agency, he was suddenly afraid to look in the plate glass window, afraid he would have no reflection.

In the dream, Alex had stolen his identity. Lived in his house with his wife and his son. Cole had tried to confront them, tried to claim what was his, but they had ignored him like he wasn't there. Frustrated by his inability to touch or talk to them, he'd looked in the huge beveled mirror in his living room and had seen nothing at all.

Forcing himself to look in the window, Cole stared at his own reflection. The man staring back at him looked tired, but no worse than the average traveler. He looked real.

"I am real, dammit," he whispered. "And when I come for what's mine, they'll know it."

Chapter 10

Jessica lay quietly with her back turned to him, and even though Alex held her in his arms, he could sense her distance. He pulled her a little closer and wished he could read her mind. Wished he could ease her doubts. Finally, unable to stand the silence any longer, he asked, "Are you sorry?"

"No."

She said it quickly, and a sense of relief stole over him.

"I love you, Jess. We can make this work."

"I want to believe that," she said, and he was shocked to hear the tears in her voice. He sat up in the bed and grabbed her shoulder. He gently pulled her over onto her back and stared down at her. Moonlight streamed through the window. It illuminated her face and the glittery path of her tears.

"Why are you crying?" he asked softly, tucking a curl behind her ear.

"I just realized that, as much as I care about you, as wonderful as it is to be here with you, nothing has changed. No matter what we do or what we feel, Cole is coming for me."

"I won't let him hurt you. I won't let him destroy us," Alex said, a little hurt by her words.

"How can you promise that? Are you going to give up your life, go on the run with Joe and me?"

"If that's what it takes." Alex blurted out the words, but as soon as he said them, he knew them to be true. He'd give up everything, walk away from his life and his job to be with Jessica.

Leaning to kiss her, he said, "Trust me."

"I'm trying," Jessica replied, and gave him a weak smile.

He made love to her again, trying to convey his feelings with every touch and every kiss.

He loved her.

As improbable as it sounded, Alex knew he did. Maybe he always had. And he knew he could never let her go.

Long after Jessica drifted off to sleep, Alex lay awake, watching her. His mind raced, trying to find a way out for them.

What *were* they going to do?

His thoughts kept coming back to his twin. Jessica was convinced that Cole was coming to kill her. Could she be right? Was his brother really a murderer? Cole had broken into her sister's house, but he had left her unharmed. Surely, if he was as intent on murdering Jessica as she thought, he wouldn't leave behind a witness, especially one that could tip them off. It simply didn't make sense.

At the hospital, Jessica had told him about her grandfather, how the man had threatened Cole in front of Jessica. How he had died the next day. But the coroner had ruled it an accident, a frail old man who'd fallen down his cellar stairs and broken his neck.

What if it had been just an accident?

Although he'd never voice the thought, he wondered if Jessica's fear of Cole had vilified him enough to go from an abusive husband to a murderer. Maybe the best thing to do would be to set up a meeting with Cole in a neutral place and feel out the situation.

But then there was Joe.

Alex had been hesitant to mention it to Jessica, but there was a very good chance she could lose custody of Joe if Cole decided to take her to court. After all, she was the one living under a false identity. She had nothing to document his abuse. It would be her word against his.

His gut clenched at the thought, because he knew Jessica would do anything to keep Cole from getting custody of their son.

Anything.

Alex was awake when the first rays of morning light

streamed through the window. He traced slow, lazy circles on Jessica's bare back with his fingers and grinned when her eyelids fluttered open.

"Good morning." He said, and began to knead her shoulders.

"Morning," she said sleepily, arching her neck like a cat to give him access to it. "Um, you know how to endear yourself, don't you?"

"I'm smart like that." He deepened his massage. Jessica gave a contented sigh as he worked out the knots in her muscles. His hands traveled a slow journey down her back, over the delightful curve of her rear end and down those long legs.

"God, you're beautiful," he murmured. He was sitting on the end of the bed, massaging the balls of her feet, when Jessica pulled away from him. She swung her legs over the side of the bed, stood, and gave him a seductive smile as she walked toward him. When she stood before him, Alex twisted around to face her, hanging his feet off the bed. Jessica climbed into his lap, straddling him, and slowly lowered herself onto his shaft.

There was something so perfect, so intimate about making love like that. Face-to-face, bare chests grazing each other as she slid up and down. When Jessica's movements became more frantic, Alex gripped the edge of the mattress so hard he thought he might rip the cover off. His mouth was on her throat, and Alex felt the cry building inside her before he could hear it. Releasing his grip on the mattress, he grasped her hips and pistoned her faster, deeper. When Jessica seized a fistful of his hair, he felt the sudden tension in her body and kissed her hard as he gave a final thrust that sent them both spiraling over the edge.

Alex rested his head on Jessica's chest, enjoying the sound of her heart pounding in his ear. She kissed the top of his head and gently raked her fingernails down his back.

"Careful," he warned. "You'll get me all excited again. It's awfully early for all this."

"What time is it?" She lifted her head to peer at the clock. "It's 5:40? You got me up at 5:40 in the morning?"

"City girl." Alex gave her a playful swat on the behind. They disentangled themselves and crawled back under the sheets. Alex cradled her against him and thought of how *right* this felt.

Reluctant to move, he said, "I need to run to town and get a few things to make breakfast. Want to come?"

"Think I'll stay here and get a shower," she said with a yawn.

"I was hoping you'd wait for me." He brushed her hair back from her forehead. "I won't be gone long. When I get back, we can shower, and I'll cook you breakfast. By that time, Joe should be up, and we'll give him a call."

"Okay." She kissed his chest before snuggling back into her pillow. "Hurry back."

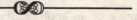

"Squirrelly Creek Road." Cole snorted.

What kind of hole-in-the-wall place was this? He'd had the presence of mind to rent a truck, but he realized his mistake now in not getting a four-wheel drive. With a frown, he looked back down at the directions he'd scribbled.

It'd been easier than he'd expected to get an address from the telephone number Jessica had given Laura. The age of technology and all that. Before Cole had left California, he'd been able to get reverse directions and a printout of the area courtesy of the county assessor's office. But as the gravel road dwindled away, Cole was beginning to wonder if he'd somehow gotten lost.

Surely, people didn't live like this, even in Backwater, Tennessee.

Cole stopped when he at the edge of a yawning mud hole that looked as if it could swallow the little rental truck whole. Cursing, he looked at the map again and realized he didn't have far to go. He'd just have to make a slight change of plans. Pulling to the side of the narrow road, Cole pocketed the keys and started walking.

Finally, he spotted it. The dead pine was close enough to the road, but it was leaning the wrong way. With some effort, Cole managed to angle it toward the road. It wasn't that big of a tree, but it took all his body weight to ride it down to the ground. It started lifting as soon as he climbed off it, and he had to wrestle with it a few minutes more until the road was blocked.

Now there would be no escape for them.

The rumble of an approaching vehicle startled Cole. He wasn't expecting any movement from them at this time of morning. He scrambled out of sight behind the fallen tree and searched for anything he could use as a weapon. Before the engine stopped, he was able to snap off a branch big enough to use as a crude club. He heard the slam of a door and dared a peek to see who was approaching.

It was Alex, and he was alone.

Cole's heart was racing, and he tried to tell himself that he had no choice. Alex deserved what he got for lying to him. Alex was stealing his life. Stealing his family . . .

Alex muttered something unintelligible as he hopped from the truck and started tugging on the tree. Cole moved quickly and rounded the tree to catch his brother by surprise. Alex's head flew around at the last instant, giving his brother a startled look before Cole slammed the club into his lower back. The blow sent Alex sprawling onto the ground, kicking up a cloud of dust. He tried to scramble under the tree, but Cole was quicker. He administered a punishing blow across Alex's shoulders.

Dropping his club, Cole grabbed Alex's leg and jerked his twin out into the open. Alex seemed dazed, offering no resistance, so Cole was surprised by the swiftness of his attack. He felt Alex's foot hook behind his leg, then found himself tumbling backward. Instinctively, he threw his hands out to break his fall and heard something pop in his left wrist.

"Cole, don't do this!" Alex pleaded as he struggled to his feet.

"You're the one who's done this!" Cole screamed, outraged.

Jumping to his feet, he lowered his head and charged.

His head caught Alex in the midsection, and Cole heard the breath whoosh out of him as they fell to the ground. Tumbling over and over in the scratchy foliage, Cole managed a swift uppercut that sent blood spurting from Alex's nose, covering them both.

Unbelievably, Alex was gaining the upper hand and for the first time, Cole was afraid. Alex straddled him, fighting to hold his arms down. A rock bit into Cole's back, making him cry out.

"It doesn't have to be like this. Don't do something you'll regret." Alex leaned over him, and Cole gave another cry of revulsion as his brother's blood dripped into his face.

With a strength born of desperation, Cole lunged to his left and threw Alex off. Reaching behind him, Cole pawed through the undergrowth and grunted with satisfaction when his hand closed on the rock. Windmilling his arm, he crashed it against the back of Alex's skull. Instantly, Alex collapsed. No faking it this time.

Cole raised the rock high above his head, intent on finishing off his brother, but he faltered when he stared into his twin's bloody face. It was disconcerting to look into the face so like his own, to know he was going to be his brother's executioner. Although he hadn't really talked to Alex in years, Cole felt a sudden rush of emotion for his twin.

Once they had been close, the Ramsey brothers against the world.

He remembered the summer of Freddie Harmon.

For some unknown reason—it sure wasn't money, because the Ramseys were as close to poor white trash as it got in their neighborhood—Freddie, a belligerent fifth grader with a cruel streak, had waited on Cole every day after baseball practice. He would demand money that Cole couldn't produce, then would gleefully knock him around instead.

Alex had been forced by their father to choose between baseball and football that year and wasn't around when Cole had to take that long walk down Lindley Avenue.

Cole couldn't tell anyone what was going on. Not that he was ashamed Freddie could get the better of him—he was only a second grader and Freddie outweighed him by about fifty pounds—but because he knew what his father's reaction would be.

Earl Ramsey expected his boys to be tough. He and Alex had learned before they were five that Ramseys never, ever cried. His father wouldn't accept that he didn't have a chance of beating the bigger boy. Earl would never let it rest until Cole had his pound of flesh, and Cole knew that wouldn't be any time soon.

Then one day, something miraculous happened. Freddie had him cornered between two apartment buildings and was threatening to beat the life out of him when Alex strode out of the shadows.

"Then you'll have to beat both of us," he'd said. Cole had never loved anyone more than he did his brother at that moment.

Of course, Freddie had, but it hadn't been as much fun with two Ramsey boys kicking, scratching and biting at him. For three days, Alex showed up when Cole was walking home. For three days, Freddie beat the crap out of them, but then it was over. As bullies often do, he moved on to easier prey.

Alex was so still.

Holding his breath, Cole pressed his fingers to Alex's throat and was relieved to feel the faint strain of his pulse.

This was Jessica's fault. All this was because of her. She had fooled his brother just like she had fooled him.

With a grimace, Cole tossed the rock aside and stared at his hands. Once again, they were covered with a sibling's blood. Although part of him was horrified by it, Cole was unable to stop the tear that slid down his nose as he smoothed his brother's hair.

"Why did you have to help her?" he asked in frustration, and pulled Alex's head into his lap.

Bleakness surrounded him, and Cole felt sick inside. Even the blue seemed to bleed from the sky, leaving it a lifeless gray. He thought again of the boys they'd been and wished he could go back to that time. There were so many things he'd change, so many things he'd say. But it was too late.

He could feel it in his bones. There was no hope for him now. No chance of redemption. The innocence of his youth had slipped away and now there was nothing left of the boy he'd been, nothing left of his mind or his soul.

In a moment of calm and utter clarity, he knew he was going to die soon. He accepted that, maybe even welcomed it. Death held no power over him. But before he died, he was going to make Jessica pay. She would pay for Alex's death.

Before he died, he wanted to hold his son in his arms and tell Joe he loved him and that he was sorry.

So sorry.

Whether he blacked out or simply fell asleep, Cole couldn't say. The only thing he knew for sure when he awakened was that Alex was gone.

Pushing himself to his feet, Cole winced at the pain in his wrist. He scanned the area and exhaled in relief when he spotted Alex sprawled face first on the ground near the truck. He hadn't been able to warn Jessica.

Stumbling over to him, Cole was a little surprised to see that Alex was still alive. The leaves around his head were stained with blood, and his face was white as chalk.

"I'm sorry, Alex," Cole said softly as he grabbed his brother's arm and dragged him toward the hill he'd spotted. It wasn't much of a drop off, but it should deter someone as wounded as Alex. Breathing hard from his effort, Cole nudged Alex with his boot and sent his brother rolling down the hill to rest in the shallow mud hole below.

Cole staggered to Alex's old truck and climbed inside. When the engine roared to life, he turned the truck around and headed back toward the cabin. Fury was building within him, and her name beat a steady tattoo in his head.

He had a date to keep with his late wife.

Jessica was awakened by the low rumble of Alex's truck. Glancing at the clock, she was surprised to find she'd been asleep for nearly an hour. Alex's massage and lovemaking had left her lethargic. She smiled to herself as she heard the front door open and rolled over on her stomach, turning her face into her pillow. That massage had felt pretty good, and she thought she could talk him into another one.

Several minutes passed before she heard the bedroom door creak open and heard his footsteps stop at the end of the bed.

"It's about time," she grumbled good-naturedly. "I'm hungry."

He sat on the edge of the bed and started massaging the ball of her foot.

"Um, that's nice." She sighed and said, "Keep that up, and I'll cook breakfast for *you*."

His hands slowly made their way up her legs, kneading her calf muscles. His mouth replaced his hand, kissing the soft flesh in the bend of her knee. Jessica gave another contented sigh, then suddenly, his hands and mouth were everywhere. Grasping, kneading, nipping. He was getting a little rough—too rough—and Jessica cried out when he bit the inside of her thigh.

"Easy!" she said, and started to twist around, but Alex's hand was on her shoulder, holding her down.

In one instant, one breath, Jessica noticed two things. The faint odor of tobacco. The absence of Alex's stubble raking across her skin as he kissed her.

Instead of a scream, the only sound she could make was a horrified whoosh as her lungs emptied. When the hand on her shoulder abruptly released her, Jessica jerked her head around . . .

. . . and found herself staring into Cole's blood spattered face.

When he grinned, her first thought was—how? How could she have ever mistaken Alex for Cole?

The face looming before hers was like a demonic caricature of Alex. The cruel smile, the madness glinting in his eyes.

He was nothing like Alex.

Alex.

Oh, God.

He was in Alex's truck.

She felt the familiar tightening in her chest.

"What—" she wheezed. "What—"

" 'What' what?" Cole said irritably, propping up on an elbow to stare at her. "Is that all you have to say after all these years? No 'hi, honey. How've you been?' No 'I'm sorry for all the years I stole from you with your son?' "

"What . . . have you done . . . with Alex?" she managed, feeling tears sting her eyes as she fought for her next breath. There was blood all over him, all over his face, his shirt, and his hands.

Alex's blood?

"Am I my brother's keeper?" Cole's voice was neutral,

and his calmness terrified her.

Black spots danced before her eyes, and Jessica made a desperate lunge for the purse she'd left on the nightstand.

Cole was quicker, however. He snatched it from her hand and prowled through it until he found her inhaler, then held it just out of her reach, taunting her with it.

"An asthma attack. That's what the autopsy report said. Do you know how I agonized over that? How I beat myself up for not being there to save you?"

"Please," she wheezed, and held out her hands in supplication.

"I think I'll watch you die," Cole said, his eyes hardening. "Right here, right now. And this time there won't be any miraculous resurrection. Maybe I'll use the ax out front, cut you into little pieces and scatter you over the property." He smiled again and said, "All the king's horses and all the king's men won't be able to put Jessica back together again."

Just when she thought it was over, that he was really going to let her die, Cole tossed her the inhaler. Jessica clutched it greedily and took a treatment.

"No, I can't let you off that easy," he said. "No passing out and fading away. You don't deserve such an easy death."

Cole frowned at the rumpled sheets. "Geez, Jessica. My own brother? Don't you think that's a little crass?" He ran a hand up her bare thigh and said, "What's the matter? Did you get to missing the real thing?"

Repulsed, Jessica jerked away from him, and his

laughter was as brittle and sharp as glass. Cole grabbed the sheet and ripped a long section from it, then attempted to seize her wrists.

"Just so you don't get any ideas."

Jessica slapped at him and tried to roll off the side of the bed to escape, but a solid uppercut to her jaw stopped her cold. By the time she was able to shake off the fog, Cole had tied her wrists to the bedposts.

"There!" he said, satisfied. "Now, we can talk."

She was still wheezing. Cole held the inhaler to her lips and nudged her with it until she opened her mouth to take another treatment.

Dumping the contents of her purse on the bed, Cole pawed through her things. Jessica's heart sank when he opened her billfold and smiled down at the picture of Joe she carried inside.

"Where is he?" Cole asked. "I thought he'd be here with you. I'm anxious to meet him."

"You'll never get him," she spat, relieved the asthma attack was fading. "He's somewhere safe . . . somewhere you'll never find him."

Cole chuckled. "Let me guess. He's with Kate and that prissy fool she married."

Jessica blanched, and he continued, "Really. Where else could he be? I know he's not at Laura's—and by the way, since she can't tell you herself, I know she was really sorry about having to help me find you. Don't blame her. I kind of forced her hand."

"What do you mean?" Jessica whispered, feeling the

blood drain from her face.

"Laura's dead," he said as casually as if he were announcing the time.

"Nooooo!" Jessica howled.

"Yessss!" Cole mocked. He lay back on the bed, resting the back of his head in his hands and staring up at the ceiling with a satisfied smile on his face. "She had it coming a long time. I hated her from the moment we met, you know that? But I tried. I tried because of you."

"But I talked to her—"

"Yeah, I know." He studied his fingernails. "I was standing right beside her with a knife at her throat. She was really pretty convincing, huh? Found out everything I needed to know."

"Kacie?"

Cole's eyes narrowed. "She's fine," he snapped. "What do you think I am?"

"Alex?" she asked, hardly daring to breathe.

Cole lunged at her and seized her by the throat. "Don't say his name. Don't say it," he said through gritted teeth. "You turned him against me. Alex paid for your betrayal."

Her heart plummeted when Cole released her throat and fumbled in his pocket for cigarettes. Jessica noticed him wince as he moved his left wrist, then dropped it to use the other one. Maybe she'd have the chance to use it against him. Maybe . . .

Cole stared at the cigarette for a long moment without lighting it, then glanced at Jessica with anguished blue eyes.

"Why?" he demanded. "Why did you do that to me? I loved you. I *trusted* you." His voice grew louder, more agitated when he said, "My father warned me about you, but I wouldn't listen. I went against him to marry you, but he was right. You're just like her. You're just like . . . *her*."

He drove his fist into Jessica's side, and she heard the sickening sound of her own bone snap. She cried out, and Cole jumped to his feet to pace in front of the bed. "Why do you make me hurt you? Did I ask that much of you? Why did you do it? WHY?" he leaned down, shouting in her face.

"I was afraid . . . you'd . . . you'd kill me," she gasped. "Afraid you'd . . . kill him."

"I would never hurt him." Cole was livid, pointing his finger in her face. "I would *never* hurt him."

He scowled at her as he gestured at the rumpled bed. "Did you sleep with Bennett too? Is that why he helped you? I wondered about that, but he swore you didn't."

"You talked to Matt?" Her stomach lurched, and Jessica thought she might throw up.

"Yes." Cole's eyes glittered. "I looked up your old buddy Bennett. I know all the details. How you faked it. How you laid there on that table pretending to be a damned corpse while my heart was being ripped out."

"I never meant to hurt you, Cole. I never—"

"I bet you laughed. I bet you all laughed at how stupid I was, how easy I was to deceive. Well, Bennett's not laughing now."

"He's dead," Jessica said flatly. She felt cold inside. Numb. So many people were dead. Because of her . . . because of Cole.

"Yeah, he's dead." Cole lit his cigarette and took an angry drag on it. "He begged for his life. Just like you are going to beg for yours."

"Will that make you happy?" she asked. "To make me beg?"

"I don't know," Cole said with a cold smile. "Why don't we find out?"

He touched the glowing tip of his cigarette to the inside of her thigh.

Water.

He was lying in water.

Alex tried to lift his head, but it was too heavy. He gagged at the taste of blood and dirt in his mouth. The putrid mud clung to him and sucked him back down when he tried to move. Clenching his teeth, Alex forced himself to sit up. The world swam crazily, and Alex fought against the blackness that sought to reclaim him. He had to get to Jessica.

How long had he been unconscious? How long had she been alone with Cole?

He tried to focus on his watch, but he was unable to discern the blurring numbers.

Move, dammit.

Move.

Grasping a handhold among the slippery leaves, Alex began the tedious climb over the hill and realized he was still near the site of Cole's ambush.

The cabin was only a quarter of a mile away.

He had to get to her.

Struggling to his feet, Alex lurched down the narrow road with his arms stretched out in front of him in an effort to keep his balance.

I must look like a zombie in a George Romero flick, he thought crazily.

But this was no movie.

And as he rounded the final bend to the cabin, he was terrified of what he would find waiting there.

Chapter 11

Jessica gritted her teeth and tried not to scream again. She was determined not to give Cole the satisfaction. A fine sheen of perspiration coated her face as she tried to ignore the mindless throbbing of the cigarette burn. The smell of burnt flesh gagged her.

"What have you told Joe about me?" Cole asked, sitting on the edge of the bed to inspect his handiwork.

"Nothing."

Cole gave her a skeptical look. "Nothing? I find that hard to believe."

"It's true." She took a deep breath, fighting nausea, and winced when a pain shot through her side.

"Is he smart? That drug you took to trick me, did it hurt him?"

"No! The drug didn't cross the placenta. I wouldn't

have risked that."

"Seems to me you risked an awful lot." He shot her an accusing glance. "Have you raised my son in poverty?"

Anger surged within her, and she forgot to curb her tongue. Forgot what a mistake it was to antagonize him.

"You think everything is about money, don't you? I've taken care of *my* son. *My* son has always had enough to eat and enough to wear. I may not have been able to give him everything, but I've loved him. And that's worth more than all your money."

"Love," Cole sneered. "Love. What a crock. I bet you really liked my mother. She was always spouting crap like that. Well, let me tell you something, Jess. Love doesn't mean a thing. Love didn't help when my brother and sister and I lay huddled in the same bed, trying to stay warm in that shack I grew up in. Love sure didn't make it any easier when the other kids made fun of us for the holes in our shoes and our Salvation Army clothes. And love didn't mean a damn thing when my baby sister was screaming because a rat crawled on the couch and bit her while she was taking a nap."

"I'm sorry—"

"Don't feel sorry for me," he interrupted, narrowing his eyes. "Don't you ever pity me. I got out. And I was determined that no child of mine would ever live like that, but the fact is, I don't know what Joe's seen. What he's had to live in. I hate you for that."

He shook his head and said, "You know, my mother's a hypocrite. She was always talking about how family was everything and we would make it if we only stayed together. Well, the first chance she got—*the first opportunity*—she high-tailed it out of there. To hell with love and to hell with me."

"She asked you to go with her."

Pain shone in his eyes, and Jessica wasn't so cold she couldn't feel compassion for the boy he'd been. What a strange realization that the man who'd dispensed such pain and horror in her life had suffered in his as well.

Cole snorted. "Yeah, that's right. She can always argue that, can't she? But you know what the truth was? The truth was she left me long before that day. I know she told you about Ka—" Cole froze for a moment, a troubled look crossing his face. He cleared his throat.

He can't even say her name, Jessica realized.

"—my sister. My mother can pretend all she wants, but she never forgave me. It didn't matter that I loved my sister. It didn't matter that I would've given anything if it'd been me instead of her. She hated me. I could sense it."

He shook his head again and gave a wry laugh. "It's kind of like when you're out walking and a strange dog jumps out in front of you, baring its teeth. And you go, 'Nice doggie. Good boy' and all the while you're reaching behind you, trying to find something to club it with. That's what I felt when my mother looked at me. She was just biding her time, waiting until she could get rid of the screw-up, the kid who got his sister killed and couldn't stop washing his fucking hands."

Jessica tried to steel her heart, tried not to feel compassion for him, but all she could think of was that little boy. A little boy maybe not much different from her own son, who felt consumed by guilt and alienated from his mother's love.

"Why didn't you ever tell me?" she asked, tears stinging her eyes. "I would've stood by you. We could've gotten you help. We can still get you help."

"Help? So, now I'm crazy." Cole raked a hand down his face and grimaced when his hand found the blood on his forehead.

The vulnerable look on his face disappeared, chased away by his scowl. "Why am I talking about this with you?" he muttered. "You're just another lying bitch, like her."

Taking a long drag on his cigarette, he blew the smoke in her face. Helplessly, Jessica started coughing. Each cough sent a white-hot bolt stabbing into her side. She hated smoke. It gagged her and wreaked havoc with her asthma. It was such a strange habit for a man like Cole to have.

Nausea burned in her throat, and she tried to fight it back, but when he blew another puff of smoke in her direction, she jerked her head and vomited. Some of it splattered on Cole's shirt. He jumped up and gave a startled cry of revulsion.

He carefully peeled the shirt off, and Jessica found herself staring at the panther. When she and Cole first became lovers, she had thought his tattoo was sexy. He could flex his chest muscle, and the big cat would look like it was going to pounce. Now, it looked demonic, a yellow-eyed creature that stalked her dreams.

Cole opened Alex's closet and jerked a black T-shirt off the rack. He stared at it for a long moment before he pulled it over his head.

"Screw this," he said sullenly. "I'm tired of talking to you. I have to find my son."

He pulled a knife from his pocket and flicked it open to reveal a shiny, wicked blade. Jessica's heart stuttered in her chest.

"Until death do us part, honey," he smiled and Jessica screamed.

Jessica's scream startled Alex. He tripped on the front steps and barely caught himself before his face smacked into the deck.

What was going on in there?

Fear spurred him on, and he stumbled toward the door. It was too late for caution. He twisted open the door, half-falling through it.

"Cole, please don't—"

The panic in her voice sickened him, but he also felt a surge of exhilaration.

Thank God, she was still alive!

They were in his bedroom.

Steadying himself on the edge of the sofa, he fumbled open the end-table drawer and removed the revolver.

Alex was halfway down the hall when Jessica

screamed again.

He rushed into the bedroom, clicking off the safety on the gun. His heart pounded, his pulse thundered.

Please, God, let her be unharmed.

The scene before him stole his breath. Cole standing over a naked Jessica, preparing to cut her throat.

"Drop it!" he shouted, and Cole's head jerked upward in surprise. He took an involuntary step backward, and seemed to realize his mistake.

"Stay away from her." Alex entered the doorway and circled around the other side of the bed. Cole hesitated, then started back toward Jessica.

"Don't do it! I swear I'll shoot you, and I don't want to."

"Alex, you're alive."

Jessica was sobbing. Alex wanted to look at her, to make sure she was okay, but he didn't dare look away from Cole, who poised like a rattlesnake ready to strike. His vision blurred for a second, and he nearly panicked. He took another step toward the bed. Cole dropped the knife and slowly raised his hands.

"Shoot him, Alex. Shoot him!" Jessica cried.

Cole winced, but never broke eye contact. He took a step backward, away from the bed.

He took another.

"Shoot him!" Jessica screamed, the fear in her voice replaced by anger. "For God's sake, Alex, shoot him."

As he looked into his twin's eyes, it tore at Alex that

they had come to this. Strangers, staring at each other across not only a bedroom, but across all the years they'd been separated. He was looking at his brother—the person who'd once been his best friend, his most trusted confidante—and his finger was on the trigger.

It would take less than two pounds of pressure to shoot his brother in the heart.

Alex would never know for sure what his twin saw in his face at that moment, but Cole smiled.

And ran from the room.

He heard Cole's footsteps pounding down the hall and the bang of the screen door. The sound of his old truck roaring to life. As the roar faded to a low rumble, Alex looked at Jessica.

She looked away.

"Jess, are you okay?" he asked softly. He climbed on the bed and used his pocket knife to saw through her restraints.

"He killed her. He killed my sister, and he killed my friend Matt." Her voice was bitter. A tear escaped her eye, tracing a path down her face before hanging precariously on her chin. Spotting the huge red knot on her jaw, Alex's guts twisted.

"He taunted me with it, how he'd forced Laura to help him."

"Maybe he was lying," Alex offered, but he didn't believe it himself. Now, it made sense. He'd wondered how Cole had found them. He finally managed to cut through the shirt Cole had used to tie her, and Jessica sat up in the bed, gingerly inspecting her thigh.

"What did he do to you?" Alex whispered, his stomach lurching. He reached for her, but she was already climbing off the other side of the bed. He scrambled after her and gently caught hold of her wrist. "Jess, talk to me."

He touched her face, turned it toward him. She only met his gaze for a second, but Alex was stunned by the fury he saw there.

Jessica opened her mouth as if to speak, and clamped it shut again. Staring into the space over his shoulder, she frowned.

"You're bleeding."

She pulled on one of his shirts and disappeared into the bathroom. She emerged a moment later with an armload of supplies.

He could feel it. The fissure in their relationship that was growing deeper by the minute. Alex let her clean his face and doctor the gash on his head, trying to think of something—*anything*—he could say to fix things before it was too late. Even though she was touching him, he could feel her distance. A coldness that wasn't there before.

"I've got it bandaged, but you need stitches. We need to go to the hospital. Call the police. He's after Joe. Maybe they can set a trap for him."

"Jess . . ." Alex was sick inside, knowing what he was about to say wouldn't make things between them any better.

"I couldn't prove he killed my grandfather, but

surely—"

"Jess, we can't call the police."

Her eyes snapped back to his, and he saw incredulity in them. Incredulity that quickly turned to rage.

"You let him waltz right out of here, and now you don't even want to call the police? I don't believe you!"

"Jess, you don't understand—"

"I understand all right. I understand that I should never have trusted you. Blood is thicker than water, isn't that what they say?"

Alex flinched, but she was too angry to care. She wanted to hurt him.

"I'm sorry . . ."

"I was stupid to think you'd choose me over him."

"That's not fair." Pain shone in his eyes. "What was I supposed to do, shoot him in the back? He's my *brother*, Jess."

"You could've stopped him. This could've been over." Hot, bitter tears scalded her cheeks. "It could've been *over*. Now, he's going after Joe." She shook her head in disbelief. "So, he's your brother. If Cole had been the one with the gun, do you think for one moment that you'd still be alive?"

When Alex spoke, his voice was tight. "That's what I've been trying to tell you all along. I'm not Cole. I'm not a murderer, and that's what it would've been. Murder. He'd dropped the knife, Jess. He was unarmed, and I didn't have a clear shot." He paused and pulled a hand down his face. "I'm sorry I hurt you. I love you. When I said we couldn't call the police, I was thinking of you."

"Me?" she scoffed, and folded her arms across her chest.

"We can't go to the police without exposing you. We have no proof. Cole is a respected businessman with no prior police record. You faked your death and have been living and working under an assumed identity. If we go to the police, it will be your word against his, and without any proof, guess who they're going to believe? They could arrest you for fraud."

"But you could . . ."

"I could what? Say he tried to kill us? A lot of people would think he was justified."

"Justified?" she repeated, hurt.

"You see it on the talk shows all the time. To them, you'd be just another cheating wife. As his brother, I'd be worse than that."

"He killed my sister. I'm supposed to do nothing?"

Her ribs hurt. She jerked a change of clothes out of her bag, unable to look at Alex. She felt like a fool.

Worse, she felt betrayed.

"Look at me," Alex commanded, and she reluctantly turned to him.

The pain her movement caused nearly stole her breath. "What?"

"Let me talk to my sources, find out if the police have any physical evidence that can be used against Cole. If they do, we'll go to them and tell them everything."

"And if they don't?"

"If they don't, we'll have to find it ourselves." He touched her again and inclined his head like he meant to kiss her, but she pulled away from him.

"I won't let him get away with it, Jess," he said as she walked away.

She stopped in the doorway and gave him a thin, cold smile.

"I think you just did, Alex."

After pulling the spark plugs from Alex's truck, Cole walked the rest of the way to his rental.

He didn't have much time left and cursed himself for not cutting the telephone line when he left.

But they probably both had cell phones. Didn't everyone?

The idea struck him as he climbed behind the wheel of the truck, and he grinned.

He knew how to get Joe.

It was a plan and a good one, even if he had to walk all the way back to Alex's truck to get the keys out of the ignition. But it didn't take too long, and soon he was on his way.

Glancing at his face in the rearview mirror, Cole was shocked by his appearance. He looked like some sort of cannibal. Alex's blood and maybe some of his own streaked his face, and his dark hair was sticking up wildly. He couldn't go to a motel—assuming a hick place like this even *had* a motel—looking like this. They'd call the police as soon as he walked in the door.

Just before he got to the main highway, he saw it. A little wooden sign pointing the way to Grundy Lakes Campground. Maybe they had a public restroom. Maybe even a shower.

Cole was glad it was a week day. The campground looked fairly deserted, no tents and only a few campers that looked like they might stay there year round. One even had Christmas lights strung in front of it.

"It's the freaking middle of August," Cole muttered in disbelief.

The narrow road made a loop, and Cole found the restrooms at the far end of the circle. Some old codger was coming out of the men's room. He hitched his pants up around his armpits and gave a friendly wave in Cole's direction, but Cole ducked his head and pretended not to see him. He made a show of rummaging through his bag.

He waited outside a few more minutes, then decided the place was empty. The smell hit him when he opened the door, and Cole resisted the impulse to bolt.

There was nothing viler than a public restroom.

The smell of human waste and mildew and God only knew what else made his stomach churn, but Cole forced himself to take a tentative step forward. There was a shower at the end of the row, and the dingy curtain was pulled back to reveal a towel rack and a slimy cement floor.

"No way," Cole said in revulsion. "Not even with my

shoes on."

The idea of standing inside that bacteria-infested chamber naked was more than he could bear. He turned back to the sinks and hesitated.

They weren't any better than the shower.

He weighed his options, even considered breaking into one of the campers, but he was running out of time. He even thought about trying to find Grundy Lake, wherever it was, and just jumping in, but the police would find him by then.

Joe.

He had to do this for Joe.

Gritting his teeth, he jerked several paper towels out of the dispenser and used them to turn on the water in the sink. Dropping them on the floor beside similar wads of used paper towels, Cole removed his T-shirt and carefully stuffed it in the back of his waistband. If it fell out and hit the floor, he'd have to leave the damn thing.

Taking great pains not to touch the sink, Cole cupped his hands and doused his head with the lukewarm water.

After he'd done all he could do, he pulled the T-shirt back on and finger combed his hair. There was nothing he could do about his dirty jeans, and he wished he could burn his shoes. He walked out of the restroom without bothering to turn off the faucet.

Two motorcycles sat parked beside his truck. Their teenaged drivers headed toward him. Cole had the paranoid fear he hadn't cleaned up enough, that they would look at him and start yelling for someone to call the cops, but they barely glanced at him. Their two passengers were a different story.

One of the girls whispered something to the other, and they both giggled. Panic surged within him.

What did they see? What had he missed?

Cole mentally gauged the distance between them. Could he kill them both before they got away, before their boyfriends came back out?

Then one of them whistled.

Stunned, Cole could only stare at them.

They were just *flirting*.

He almost laughed. Dear God, was he that far removed from reality? He'd been ready to kill them . . .

Jessica had destroyed his self-confidence. It was nice to remember that some women didn't look at him like he was a monster. Some women wanted him. A slow grin spread across his face as he strolled over to them.

"Hey, girls. Can you give me directions to Monteagle? I'm sort of lost."

"I'd rather *show* you," one of them said, and gave him a bawdy wink.

Cole laughed.

"Where were you when I was seventeen?" he teased. "I think I'm a little old for you, and I don't want to go to jail today."

"I'm eighteen," the girl piped in, and the other one muttered, "Liar."

Cole heard their companions coming out of the

restroom. Their conversation died when they noticed him. The girls, realizing they'd been caught, gave him hasty directions. Cole thanked them and nodded at their boyfriends as he walked away.

He didn't need any trouble. Not now.

Alex and Jessica thought he was running. They'd never expect him to take the offensive. But he was through playing games.

He wanted his son, and he was prepared to destroy anyone who stood in his way.

The directions he'd been given were surprisingly good. In no time, he was standing in front of Ramsey/Boyd Detective Agency. A glance at the posted hours of business told him he had nearly forty minutes before the place opened. He wouldn't need that long.

Although Alex's key ring was huge and annoying because none of the keys were labeled, the third key slid smoothly into the lock. With a grunt of satisfaction, Cole twisted the knob and went inside. After taking care to lock the door behind him, he hesitated at the receptionist's desk and tried to guess which office was Alex's.

He tried the door on the left first. None of the keys fit.

Moving on to the door behind the reception area, he was beginning to wonder if Alex had another key ring somewhere when the last key turned the lock.

It was a nice office, decorated in soft grays and greens. His brother apparently did pretty well for himself. The big desk was a little messy, though. Cole wandered over and absently-mindedly straightened the haphazard stack of files while he scanned the room.

There it was. Alex's rolodex.

Cole faltered when he saw the picture beside it. It was the three of them, in their Halloween costumes.

Forgetting about the rolodex, he picked up the little gold frame. He remembered that Halloween. It was right before the end, right before his life went to hell.

He and Alex were a little big for trick or treating, but they'd gone to walk Kaitlyn around the neighborhood. She was so beautiful with her golden hair falling around her shoulders, dressed in a pink princess gown. She stood between a Zorro with a crooked moustache and a rakish looking pirate.

Cole chuckled, recalling how Alex had spent half the night chasing that damn little moustache around. It kept coming loose on one side, hanging like an exclamation point on his face. If he closed his eyes, he could still hear Kaitlyn's laughter.

God, it hurt to think of her.

He set the photo back, then picked it up again. He surprised himself when he slid the picture out and stuck it in his wallet.

A talisman, but one of good or evil?

Flipping through the rolodex, he frowned when he couldn't recall Kate's husband's name.

Wilson, Walker...

Watson. There it was.

He had to do this right. Pacing around the room, Cole

started talking to himself. It took him a few minutes, but he finally slowed the cadence of his speech to match Alex's drawl.

Cole knew it was close, but was it close enough?

He had the benefit of surprise. Kate would never expect him to call her. Taking a deep breath, he lifted the receiver and dialed his mother's cell phone number.

"Hello," she said, and Cole's heart fluttered. He didn't know if he could do this. He didn't know if he could talk to her.

"Hello?" she said again, and Cole forced himself to speak. He was grateful for the static crackling over the line.

"Mom? Mom, it's Alex."

"Alex. Is everything all right?"

So far, so good. Don't freak out. *Don't freak out.*

"Cole found us. We've got to get Joe and get out of here."

The other end of the line was silent, and Cole almost thought they'd been disconnected.

"Are . . . are you okay?"

"I'm okay."

Then she stunned him by asking, "Your brother? Is he okay?"

Swallowing over the lump in his throat, Cole said, "He's fine."

"Thank God," she whispered. "It kills me to think of either of you being hurt."

He couldn't stand this.

"Joe," he interrupted. "We need to get Joe. Tell me where to meet you."

"How about Jasper? Outside The Boxcar? We can be there in a couple of hours."

"Fine." He remember passing through Jasper on his way into town. He could find The Boxcar.

"I love you. Please be careful."

Cole hesitated. "I will."

Talking to her unnerved him, and Cole nearly forgot a crucial part of his plan.

"Mom, ditch your cell phone. I think that's how Cole tracked us down. Don't take it with you."

"He can do that?" she asked.

"I don't know, but I'd rather not take a chance."

"Of course. I'll leave it here."

He hung up with an audible sigh of relief. It had worked. He couldn't believe it. By the time Alex figured out what was going on, it would be too late.

He'd have his son.

Chapter 12

"Hurry up, will you?" Jessica muttered, and glared at the closed bathroom door. Her hasty shower had done little to wash away the contamination she felt from Cole's touch.

And then there was Alex.

What was wrong with her? What had she been thinking? It had been stupid to think she could be involved with someone that close to Cole and not be hurt.

Stupid, stupid, stupid. Would she never have any common sense at all where men were concerned?

Yes, she thought. *Because this is it. I'm never going through this again.*

Joe was the only thing that mattered. She was anxious to get to him. To hold him in her arms and know that he was safe.

But that was an illusion too.

Neither of them would ever be safe until Cole Ramsey was dead.

It didn't help her mood any that Alex hadn't been able to get his mother on the phone. There was no way Cole had time to find them yet, but her shattered nerves were screaming.

Walking to the living room, she looked at the phone. Tears stung her eyes as she lifted it to make the call she'd been avoiding.

"What city and listing?" the recorded voice asked.

"Los Angeles. Whelan Industries."

Her hand was shaking as she punched in the number and asked for Daniel Harmon.

"May I ask who's calling, please?"

"A friend," she blurted. "I heard about Laura."

"She's doing a little better," the woman said. "Daniel said she opened her eyes this morning, but she hasn't been able to talk yet."

Jessica fumbled the phone and nearly dropped it.

"What? What did you say?" she stammered. "Laura's alive?"

"Oh, honey, you thought she was dead?"

Overcome with emotion, Jessica tried to say something, but all that emerged was a squeak.

"She's at Memorial," his secretary said quickly. "Room 614. Do you want the number?"

"Yes," she managed, after realizing the woman couldn't

see her nod. She jotted it down on her hand and thanked the secretary.

"Thank God," she exclaimed, and punched in the number.

"What's going on?"

Alex appeared in the doorway, watching her with wary eyes, and Jessica forgot for a moment that she was mad at him. Forgot that she was never going to touch him again. She hurled herself in his arms.

"Laura's alive!" she said, hugging him. She still had the phone cradled against her ear and pulled away when the hospital switchboard picked up.

"614, please."

Daniel answered on the second ring. "Laura Harmon's room."

"Danny, it's me," Jessica said, relieved just to hear his voice.

"Jess! I'm so glad you called. I've been trying to find you, but nobody knew how to get in touch with you."

"Is she okay?"

"Hang on a sec," Laura's ex-husband said.

Jessica heard clattering in the background, then he was back. When he spoke again, his voice was low. "Sorry. I think Laura's asleep, but I moved over here just in case. She was in a coma when they found her, but started coming around this morning. She's lost about two weeks of prior memory, but she seems alert. She knew me and Kacie right away, but she's still a little foggy. We're waiting on the results of the latest EEG."

"Do you know what happened?" Jessica asked, her stomach rolling.

What had Cole done to her?

"Not yet," Danny said, and she heard the hesitation in his voice. "Someone broke into the house, but didn't seem to take anything. She wasn't . . ." Danny's voice trailed off, and Jessica heard him swallow. She knew how hard this must be for him. It was no secret that he was still in love with Laura.

"She wasn't raped, but someone threw her against the wall hard enough to crack her skull. Then he took Kacie."

The living room swam before her, and Jessica would've fallen if Alex hadn't grabbed her.

"Kacie?" she gasped.

"She's okay," Danny said. "He took her to some store and set her out unharmed. She didn't see Laura. Didn't know she was hurt."

"Are you sure?"

"I'm sure. He didn't do anything to Kacie, or she would've told me. She thought he was . . . nice." Jessica caught the bitterness in the last word, and her heart ached for him.

"Do they know who did it?"

"No. Kacie told the police the guy's name was Jose, and that he was her mom's boyfriend, but Laura wasn't dating anyone. At least, I don't think . . . I mean, we were even talking about getting back together."

"Maybe he only told her that to throw off the police."

Jessica tried to keep her voice neutral. Tried to keep her anger at bay.

"Maybe." Danny sounded dispirited. "But the police didn't find any sign of forced entry. In fact, they haven't found much of anything. No witnesses, nothing."

"Talk to Kacie. I bet she'd never seen the guy before. I bet he told her all that stuff to confuse the police."

"It's okay, Jess. You don't have to convince me to stick around. I love her. Even if he was her boyfriend, who am I to place blame? I'm the reason our marriage ended. If I'd been home more, been there for her and Kacie . . ."

"Don't do that, Danny. Don't beat yourself up."

He exhaled and said, "Okay. Hey, are you coming up? I know Laura would be thrilled to see you and Joe. So would Kacie and I."

"I'll be there as soon as I can," Jessica promised, irritated by the look of protest on Alex's face. If he thought Cole would frighten her away from her only sister, he had another think coming.

After a murmured goodbye, she hung up the phone and turned to Alex. She gave him a terse summary of what Daniel had told her.

"I'm so glad Laura is alive, but . . ."

"Let's go." Jessica cut him off. She was through doing things his way. "I want to see my son."

"You can't go to California. If Cole knows Laura is alive, he'll know—"

"I don't care what Cole knows or what he doesn't. My sister needs me, and I'm going to her."

She slung her bag over her shoulder and pushed past him. He trailed along behind her, punching numbers on his cell phone as they stepped out onto the deck.

"Still no answer," he said with a frown, and Jessica took a gulp of fresh air, trying to ease her sudden queasiness.

Since Cole had stolen the truck, they were forced to ride Alex's ATV out of the woods. Although she'd known the ride would be rough, Jessica hadn't anticipated how the bumps and jerks would affect her ribs. She had to bite her lip a couple of times to keep from crying out. Alex, although refusing to get stitches for himself, would force her to go to the nearest hospital to get checked out, and she didn't have time. Besides, she'd once been a nurse. She knew what little could be done for broken ribs and what symptoms to watch out for.

As long and horrible as the ride to town was, it was nothing compared to their wait at the rental agency. She was ready to throttle the snide little man behind the counter who kept shoving paperwork at them and staring at her breasts.

Finally, remarkably, they were on their way.

Alex cast a worried glance at Jessica. She was too pale. She sat ramrod straight in the seat with her lips pursed in a thin, grim line.

Every time he spoke, she bit his head off, but he couldn't blame her. He had begged her to trust him, and he had let her down.

But he didn't regret not killing Cole.

How could he want his twin to die? Alex wished he could've done more to protect Jessica. Wished he could figure a way out of this mess. He didn't want Cole to die, not when there was a chance he could be helped.

His blood chilled when he thought of what Cole had become. They were twins; they shared the same genetic make-up.

It could've been him. If he'd been the one watching Kaitlyn that day, would his and Cole's roles be reversed?

It wasn't a pleasant thought, but it was one he had to acknowledge. Cole had been normal before her death. A normal little boy who was no more prone to violence than any other boy, including himself.

The accident had changed Cole; it had scarred his soul. Alex had always believed people were responsible for their own actions, but now he had to question his beliefs. How much of Cole's future had been decided that day?

Was the line between sanity and psychosis such a thin one? He'd been shocked when Jessica had told him what his brother had become and even now, faced with proof of Cole's violence, he couldn't hate him. He could only feel sorry for the brother who had sentenced himself to his own personal hell and had never gotten out. He felt guilty for being normal.

Jessica didn't trust him now, and there was nothing he could say to change her mind. She would never realize how close he'd been to pulling that trigger. How he would've done it if Cole hadn't backed away from her. He would've shot Cole if that had been his only alternative, but he didn't blame her for thinking that wasn't good enough.

Jessica picked up his cell phone and hit redial, only to click it shut in frustration a moment later.

"He's okay," Alex said. "Cole has no way of knowing where they are. They didn't even know where I was sending them. He couldn't have found them."

"Gee, that sounds familiar." Jessica cocked her head, and anger flashed in her green eyes. "I think you said the same thing about us."

"What can I say to make things better?" Alex asked, pained. "Tell me what to do, and I'll do it."

"There's nothing you *can* say or do. It's too late. You've proven where your loyalties lie."

"That's not true."

"The hell it isn't. I believed you. Against my better judgment, I trusted you. And you threw it in my face." Her lower lip trembled as she said, "All I want is my son back. And then . . ."

She hesitated, and Alex's heart sank. "And then what?"

"And then I never want to see you again."

Cole arrived at The Boxcar with forty minutes to spare. He parked across the road in a drugstore parking lot and waited, half-sick with excitement and fear.

His son. He was finally going to meet his son.

His stomach churned uneasily, and Cole regretted the fast food burger he'd just demolished. It was important to keep his strength up, and he couldn't even remember the last time he'd slept. The airplane? He wasn't sure. Everything was a little hazy, a little out of focus. But it would get better. Joe would make it better.

Then there was his mother. There would be no way to avoid seeing her. He might even have to hurt her. Even though he knew he had to face it, Cole was too nervous to think about her right now. The multiplication tables didn't work. Nothing did. Cole barely made it out of the car before he began to retch.

Glancing up, he saw an old woman watching him. She quickly averted her gaze and hurried inside the drugstore. From her look of disapproval, she undoubtedly thought he was a drunk.

He felt worse than drunk. He felt weak. Drained.

Cole fished a dollar bill out of his wallet and fed it into the soda machine outside. He used the first gulp as mouthwash, trying to rid his mouth of its acrid taste.

He couldn't sit anymore. He needed to *move*.

Crossing the road, he paced the sidewalk and cased The Boxcar. Since it didn't open until noon, the parking lot was empty except for a few vacant cars that probably belonged to employees.

To get Joe, he needed the element of surprise. Kate couldn't see him until the last possible moment, or she'd just drive away. She probably had her husband with her. Cole almost hoped she did.

He owed that bastard.

In the end, Cole decided to hide behind the green

dumpster. He took another glance at his watch. Ten minutes to go, at least. Cole held a cigarette between his trembling fingers and tried to look casual in case he was being observed by anyone on the street.

Forty-five minutes later he was still waiting.

He was panicky, ready to bolt when the sedan pulled up. From his viewpoint, he recognized the back of his mother's head when she climbed out of the car.

Something was wrong. Where was Joe?

Maybe he was asleep in the backseat.

"Cole?" his mother called, and walked around the front of her car. "Cole, are you here?"

His heart froze in his chest.

"Cole?"

She was still beautiful. Still looked the same after all this time. A thousand thoughts flooded his mind, and Cole didn't even realize he'd stepped into view until it was too late.

"Cole!" she exclaimed. Kate cupped her hands to her face and blinked back tears.

"Where's my son?" he demanded.

"There was an accident—on the freeway in Chattanooga—"

Cole's knees buckled, and he had to grab the side of the dumpster for support.

"Joe?" he gasped.

"No, no, no," his mother said in surprise, realizing what he was thinking. She advanced toward him.

Cole held up a hand to ward her off, and she stopped.

"Joe's not hurt—uh, we were caught in traffic for awhile. Once we were moving again, Mason stopped at a gas station to call Alex to tell him we'd be late, so he wouldn't worry."

"And you found out it was a trick." Bitterness rocked him.

He had lost again.

"So, what are you doing here? Leading the police to me?"

He scanned the area, but it looked quiet.

"No. No police. I just wanted . . ."

"You just wanted to what?" he snapped. "To gloat? To what?"

"To see you," she said simply.

Tears sprang to his eyes, enraging him, and he started to walk away.

"I love you," she sobbed. "I love you. That's why I'm here."

"Yeah, you love me," he stormed. "That's why you're helping them keep my child away from me."

"I don't want to keep him from you, Cole. You have to believe that. But I have to do what's best for him. You need help."

"Don't," Cole warned, pointing at her. "Don't."

"No matter what's happened, no matter what you've done, we can get through this together. I'm here for you. I'll be here for you no matter what. I'll do whatever it takes to get help for you, and so will Alex."

"Yeah, he loves me too. So much that he's sleeping with my wife."

He tried to walk past her, and she grabbed his shirt.

"Don't touch me!" he cried, but Kate clung to him. She wrapped her arms around his waist. The scent of her was so sweet, so achingly familiar.

"I don't want to hurt you," he hissed in her ear, his tears wet and hot on his cheeks.

"Then don't," she said, pressing her head against his chest. With a huff, he released the breath he was holding and for a second, he buried his face in her hair.

For a second, he let her hold him.

"He's a wonderful boy. Smart like you were at that age. If you'll let me help you, I know we can arrange for you to see him. You'll be able to know your son. Be a part of his life."

Her words were sweet, lulling, and he could almost believe them. Could almost believe in her. Then it hit him like an electric shock what he was doing.

Cole jerked away from her.

"Liar!" he said as he backed away. "It's a trick. You blamed me. You hate me."

"The only one who ever blamed or hated you was you," she said.

Cole ran across the road without even looking. A horn blared, and he felt the wind off the car as it swerved to avoid him, heard the squeal of its brakes. His mother screamed, but Cole kept moving. He'd rather die than listen to another word she said. It hurt too much.

His life was a joke, something to be endured.

All he wanted was to see his son, and all everyone wanted was to keep him from it.

Peeling out of the parking lot, he could barely see the road ahead.

"I would've been a good father. I would've taken care of him," he whispered. He could smell his mother's scent on him. Part of him wanted to pull to the side of the road and jerk off his shirt. But another part wanted to be back in her arms again.

Weak. He was so damn weak, and he didn't need Earl Ramsey to tell him that. His father loved him, in his own way. Cole knew that. The old drunk might've been the only one who ever did besides Kaitlyn.

"Dammit!" he cried, and banged his hand on the steering wheel. He'd thought her name again. For years, he'd avoided it. And he'd felt safe.

He'd felt sane.

Now, he dangled from the ledge, and there was no going back. No one could save him. No one wanted to.

He was scared, maybe more scared than he'd ever been. The monster, long dormant, was awake, and it was hungry.

When he was a kid, after Alex and Kaitlyn were gone, he'd found ways to ward it off. Cole had dozens of rituals. They had protected him all those nights when he was alone in the house and heard the whisper of the beast. Cole would lay awake, petrified. He'd pray for his father to hurry home from the beer joint, even though he knew no one could help him. The monster wasn't under his bed or in his closet. It was in his mind, and that was the most terrifying thing of all.

Never say her name

Never smoke the last cigarette in a pack

Never leave the house without tapping my watch

He knew it was crazy, but the rituals had made him feel better. Now, nothing did.

He'd forgotten to fear it, hadn't felt the blackness for years. It had been easy to imagine it was weak now, a figment of his childhood fears that no longer had power over him. The mistake was in thinking it was harmless, like a toothless old man, because Cole could see it now, and its teeth were long and razor sharp.

Chapter 13

Jessica sat in the backseat with Joe, her mouth pressed in a grim line. She hadn't spoken a word during the half-hour trip to the airport. Although she wouldn't say anything in front of her son, Alex knew she was furious.

He had failed her again. If not for sheer, dumb luck, Cole would have taken Joe.

Alex had never felt like such a loser in his life. These past few days had taught him about helplessness. About having to second guess every move he made. And the worst thing was, it was only a taste of what Jessica dealt with every day. Her life was a living hell, and he'd only contributed to her pain.

Jessica's gaze burned into the back of his head as he drove past the short-term parking lot. His fingers tightened on the steering wheel as he braced himself for the confrontation to come.

"What do you think you're doing?" she demanded when Alex pulled into the rental car drop-off area.

"I'm returning the car."

"I can see that," she snapped. "*Why* are you returning the car?"

Alex sighed and twisted in the seat to face her. With a pointed glance at Joe, he said, "Step outside, and we'll talk."

Jessica's frown deepened, but she whispered something to Joe and climbed out of the car.

She shut the door and folded her arms over her chest. "Talk."

"I'm going to California with you."

She looked astounded. "The hell you are!"

"I'm going to investigate Matt Bennett's murder and your sister's assault. I can get further with the police than you can. If I can link the murder and the assault to Cole, I can put him away without you having to come forward. He'll be in prison, and you'll be safe."

"How can I believe you? How do I know you won't destroy evidence to save him?"

Alex blanched. "You think I would do that?"

Jessica wiped a tear from her eye and turned her back to him. "I don't know. I don't know anything anymore."

Alex reached for her. She didn't want him to touch her, but he didn't care. He threw an arm around her and hugged her to him.

"Stop it," she hissed, but she was crying. Trembling.

So was he.

"I love you," he whispered. "I love you, and I'll do whatever it takes to prove it. I'm sorry I failed you. I'm sorry I hurt you. Please don't say there's no chance for us."

"What do you want from me?" she sobbed, but she quit struggling against him.

"Just hold on. Don't give up on me. On what we have. Don't shut me out of your life. I know it's my fault we've come to this, but I'll make it up to you, I swear it."

"God, Alex, don't do this to me." She hugged herself and turned to face him. He cursed himself for the tears sparkling in her green eyes. "I can't . . . I don't know . . ."

"Shhh, I know." He enveloped her in his arms. "I'm not asking you for anything other than the chance to prove myself to you." Alex kissed the top of her head and said, "Let's get Joe before we miss our flight."

Jessica couldn't look at Alex. She didn't know what to say or what to do, so she tried to ignore him. That proved to be impossible, especially when Joe made her trade the window seat for the middle. Alex's arm brushed against hers and his scent surrounded her.

He had called her strong, but she wasn't strong at all. Even though Jessica knew—she *knew*—there was nothing in their future but pain, she wanted to lay her head on Alex's chest and beg him to be what she wanted him to be. What she needed him to be.

Jessica shifted in the seat and leaned to wrap her arm

around her son. A pain ripped through her, and her hand involuntarily shot to her side.

Alex frowned. "Jess? What is it?"

The stewardess saved her from answering when she suddenly appeared at Alex's side.

"You guys doing okay?" she said. "Can I get you anything?"

"Juice?" Joe asked, finally tearing his gaze from the window.

"Sure thing." She beamed at him. "Wow, I don't know if I've ever seen a father and son who looked as much alike as you two do."

Alex smiled and didn't bother to correct her, but Jessica's stomach lurched. She didn't like to be reminded of the fact that Joe shared anything with Cole. For the first time, she allowed herself to think about what Alex had said.

Dear God, what if Cole used the law to take her son from her?

Jessica took a deep breath. She couldn't think about that right now. If she did, she might start screaming and never be able to stop. She was tired. Frazzled. How did she expect to outthink Cole when she was such a wreck? The cigarette burn chafed against her jeans, and the mindless throb of it reminded her of what she was up against.

Cole was ruthless. Willing to destroy anybody or anything to get what he wanted. To defeat him, she would have to be ruthless too.

Alex leaned over and whispered, "Jess, what's wrong with your side?"

"It's nothing. I . . ." She gasped and threw her arm up protectively when he reached to touch it.

"Nothing, huh?" Alex asked, his voice grim. "Let me see."

Realizing she had no choice—he'd keep badgering her until she did—Jessica twisted so Joe couldn't see, and lifted the hem of her shirt. Alex flinched at the sight of the bruise. Black, purple, green, yellow . . . her side sported more colors than a box of crayons.

"Are you my daddy?" Joe said suddenly, and Jessica jumped. Her panicked eyes flew to Alex's face.

Oh, please, Joe, not now, she silently begged. What could she say? What *should* she say?

Alex cleared his throat. "No."

"Where's my real daddy?"

Jessica found herself afraid to look at Joe's little face. A quiet kid anyway, he'd had very little to say since they'd picked him up from Kate. Jessica supposed he sensed the tension between the adults.

"Your real daddy's sick, honey," Jessica said, and took Joe's hand. "He can't take care of us. So we take care of ourselves, right, kiddo?"

"What's wrong with him?" Joe asked.

As Jessica tried to form an answer, the stewardess brought Joe a glass of juice. Alex started asking her questions about the plane to draw Joe off the subject, but Jessica knew her respite was only temporary.

How could she explain things to Joe that she couldn't understand herself?

Every time she looked at Joe, she felt a tightening in her chest that had nothing to do with her asthma. Cole was coming for what was his, and no matter what Alex said about the law, she knew this whole mess could only end one way.

Either she or Cole would be dead.

Cole pulled the T-shirt over his head with one vicious yank and threw it on the hotel room floor. It smelled like Kate, and he couldn't take it anymore. He rubbed a hand down his face and tried to figure out his next move.

He couldn't concentrate. His mind kept replaying the meeting with his mother, the look on her face.

"Stop it!" he said, and clamped his hands over his ears, as if the scenes came from some outside source, not inside his head.

Cole was exhausted, but he didn't know how in the world he could make himself go to sleep when he was this wired. As he paced, the sight of the black T-shirt irritated him. He picked it up and threw it in the trash.

The colors in the room irritated him. Soft greens and mauves. It didn't look clean, even though this was the nicest place he'd found.

He hated staying away from home. Couldn't stand the thought of not knowing who had used this bed before him.

After he'd checked in, Cole made a stop at the local Dillard's, where he bought some sheets and a new blanket. He always did that when he had to sleep in a strange bed. Bought his own pillow and towels too. In the morning when he checked out, he would leave his new sheets behind.

Cole used the plastic Dillard's bag as a glove and ripped off the hotel sheets. Then he carefully put the new ones on and stretched out on the bed.

No good.

Cole tried to shut his eyes, tried to get some sleep, but he kept thinking about the mattress and the little germs crawling on it.

Could they get through his sheets? It had never bothered him before, but now he started itching.

Dammit, he knew this wasn't normal. Normal people weren't afraid of hotel mattresses, but he was miserable. His skin crawled, and he finally jumped to his feet. He thought about lying on the floor, but it was probably worse than the mattress. Frustrated with himself, Cole went to take a shower.

The room had both a shower stall and a garden tub. Cole hesitated with his hand on the glass door, then turned to prowl under the sink.

Nothing.

He wandered out in the hall and started to walk to the courtesy desk when he spied the housekeeping cart. Cole stood at the door and listened. Two maids laughed as they cleaned the room.

Cole glanced at the cart. There was a bottle of disinfectant on the top rack. He grabbed it and hurried back to his room.

An hour later, the bathroom sparkled.

Exhausted, Cole stripped off his clothes and stepped into the shower. He almost fell asleep standing under the hot spray. Finally, he got out and put on a fresh shirt and boxers. Then, with another scowl, he took his new pillow and blanket and crawled into the garden tub. He got a couple hours of fitful sleep before the chirp of his cell phone awakened him.

Cole grimaced as he climbed out of the tub. If at all possible, he felt worse than before. He rubbed his eyes and snatched up the phone.

"Yeah."

"Where are you?" his father barked.

Too far away to give you a loan, old man, he thought. But he didn't say that. Even though Earl was old now, Cole knew better than to talk back to his father.

"I'm not in California. I'm traveling."

"Good."

His father sounded relieved, and an uneasy feeling tickled at Cole's stomach.

"What's up, Pop?"

"Your sister-in-law was on the six o'clock news."

"What about her?" Cole kept his voice casual, but the uneasy feeling had begun to turn to panic. Earl wouldn't call him with this if he didn't have some reason to suspect him.

"Somebody broke into her place, put her in the

hospital, and took her kid."

"She's not dead?" Cole pinched the bridge of his nose. He should've made sure she was dead.

"Was in a coma, last I heard. The girl was dropped at a department store." Earl's voice sounded funny, tight. Almost hesitant.

Well, the coma was a relief. Laura wasn't talking to the police, or his picture would be plastered all over the news by now.

Earl coughed. "Son . . . are you in some sort of trouble? I could help."

"What makes you ask that, Pop?"

"Cole, I . . . I saw the security tapes on the news. Guy kept his head down, had on a cap. He never showed his face, but he walked like you."

Cole opened his mouth to deny it, then shut it again. His father already knew, or he wouldn't have called. And Earl wasn't going to tell anybody. "Look, Pop. I gotta go right now, but I'll be home soon and we'll talk, okay?"

"Okay." Earl paused and said, "Take care, son."

Cole clicked his phone shut and grabbed a pair of jeans from his bag. If his father had seen all this on the news, surely someone would tell Jessica. And if Cole knew his little wifey at all, she'd be on the first plane to California.

That was where this would end. Right back where it had all started.

Jessica walked out of the airport and lifted a hand to shield her eyes from the afternoon sunlight. As she watched the people bustle around her, she was a little surprised by what she *didn't* feel. Thomas Wolfe said you can't go home again, and maybe he was right.

Too many people, moving too fast.

When she first moved to Tennessee, Jessica had wondered if she could actually die from loneliness. She missed her sister, her friends (the ones that she still had left, anyway), and the excitement of the city. Pru tried to help, but she had a family of her own to care for. She couldn't spend her days playing social director for a timid pregnant woman who scurried home from work every day to lock herself in a miserable, tiny apartment.

Jessica frowned when she thought of the girl she'd been five years ago. Young and cowed and scared out of her wits.

God, she could never let herself get back to that place.

Cole had taken care of everything. She hadn't even known how to use the ATM card Laura gave her. If she closed her eyes, she could remember what it felt like that day. How the wig had itched and how she might've turned around and run back had there been anything to run back to. But Jessica had known the uncertain future that stretched before her had to be better than the certain one she was leaving behind.

On the airplane, she'd gripped the armrests so tightly the flight attendant had sat in the empty seat beside her. When the woman had asked if she was going to be okay, Jessica hadn't known what to say.

But I am okay, she thought. I'm not her anymore. I am not that girl.

Her life was quiet, but it was hers. The house she lived in was hers. She'd bought the clothes on her back with her own money and raised the little boy beside her with love. If Cole thought he could take those things from her, he had another think coming.

Alex hailed a cab. Both he and Joe seemed a little unnerved by the crowd, though they were trying hard not to show it. Strange to think this city had once been Alex's home too.

"Are you okay?" Alex asked as he helped her into the cab.

Jessica met his eyes for a moment and saw concern there. She wished she could trust him. Wished there could be some fairy tale happy ending for them, but how could there be?

"Jess?" he said again, and she realized she hadn't answered him. She nodded and turned to Joe, who pointed at the shining silver buildings outside the window. His father worked in one of those buildings. But she knew Cole wasn't working now. He was hunting.

They checked into separate rooms in a hotel near St. Agnes Memorial Hospital and caught the tram to the medical complex.

When the elevator lurched upward, so did Jessica's stomach. Although she knew this wasn't her fault, Jessica couldn't help the guilty feeling that nagged at her. Her sister was here because of her, because she'd once believed the promise in a stranger's eyes.

The elevator doors swung open on the sixth floor, and Jessica blinked. She took Joe's hand and forced her feet forward.

"Do you know the room number?" Alex asked.

"It's 614." Jessica took a deep breath and turned down the long corridor. This wasn't the hospital she'd worked in, but she was struck by a sense of déjà vu as she wandered down the hallway. It smelled the same, like rubbing alcohol and floor wax, and Jessica found herself thinking of the first time she'd seen Cole. In his groggy half-consciousness, he'd asked her if she were an angel. He had completely and utterly charmed her. Hid what he really was. Jessica cast a sideways glance at Alex. She wondered if she was being tricked again and was simply too stupid to realize it.

Jessica took one more deep breath as she placed her hand on the door. Forcing a smile, she pushed it open.

"Oh!" Jessica couldn't stop the startled gasp that burst from her lips when she saw her sister. She felt Alex's hand on her waist and blinked back tears.

Laura was asleep. The top of her head was completely bandaged, and bruises darkened the area underneath her eyes. Laura's swollen face was hardly recognizable.

"Jess?" Danny stood quickly, letting his magazine fall to the floor. He crossed to her and swept her in his arms. Jessica gritted her teeth to keep from crying out at the pain in her ribs. Danny let her go and smiled down at her. His smile disappeared when he noticed the knot on her jaw.

"What happened to you?" he asked. Jessica saw his gaze flicker past her and lock on Alex, then Joe. His brown eyes narrowed, and she knew what he was thinking. Only a blind man could miss the resemblance.

Danny's fists clenched, and he advanced toward Alex.

"No, Danny, it's not what you think." Jessica grabbed his arm.

A strangled sound from the hospital bed startled her. Laura was trying to push herself up in the bed.

"Get . . . away . . . from her," Laura growled, her raspy voice barely audible. "Cole . . ."

Jessica let go of Danny and rushed to Laura's side. One of the machines hooked to Laura began beeping.

"Honey, calm down," Jessica pleaded. "It's not what you think—"

"Go away!" Laura yelled at Alex. "Go away!"

Laura's face changed colors, her pallor replaced by a mottled purple color that scared Jessica to death.

"Get out, Alex," Jessica cried. "You're frightening her."

Alex immediately backed out the door. After a moment's hesitation, Joe followed.

"Jess, what are you doing?" Laura gasped.

Jessica sat on the side of the bed and tried to calm her sister. "Shhh. Shhh. Calm down. He's not Cole. He's Cole's brother. He's helping me."

Jessica turned toward Danny. "I'm so sorry. I wasn't thinking when I let him in here."

"What are you doing with him?" Laura demanded.

"It's a long story, but I promise I'll tell you everything if you just relax."

A nurse came in and frowned at them. "What's going on in here?"

"I'm okay," Laura said, and tried to push herself up in the bed again.

"You are most definitely not okay." She glanced at Jessica and Danny. "I need everyone to clear out for a moment."

Danny's arm dropped across her shoulder, and Jessica let him lead her outside. She leaned against the wall, then slid down it. Hugging her knees, Jessica burst into tears.

"Jessica, what's going on?" Danny crouched beside her. "Whatever it is, let me help you."

"Mama, what's wrong?" Joe's voice brought her back to herself. She had to keep it together for him. Jessica wiped her tears away and tried to smile.

"Aunt Laura was hurt, and Mommy's just scared. She's going to be okay, though. Uh, Danny, could you take Joe to get something from the vending machine? I need to talk to Alex for a minute."

Danny gave her an 'are you sure' look, and Jessica nodded.

"C'mon, Joe. Let's get a coke." He took Joe's hand and said, "I told Kacie you were coming, and she can't wait to see you."

Alex sat down on the floor beside her, but Jessica waited until Joe was out of sight before she spoke.

"I'm sorry I screamed at you, but I can't handle all this right now."

She forced herself to look at him and dreaded what she had to say. "You have to go. I need some space so I can figure out what I have to do next. You said you wanted to investigate Matt's murder. Maybe—"

"I don't want to leave you. What if Cole finds you again?"

"Then I'll have to be ready."

"What does that mean, Jess?" Alex asked in frustration. "You can't do this alone."

"If you prove Cole murdered Matt, you can stop him. Danny will help me. I still have friends here. If you really want to help me, you'll do what you said. You'll help build a case against Cole."

"Can I at least call you? See if you're okay?"

Jessica squeezed her eyes shut. "Alex, when I said I needed space, I didn't just mean from this. I need to sort us out. To be honest, I don't know how I feel about you right now. I want to believe there's something there we can save, but . . ."

"There is, Jess." He took her hand, squeezed her fingers.

"But we have no future as long as Cole is stalking us."

Alex sighed. "Okay," he said finally. "If that's what you want. I'll go find out what I can about Matt Bennett. Just promise me you'll be careful. Promise me you won't take any stupid chances."

"Okay," Jessica said. He placed a kiss on her forehead and stood. Jessica extended her hand. He helped her up, and folded her in his arms.

"We're going to make it through this, Jess. I promise you. And get those ribs checked out, okay?"

Jessica nodded against his chest. His arms felt so good around her, and for a moment, she wished she could take back everything she'd said and ask him to stay. She said nothing, however. Alex released her and she watched him walk away.

Danny and Joe returned a moment later. Danny pressed a soft drink can in her hand, and Jessica accepted it gratefully.

"Where'd Alex go?" Joe asked.

"He had to go do some work stuff, hon."

"But I didn't get to tell him 'bye," Joe complained.

Danny cleared his throat. "Uh, Jess. My sister is keeping Kacie right now so I can stay here with Laura. I know they'd love to have Joe over to play."

"Ah, I don't know."

"Theresa loves kids. I know she wouldn't mind. They haven't seen each other since—when? Orlando last summer?"

"Laura and Kacie flew to Tennessee for a week last December." Jessica smiled when she remembered how much fun they'd had decorating her Christmas tree.

"Oh, yeah. I forgot. But anyway, that's been eight months."

Jessica exhaled. "Okay, if she doesn't mind. I really need to talk to you." She turned to Joe. "How about it, sport? You want to go see Kacie?"

"Yeah!" His blue eyes lit with excitement, and Jessica felt sorry for him again. Joe was so patient and quiet. He was a great kid.

Danny went to call his sister. Jessica looked at Joe and said, "Come here." She hugged him and said, "I love you. You know that?"

"I love you too. Is everything okay?"

"It's going to be," she said, and smoothed back his dark hair.

"You can go back in now." The nurse's voice startled Jessica. "She's okay."

Jessica jerked her head around, and nodded her thanks. She really had to get her nerves settled. She felt like that cat on the Bugs Bunny cartoons Joe watched all the time. Jessica took Joe's hand, but he pulled away from her.

"Mama, I don't want to go back in there," he said hesitantly. "Aunt Laura looked scary."

"Oh." Jessica sat back down. "But you know Aunt Laura would never hurt you."

"I know, but I just don't want to go back in there."

"Well, you don't have to. We'll wait right here for Uncle Danny."

"What happened to her?" Joe held his shoe up for Jessica to tie.

"She hurt her head, baby. But she's going to be okay."

Danny returned with a smile. "Theresa says she'd be glad to keep him. She only lives a few minutes away, so

I'll take Joe to the lobby to wait for her."

"Be good." Jessica brushed a kiss on his cheek. "I'll come get you in a little while."

"Did the nurse ever come out?" Danny glanced at Laura's door. His brown hair had more gray than Jessica remembered, and worry lined his handsome face.

"Yes. She said Laura is okay."

"Good. I'll be back in a few minutes. You can keep her company."

Jessica waved goodbye and slipped back into Laura's room.

"Hey," she said, and sat beside Laura.

"What's going on, J.J.? Does Cole know you're alive?"

Jessica hesitated, but she couldn't lie to her sister. "Yes."

"Then, what are you doing here?" Laura demanded. "You know he'll come after you."

"He already has." Jessica squeezed her eyes shut. "Laura, do you remember anything about the attack?"

"No." Laura frowned. "The last thing I remember is Kacie's dance recital. They tell me it was two weeks ago. I don't even know anyone named Jose."

Danny opened the door, and Jessica waited until he was seated to say, "Cole did this to you."

"What?" they asked in unison.

"He told me when he caught up to us. He told me he'd killed you."

"Did he do that to your face?" Danny asked. "And the cuts on Alex's face?"

"Yeah." Jessica leaned forward and rested her face in her hands. "He ambushed us in Tennessee. He . . . got away. Now, he's after Joe."

Danny sat up straight. "The police have a surveillance tape of the man who took Kacie."

"I saw it, but I didn't recognize him," Laura said. "I wasn't thinking about Cole at all. I thought that nightmare was gone from our lives. But I can tell the police it's him. They'll arrest him."

"Not enough." Jessica sighed. "If the whole thing comes out, I could lose Joe, and Cole might get nothing more than probation or something. He'd be free to come after me. After Joe."

"What do you mean?" Laura pushed herself up in the bed with her elbows.

"I faked my death. Fraud. And I've been living and working under a false identity. Danny, you're a lawyer. How much trouble could I be in?"

"Ah, Jess. I've been doing corporate law for so long, I'm not sure."

"But you think the state could take custody of Joe?" Laura prodded.

"It's possible," he admitted, rubbing a hand over his chin. "Cole has no prior record?"

"Not that I know of," Jessica said. "But there's something you don't know." She took a deep breath. "Cole murdered Matt Bennett."

Laura gasped, and Danny asked, "Who's Matt Bennett?"

"He was my friend. The morgue worker who helped me," Jessica explained. It was hard to believe Danny hadn't been around back then. Hard to believe he wasn't Kacie's real father. Laura had struck out her first time at marriage too, although not as spectacularly as Jessica had.

"Alex is investigating it."

Laura sighed. "Of all the people in the world to have a twin, it would have to be Cole Ramsey. Can you trust him, Jess?"

"I'm not sure," Jessica admitted. She told them the whole story, starting with the meeting in the restaurant. Laura watched her with pitying eyes, and Jessica realized how stupid she must sound. She'd escaped the devil, then bedded his brother. Laura had always been vocal about her disapproval of Cole, and Jessica dreaded the lecture that was coming. Laura surprised her.

"Honey, just be careful. He doesn't seem anything like Cole, and it does sound like he cares for you. I would wait, though, and see if he comes through with his promises before I got in too deep."

Too late, Jessica thought, but she forced a smile and said, "Okay."

"Jess, I was thinking about the fraud thing. Does Cole know the identity you were living under?"

She shook her head. "I don't think so."

"Okay." Danny leaned forward eagerly on his elbows. "Then he can't prove you've been living under one. We could've been supporting you. He doesn't have anything except the fake death certificate, right?"

Jessica rubbed her head. "I'm not sure what you're getting at."

"If Cole didn't have the fake death certificate, how could he prove anything? Laura said your funeral was an outdoor memorial, very small. Nobody there but your family. No real funeral director, either. No actual person's ashes in the urn he has. Who's to say that you didn't just pack up and leave one day? That's not a crime. You had no idea Cole told everyone you were dead."

Jessica finally got what he was saying, "And my family would deny the funeral ever happened. But what about the death certificate? I don't want to get anyone who helped me in trouble. Matt's signature was on the paperwork, along with that of another nurse who helped me. I know Matt's dead, but I don't want to destroy his reputation or her career. And I don't want it to be traced back to Laura."

Danny pursed his lips. "Does Cole have a safe deposit box that he keeps his papers in? Maybe Alex could impersonate him. Get the death certificate and destroy it."

Jessica thought about it for a minute. One little paper. She could get it.

She jumped to her feet. "I've got to go. I'll be by to get Joe soon."

"J.J., please be careful," Laura begged.

"I will," she promised, and shut the door behind her. Jessica leaned on it for a moment and gathered her nerve. She thought about calling Alex, then decided against it. She could do this, but she would have to move fast.

Cole wouldn't keep the death certificate in a bank. It would be in his wall safe at home.

Chapter 19

It took nearly forty minutes to reach her old neighborhood by cab, but Jessica was grateful for the time she had to prepare herself. Even though she knew it was silly, she was as terrified of that house as she was of Cole himself.

Her hands shook as she paid the cabby. He asked her if she wanted him to wait, and Jessica debated it for a moment before sending him away. She had lived frugally the past five years, but a secretary's salary was still just a secretary's salary. The thought of running out of money before this mess was over made her stomach knot.

Jessica had instructed the cab driver to drop her a block from Cole's home. She'd have liked to have been further away, because people tended to notice strangers climbing out of cabs, but she couldn't risk running into any former neighbors out walking their dogs.

Slipping on her sunglasses and ducking her head, Jessica walked briskly down the sidewalk. A giggle rose in her throat at the thought that this wasn't different at all.

While married to Cole, she'd done a lot of walking with her head down. With shades and long sleeves to cover the bruises when make-up couldn't.

After the first year of marriage, Cole had grown more refined in his technique and didn't hit her in the face as often. Plenty of places hurt just as much without all the mess. By then, even the sixteen-year-old bag boy at the Shop and Save had figured out what was going on. He'd slipped her a card one day that listed a phone number for a home for battered women.

"My sister runs it," he said, and walked away before Jessica could tell him that he was mistaken, that she'd just run into the door again. But that boy was the only person other than her family who'd ever said a word about it.

The few that asked for explanations for her bruises blithely accepted whatever excuse she gave them, but most pretended not to notice. When Jessica first moved to Tennessee, it had taken her awhile to figure out why the people at work made her so uneasy. The answer was as simple as it was startling.

They looked her in the eye.

Jessica realized that, for the three years she was married to Cole, the people she'd dealt with every day, her neighbors and friends, had managed to stare at her forehead when she talked, or over her shoulder, but no one looked her in the eye. And the scariest thing of all, she hadn't wanted them to.

Jessica was so caught up in her thoughts that she nearly walked past the house. After a quick glance to see if she was being observed, Jessica took off her shades and stared up at the white, split-level townhouse that had been her home for three miserable years.

Her own little piece of hell in the city of angels.

Gulls squalled overhead. Waves crashed against the golden sand, scenting the air with their salty spray, but Jessica could suddenly hear nothing but the pounding of the pulse in her ears, and the only thing she smelled was the coppery scent of blood. Even the ocean and the sky, which had once rivaled each other in their brilliant blues, looked desolate and gray. The house loomed against the skyline, taunting her, reminding her that she was back again. Back home.

"This is not my home," she muttered defiantly. Gathering her courage, Jessica started up the cobblestone walk.

The key won't be there, an inner voice whispered. *Cole never forgot his keys. You did. Now what are you going to do?*

But the key was there. Right where it had been years ago, where Cole had put it when he'd had to come home from work to let her in to put the groceries up.

Jessica wiped her sweaty palms on her pants and remembered how it had felt that day, to agonize over whether it would be worse to call Cole home or to let the groceries ruin.

How it had felt to sit on the front steps watching for his black Jaguar pull up. She'd paid for her stupidity that day, a lesson bought with blood.

Cole was a great teacher. To this day, she'd never locked herself out of her house again.

Jessica removed the key from the fake stone in the flowerbed and hurried up the steps before her nerves failed her completely. Her trembling hands made three stabs at the lock before she managed to insert the key. With a vicious wrench, she threw open the door and walked inside.

Nothing had changed. Not one damned thing.

Even though she knew what to expect, it took her breath away. No dust, no cobwebs. Not even spiders dared enter this place.

Cathedral ceilings with a huge dormer; sliding glass door in the living room that showcased the ocean. Pristine white walls and furnishings, spotless white carpet. Some part of her mind began to scream. Jessica stuffed her fist in her mouth to keep from wailing aloud. Tears streamed down her cheeks and she froze in the doorway. She'd broken the first rule.

One did not cry in this house.

She'd broken that one thousands of times, but never when Cole was around, unless the silent tears absorbed by her pillowcase counted. But the house knew.

Stop it, dammit, the tough Jessica hissed. *It's just a house. Just a Godforsaken house. It can't hurt you. Shut the door and do what you have to do. Think of Joe.*

That snapped her out of it. She could do anything for Joe.

Jessica moved inside and was about to slip out of her shoes when she realized what she was doing.

Rule two. One did not wear shoes in this house unless one wanted to be slapped upside the head with them. This rule she'd only broken once.

Defiantly, Jessica slipped her shoe back on and took another step onto the carpet. She almost expected the whiteness to open up, to seize her like a mouthful of gigantic white teeth, but nothing happened. She took another step. Rested her hand on the white leather sofa.

She'd watched a program on TV one time where the detective sprayed a clean-looking wall with a substance called Luminol. The killer had painted over the wall in an attempt to hide the evidence, but the chemicals in Luminol reacted with minute traces of iron in the hemoglobin anyway. Bloodstains invisible to the naked eye glowed a ghostly blue under the detective's light.

What would this place look like, she wondered, under one of those lights?

Quit acting so stupid, she told herself. *Move.*

She walked through the living room into the kitchen. It too, was sparkling white. White cabinets, white countertops with nothing sitting on them. It looked like a clinical lab. Sterile, spotless.

Jessica opened the cabinet to the left of the sink and carefully removed the glasses inside, stacking them neatly on the counter. Then she pulled out the shelf and opened the false back, revealing the small fireproof safe built into the wall.

Jessica twisted the dial and listened for the soft click. 00929. Their anniversary plus a zero. She pulled on the door and nothing happened. Panic deflated her hopes like a pinprick in a balloon.

Why had he changed the combination?

Taking a deep breath, Jessica tried again. This time, it opened.

Relief flooded her, nearly stealing her legs. Jessica reached inside and pulled out a heavy manila folder, shaking the banded stacks of twenties off the top and ignoring them. She was no thief and wanted nothing from Cole Ramsey but freedom.

Cole was a meticulous recordkeeper. The death certificate was right there, right behind her marriage certificate. She folded it and stuffed it into the pocket of her jeans.

A small caliber revolver lay inside the safe, and after a moment's hesitation, she picked it up. It wasn't loaded, and Jessica didn't see any cartridges anywhere. She stuffed it in her waistband and started replacing the papers. The sight of her marriage license brought her up short. As she gazed at their names, listed in black and white by a bored county clerk, something inside Jessica snapped.

Viciously, she ripped into the license. Shredded it into confetti and tossed it in the air. The pieces floated down, littering the kitchen floor like snowflakes. Jessica watched them with horrified fascination and had to resist the impulse to clean them up.

"Clean it up yourself, Cole." She grinned.

God, it felt good.

Impulsively, Jessica threw open the refrigerator door.

Surprise, surprise.

It was immaculate. All the jars were perfectly aligned, labels facing outward, tallest to shortest. Jessica hefted a jar of pickles and tossed it at the stove.

"Ohh!" She jumped as it shattered and sprayed the floor with green juice, glass, and dill slices. The acrid scent of vinegar filled her nostrils.

Jessica grabbed a bottle of ketchup and doodled a row of red squiggles on the countertop. With a frown, she dropped the bottle. Too red. Too red against the white, like blood. Snatching the mustard from the refrigerator shelf, she dashed toward the living room. It was a full bottle and squirted well.

Jessica danced around the room, painting the couch and walls with mustard yellow. A picture of her and Cole, dressed in their wedding clothes, hung above the fireplace. Jessica painted him a yellow mustache before she jerked it off the wall and stomped on his face.

Cackling madly and leaving mustard tracks in her wake, Jessica ran back to the kitchen and came back out with an armful of ammunition. She dashed through the house and left no room untouched. She squealed as she dumped a jar of olives on Cole's black satin sheets and stuck her hand in the mayonnaise jar. Jessica slapped a handful of the stuff on his pillow and smeared it over the top, as carefully as if she were icing a cake. Throwing open his closet door, Jessica fired on his suits with a can of Redi-whip. It took an extra trip, but she ran to get the milk and poured it in a wide swath on Cole's bedroom carpet. Hopefully, it would be a few days before he came home.

She trashed the bathroom, squirted shampoo and shaving cream on everything. Jessica threw an entire roll of toilet tissue in the commode and flushed it. She clapped her hands in delight when it backed up, and the blue water sloshed onto the white tile.

Jessica grinned at herself in the bathroom mirror. There were mustard splatters in her hair and a dab of whipped cream on her cheek, but she felt great.

"The place never looked so good," she said, beaming at herself in the mirror before she drew a picture on it with Cole's toothpaste.

She raced back to the kitchen and was gathering supplies to finish up in the spare bedroom when she heard the living room door crash against the wall.

"What the *fuck*!" Cole screamed.

Instantly, Jessica's euphoria washed away in a wave of icy terror. She might have screamed if she could have sucked in any air at all.

Glass shattered in another room, and she heard the dull thud of Cole's footsteps on the living room carpet. Jessica glanced at the sliding glass doors across the kitchen that led to the patio.

There wasn't time. Cole would see her cross the doorway and would be on her before she got the door unlocked. The pantry was the only place she could hide.

Jessica scrambled under the bottom shelf seconds before Cole burst through the doorway. She hadn't even had time to shut the doors all the way. Jessica hugged her knees to her chest and began to pray.

"Oh, you bitch," he muttered, his voice thick with rage.

The safe was standing wide open.

The pantry was on the wall opposite the sliding glass doors, and it gave her a view of the entire kitchen through its slatted doors. She saw the blur of Cole's legs as he ran toward the safe. Toward her.

Jessica watched in horror as Cole lost his footing on the messy kitchen floor and started to slide. She jerked when he crashed into the door she hid behind and fell to the floor. He screamed as he clutched his injured wrist.

Jessica groped blindly at the shelf above her head, searching for any weapon. Her hands closed on a can, and she drew it to her.

Less than a foot separated her from Cole. The flimsy slatted door was the only barrier between them. She could see his face, flushed with rage and pain. Could hear his ragged breaths.

She'd had a friend once, Trina, who hadn't liked to drive a particular stretch of highway. Trina would go miles out of her way to avoid this road, and Jessica had asked her why.

Trina had given her an abashed smile and said, "Because it gives me this creepy feeling when I'm on it. I don't know why. I just get the feeling that if I travel on it, I might die there. Do you know what I mean?" Jessica had nodded, because she did know what that superstitious feeling was like. She had felt the same way about this house. Jessica had thought when she'd escaped Cole that she'd never have to come back here, that she'd never have to die here.

Maybe she'd been wrong.

She glanced down at the can of spinach in her hand. Cole struggled to his knees and Jessica wondered if she could surprise him, brain him with it before he could kill her.

I'm strong to the finich cause I eats me spinach, Jessica thought crazily, but unlike the crusty old sailor Popeye, she couldn't put a lot of faith in that can. Her heart was in her throat while he struggled to his feet and staggered out of the room.

Where was he? Could she make it to the patio doors?

Jessica squeezed her eyes shut and wondered what to do. Her legs cramped and pickle juice ran underneath the door. It pooled around her bottom and soaked through her pants. Jessica heard a dull crash from somewhere else in the house and decided she had to try to escape.

Cautiously, she crawled out of the pantry and made her way over the slick tile to the doorway. Jessica paused and dared a peek toward the living room, ducking back when she saw Cole standing in the ruins of his precious white sanctuary.

His back was to her however, and Jessica padded past the doorway. No turning back now. Her hand was on the patio latch when she heard him coming back. Panicked, she jerked it open and squeezed outside. Her first breath of salty air was like the promise of freedom.

Jessica hurried to the side of the deck, out of Cole's view, and threw a leg over one section of the railing. It was a twelve foot jump—not the most fun proposition with a broken rib—but she'd jump off the Empire State building before she'd go back in there with Cole. She dropped to the soft sand below.

As expected, a ferocious pain stabbed through her ribs, and Jessica grabbed her side. Even though she'd tried to brace herself for it, the pain left her doubled over. She heard the squeak of the door being pushed further open and shrank back underneath the deck. Above her head, she heard the creak of Cole's footsteps.

Finally, he walked back inside. Jessica forced herself to wait another five minutes, then took off across the sand. She still clutched her side and was scuttling sideways like a crab, but she was smiling.

Cradling his injured wrist against his body, Cole used his foot to slide the door shut. It had given him a start, but the damn door had probably been open before, and he just hadn't seen it.

No wonder. Cole had to close his eyes at the visual assault that had been his kitchen.

If he'd caught Jessica in here, the police would've had to carry whatever was left of her out in a bucket. He'd known it was Jessica when he'd seen the safe open. But what had she wanted?

Cole tried to think, but his wrist felt like it was teeming with red fire ants, and the pain was making its way up his arm.

Where was Alex?

Cole stumbled back to his living room, just to double check, but there they were, only one set of footprints across his carpet. Small feet, definitely not his brother's.

"When I catch up with you, you're going to beg me to kill you," Cole muttered. He stared down at the ruins of their wedding picture. How dare she do this to his house, to him? Nobody screwed with Cole Ramsey like this.

The blinking red eye on his answering machine flashed furiously, and for some reason it irritated him. Cole picked up the answering machine and started to hurl it into the trash can, but he thought better of it.

What if his father's voice was on there with another heads-up?

With a sigh, Cole jabbed the play button and listened to what turned out to be a barrage of calls from his office. Mostly from his vice president, Deke Sampson.

If he didn't call them back, they might report him missing. And police attention wasn't something he wanted right now. He punched in the number to Sampson's direct line.

"Sampson."

"Yeah, it's me . . ."

"Where have you been?" Sampson demanded.

The tone of his voice provoked Cole to a new level of fury. Obviously the little twit needed to be reminded whose name was on the bottom of his paychecks.

"Sampson!" he barked. "Do you like your job?"

"Y . . . yes, sir," he stammered, the bravado gone from his voice. Just a scared little rabbit under all that bluster. Cole hated rabbits.

"Then, you will never use that tone of voice with me again, you got that? I'll kick your ass all the way to the unemployment line."

"Sir, I just meant that we've been worried about you. We couldn't get you at home or on your car phone."

"Death in the family," Cole said shortly, and rubbed his forehead. "I don't know when I'll be back. I have a lot of loose ends to take care of."

"Sir, I'm sorry. Who died?"

"I trust you can manage a few days without me?" Cole demanded, ignoring him.

"Yes, sir, but . . ."

Cole slammed the phone down without waiting for him to finish. He called his normal cleaning crew and told them vandals had broken into his house. Yes, he needed them to come this afternoon. When he hung up, Cole went to his bedroom and prowled through his closet.

She'd sprayed all his suits with something, but the clothes in the back seemed clean. He snatched a pair of jeans and a Henley off the rack and stalked toward his bathroom. When he opened the door, Cole gave a startled cry of revulsion when he saw the overflowing toilet.

God, he was going to kill her!

He stepped gingerly in the puddle of blue water, and turned the water off to the toilet, frowning when he got his fingers wet. His wrist was swollen, no doubt broken. As soon as he took a shower, he'd have to go to a hospital.

Laura's hospital.

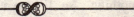

Alex glanced at his watch and sighed. Two hours and counting. He shifted in the stiff metal chair and leaned his head back against the concrete block wall of the precinct. Sandwiched in the waiting area between a derelict and a prostitute, he wondered which would overpower him first, the derelict's body odor or the prostitute's cheap perfume. Not that he should've expected any better; a lot of cops had a general disdain for P.I.'s. Assuming he ever got back to see Detective Kazeraski, he doubted the detective would be very eager to share info.

That's why he'd called Rachel. She had pretty much chewed him out for not keeping her in the loop, but once he'd explained what was going on, Rachel had jumped into action. Knowing she was on the job made Alex feel better. There were very few people in whom Alex had ever had more confidence than in Rachel Boyd. She could get information out of a rock.

His pager beeped, and Alex checked the number. It was Rachel. After he told the bored-looking desk officer he had to make a call, Alex walked outside and punched in Rachel's number.

"Hey, it's me."

"Alex, where are you?"

"I'm still at the precinct," he said, squinting in the afternoon sun. It was blindingly bright to eyes that had grown accustomed to the dingy gray interior of the police department.

"Well, get out of there. I've got what you want, which is a lot of nothing. But I'll fax it to you when you give me a number."

"How . . ."

"If I tell you, I'll have to kill you." She smacked a loud kiss in his ear and hung up.

Alex grinned as he ran to his car. Twenty minutes later, he sat in his hotel room and connected the fax he'd requested from the desk. He called Rachel and gave her the number. As the pages started spitting out, she said, "For the record, you don't have this. Did you give the desk guy at the precinct your name?"

"Nope. He cut me off as soon as I told him that I was a private investigator." Alex stretched. "I've been sitting in the waiting area on my rear end ever since."

"Good, because I'm thinking it wouldn't look good if they arrest Cole to have a P.I. with the same face poking around the evidence, asking a lot of questions. They could think you're just covering your own trail."

"Do they have DNA evidence?" Alex's pulse quickened.

"No. To be perfectly honest, they've got squat. They're treating it as a botched robbery. One old lady down the street, a neighborhood watch gal, saw a dark-colored sedan parked in front of Bennett's place that night. It was parked out front, bold as brass. So, I'm thinking this isn't your brother's personal vehicle."

"A rental," Alex said, his mind clicking. This would

be great news in Tennessee, where there weren't as many rental car agencies, but they were a dime a dozen in LA.

"Bennett's driveway was a mess. He was leveling it off, fixing to get it paved. The police have a pretty good set of tire treads taken from the scene. It had twenty-inch, SBR BSW touring tires. Based on the wheel base, Mike guesstimates it's a Ford Taurus or something similar." She hesitated. "I didn't tell him about Cole. Just that it was very important."

"It's okay, Rach." Alex paused to look at the digital images pouring from the fax. "Great. It's already been enlarged."

"Rotated, enlarged, and cropped. Go on, tell me I'm the best."

"You are definitely the best. Now I just need to figure out where Cole rented it from."

"What's his home address?" Rachel asked.

"Hang on a sec." Alex dug into his wallet and gave her the information.

"Okay," she said, and in the background Alex could hear the rapid clack-clack as her fingers flew across the keyboard.

"Depending on how confident he was, he probably used a rental agency within fifty miles of his house. It had been five years since he'd seen Bennett, so I don't think he'd worry about being connected." Alex's mind raced ahead, trying to figure out the quickest way to do all the groundwork.

"Try thirty-five miles. Galen Rental, 4502 Westmore

Street. They queried his credit card the day of the murders, but he paid in cash."

"Does your boyfriend know what a little hacker you are?" Alex asked in astonishment. He really shouldn't be surprised anymore, but she still amazed him. He'd met Rachel in college in a computer programming class. By the end of the semester, she was running the show.

"You're welcome."

"You're amazing. I can't believe he used his own credit card."

"Well, he didn't, really. Probably didn't know the queries left a trace and didn't see the need to get a fake ID anyway. You know how it is with these rental agencies. No matter how much cash you flash, they gotta have a driver's license and credit card number."

Alex exhaled. "Well, off to Galen Rental, then. I owe you, girl."

"Damn straight, you do. I'm thinking a month off this winter. Me and Mike getting all toasty on the beach in Jamaica while Tennessee's up to its armpits in snow."

"You've earned it."

When she spoke again, her voice was soft. Serious. "Alex, let me know what's going on, okay? You know I'll be on a plane if you need me."

"Why do I need you here?" he teased. "You can run the world from your desk, apparently."

She laughed. "And don't you forget it. Be careful, partner."

He hung up and scanned the fax. Rachel was right.

Other than the treads, the police had nothing. No suspects, no witnesses.

Alex hailed a cab and headed to the rental place. He wondered where Jessica was and what she was doing. She probably didn't want to talk to him, but he was going to try anyway. He dialed the hospital and asked for Laura Shanahan's room. Her ex-husband answered the phone.

"This is Alex," he said. "Is Jess around?"

"No, she's not here right now."

Something in the man's voice made Alex uneasy. He cleared his throat. "Where is she?"

"I don't know. Said she had some business to take care of."

"How can I find her?" Alex asked.

"Leave your cell phone number, and I'll have her contact you. No offense, buddy, but I don't know you. If Jess wants to call you back, it's her choice."

Alex gave him the number and hung up. His nerves were jumping, and he wondered what Jessica was up to.

At the rental agency, he found a wide variety of dark sedans to choose from, and there was no telling how many were out on rentals right now. Alex didn't know what the police would make of this later, but he did what he had to do. He went inside.

"The name's Cole Ramsey. I rented a car here Friday. I'd like to see if the same car is available again."

"Yes, sir. Just a moment." The girl pushed her glasses up on her nose and peered at the computer screen. "Yes, it's here. For how many days . . ."

"Can I see it? It was a Taurus, right? Black?" he interrupted.

She gave him an odd look, but pointed outside. "Navy blue. The new model by the sign. It's one of them in that color. Wally out there will help you find it."

Alex thanked her and walked outside. Wally was busy talking, so he ducked around him and walked down the line, inspecting the cars. He found the Taurus and started to pull the fax pages out of his folder when he noticed the tires. They were brand new, stickers still white. Alex swore under his breath.

"Hey, there!" A heavy man he assumed was Wally jogged up to him. "Help you with something, fella?"

"The tires on this car are new."

"Oh yeah, we strive to keep our rentals in tip-top shape."

"Where are the old ones?"

Wally looked puzzled. "Why do you want to know?"

Alex flipped open his P.I. badge. "I'm conducting an investigation, and I have reason to believe this car was used to commit a felony."

"I need to call my supervisor," Wally said nervously. "He can tell you more about it."

"You tell me." Alex opened his wallet and withdrew a hundred-dollar bill. "I really need to find those tires, Wally. I'll be happy to pay for your time. Two more of these if you help me find them."

The man licked his lips, then snatched the bill from Alex's hand.

"Just a sec," he said, and hurried to the door. Throwing it open, he bellowed, "Ann, I'm taking a break! Tell Sandy to get out here."

He motioned for Alex to follow him, and they walked around the side of the building to the garage. Wally pecked on the hood of a Chrysler, and a mechanic rolled out from underneath, giving them a 'what now' look.

"James, where are the tires you pulled off that Taurus yesterday?"

James pointed to the corner, where three stacks of tires were piled. "Salvage guy's coming after lunch. Put them back like you found them."

He rolled back under the car, apparently not caring why they asked.

There were twenty tires total, and of course, the tires Alex needed were in the last stack. Wally leaned anxiously over his shoulder as Alex matched the tire treads to the digital images taken at the crime scene.

Perfect match. They had him.

At least Cole could get the help he needed now, before one of them got killed. Alex hefted two of the tires, and Wally grabbed the other two. When they'd secured them in the trunk of the Taurus, Alex gave Wally his money and instructed him not to let the car go back out. The police would be coming to check on it.

Alex caught another cab and had it stop at a nearby pay phone.

"I need to leave a message for Detective Kazeraski. Tell him to go to Galen Rentals at 4502 Westmore Street.

He'll find evidence there pertaining to the Matthew Bennett murder. Tell him to ask for Wally." The woman on the other end was asking questions, but Alex hung up.

He had to talk to Jessica. He'd delivered his brother to the police. Now, all he had to do was keep her and Joe safe until they picked Cole up.

Chapter 15

Jessica wandered through Daniel's apartment. As she tidied up, she thought of Alex and debated on whether to return his message. She really couldn't handle any discussion about their relationship right now, and that was probably what he wanted to do. But the house was too quiet—Theresa had taken Joe and Kacie to the movies. With a sigh, she picked up the phone and called Alex.

"Jess! Thank God. I was worried about you."

"I'm okay." She cradled the phone with her shoulder and started putting up dishes. She tried to pretend it wasn't good to hear his voice.

"I need to talk to you. Can we meet somewhere?"

"Alex, I don't know."

"We've got him, Jess. I can link Cole to Matt Bennett's murder."

The glass Jessica held slipped from her hands and shattered in the sink.

"Are you okay?" Alex asked.

"What?" she gasped. It was too unbelievable, too good to be true. "How?"

"Meet me for dinner and I'll tell you about it."

"Okay," Jessica said. "The China Rose. It's about seven blocks from the hospital, on the corner of West and Main. I can be there in twenty minutes."

"See you then."

Jessica hung up the phone and stared at it in wonder. She knew it was dangerous to feel optimistic where Cole was concerned, but she couldn't squelch the excitement that rose within her. Maybe Alex had really come through for her, after all.

Pulling clothes out of her bag, Jessica regretted telling Alex to meet her at the China Rose. None of the wrinkled items seemed nice enough. Knowing he wouldn't care, she opened Danny's closet. She hoped Laura might've left something, but no such luck. In the back, she found a dark blue silk shirt that she couldn't imagine Danny wearing. It was a little big, but desperate times called for desperate measures.

Jessica belted it around her waist and pulled on her black slacks. Then she called to tell Danny where she was going and headed for the door. Jessica peered at her reflection in the shiny elevator doors and finger-combed her hair. Presentable, but not much more.

She made it to the restaurant first and asked for a back

booth. Alex arrived as the waiter brought her water. It was still early for the dinner crowd, and they practically had the place to themselves. Her smile faltered when she stared at his face.

"You shaved," Jessica said quietly, and took a sip of her water. She saw the hurt flash in his eyes and wished she hadn't said it. She knew it shouldn't matter, but somehow it did. Some part of her needed him to not only act differently than Cole, but to look different too. Seeing Cole again had been such a shock to her system that Alex's face started her nerves jumping again.

"Yeah." He sighed. "I shaved."

"So, what did you find? Tell me!" She leaned forward and listened with increasing astonishment as Alex told her about the rental car.

"Oh Alex, you did it!" She grasped his hands. "You really did it."

Alex looked troubled, but he didn't pull away. "Daniel told me you were out taking care of some things today. What were you doing?"

Jessica hesitated, then stared down at the table. She told him everything, from Danny's plan, to her near confrontation with Cole.

"Dammit, Jess, you could've gotten yourself killed."

Jessica finally dared to look at him. His handsome face was etched with exasperation, but not the anger she expected.

"I know," she said. "I know it was crazy, but this is my life we're talking about. My son's life. I was desperate."

Alex frowned. "And your brother-in-law, I thought he was a smart guy. How could he let you go in there like that?"

"Danny doesn't know," she admitted. "He thinks you helped me get the certificate from a safe deposit box. He's got enough to worry about right now."

"Do you realize you've put them both in danger?"

Jessica stiffened. "Cole never saw me. I won't go back to the hospital."

"But he knows you're the only one who could've gotten into that safe. Where do you think he'll look next?"

"I wasn't thinking . . ." Jessica's hand trembled when she lifted for her water glass.

"It's time for Laura to tell the police she wants to watch the surveillance tape again. This time she can ID Cole. The police will be looking for him anyway. Make Danny insist they put a guard at her door."

Alex leaned back against the red vinyl seat and let his mind shift the pieces around. "Did you destroy the death certificate?"

"I burned it in Danny's sink," Jessica said.

"Good. Make sure Danny and Laura have their stories straight. You left Cole, have been living with various relatives for the past five years. They don't know where you are, only that you're in hiding. When they catch Cole and he mentions anything about your death, they act like they don't know what he's talking about. What about anyone else that was at the memorial service?"

Jessica shook her head. "There wasn't anyone else

ther than my family."

"What about your friends?"

"What few I had left?" Jessica gave him a pained smile. "Laura didn't invite them."

"What about my family?"

"Your Aunt Gina was in the hospital, and your father didn't show. They were the only ones who might've bothered."

Alex looked relieved. "Ok, here's the plan. We're going to get Joe and get out of town tonight, go somewhere safe until Cole is in custody."

"Okay," Jessica agreed. "Whatever you say."

Cole punched the elevator button and hefted his new cast gingerly, trying to get used to the heavy tug. He was in a foul mood from two hours spent in the emergency room, then x-ray. When that stupid nurse had asked if he wanted a smiley face sticker on his new cast, Cole had thought about braining her with it.

He'd never had a broken bone in his life, and Jessica was going to pay for this one. He'd start with her fingers and snap them like twigs. Then maybe her toes.

Cole didn't pay any attention to the man who got into the elevator behind him until he spoke.

"Hey, what happened to your wrist?"

Cole disliked making conversation with strangers, but he didn't want to draw attention to himself. "I fell," he said shortly, and hoped the man would take the hint.

"Is that why you're here?"

What kind of dumb ass question was that? Cole wondered.

If this little faggot was looking for a friend, he was most assuredly barking up the wrong tree. He opened his mouth to tell him so when the man said, "Does Jess know? I thought she was meeting you at the China Rose."

Cole clamped his mouth shut again, stunned. He stared at the man and realized he was looking at Laura's ex-husband, the man in the pictures hanging on her walls.

Cole had always been able to think on his feet. He started talking before his brain even processed what he was going to say. "Why? Has she called in the last ten minutes? I called to tell her I was running late. Thought she might've come back here."

"Oh, no. I guess I talked to her a half hour ago. haven't seen her."

Cole thought briefly about forcing the ex to go with him, but the idiot had already provided him with what he needed. The elevator doors dinged open on the sixth floor, and the man stepped out.

"See you later." Cole gave him a cheerful wave. "Don't want to keep Jess waiting."

The elevator doors slid shut, and Cole sagged, smiling.

When the elevator opened, he sprinted across the lobby to the pay phones. Cole called the China Rose and got directions.

Cole grinned as he replaced the phone back in the cradle. The China Rose was just a few blocks away. Fe the first time in days, he felt hopeful.

Some of that hope evaporated while he sat in the parking lot of DeRico's Italian Restaurant and watched the entrance of the China Rose.

Cole turned on his radio, scanned the stations, and turned it off again. What if he was too late? They could've already been there and gone. He willed himself not to panic. If they were gone, so be it. He'd find them again. Still, it was hard to resist the temptation to have a look inside.

At that moment, Jessica stepped out the door. She smiled up at Alex, who walked out behind her. Alex threw his arm across her shoulders as they walked down the sidewalk.

Bitterness scalded Cole.

Dammit, she was still his wife. Alex was his brother. They could try to justify it all they wanted, but he was the one being betrayed here. He was completely, utterly alone. The only person in the world who really needed him was a little boy who didn't know his father existed. Joe was the only reason he hung on now. His only reason for living.

Cole stared at Alex's rental car when it pulled out of the parking lot, memorizing it. Cole let it take a moment's lead before he pulled out onto the highway in pursuit. He wished he'd had time to get a rental—a black Jag was not exactly inconspicuous—but he had to take the hand fate dealt him.

Where was Joe? Did she never take him anywhere

with her?

Cole's anger grew at Jessica's irresponsibility. She'd better not be leaving Joe alone. He prayed his son didn't know what it was like to feel scared and abandoned, as he once had.

Agitated, Cole shook out the last cigarette in the pack and jammed it between his lips. He lit it and took the first, sweet hit of nicotine into his lungs.

"Doesn't matter," he said, exhaling. "Joe has me now. I'll take care of him."

Cole didn't know where they'd go. Mexico, maybe. He had a lot of money saved up. He'd buried himself in work after Jessica's "death," to keep from coming home to an empty house. All that work was about to pay off, even though he'd have to walk away from his business and his home.

He was so caught up in his plans he didn't notice Alex was stopping until he was nearly upon them.

Cole cursed and whipped the Jag into a service station, earning a short blast from the horn of the driver behind him. He hoped Alex hadn't spotted him.

Alex and Jessica never looked back however, as they stepped onto the curb and entered the brown apartment building.

Once again, Cole waited.

Cole fidgeted in his seat and stared longingly at the coffee shop across the street. He hated waiting. Hated that antsy feeling of having so much to do and not being able to do anything. He recited his multiplication tables, but he gave it up after a few minutes because he couldn't concentrate.

Intent on watching the people leaving the apartment complex, Cole barely spared a glance at the woman who walked up to the entrance of the building with her children. Bored, he looked away, then something caused his gaze to snap back. The little girl dropped her doll and bent to retrieve it.

It was Laura's daughter. Kacie.

Startled, Cole's eyes darted to the little boy beside her. He sucked in his breath as he stared at his son for the first time.

"Joe," he whispered, and fumbled for the door handle.

His brain barely had time to register the boy's image before the trio disappeared inside the apartment building.

Alex watched Jessica twist the phone cord. No one answered the phone in Laura's room, and Jessica was about to panic. Alex wished he could take back his words from the restaurant. He took the phone from her hand.

"Cole surely couldn't have done anything to them, not there in front of all those people," she blurted.

"Let me see." Alex redialed the hospital's number, conscious of Jessica's worried gaze. "Yes, I'm trying to get Laura Shanahan's room. There's no answer."

He cupped his hand over the receiver and whispered, "Physical therapy."

Jessica visibly relaxed. Alex thanked the nurse and hung up. "She said they were walking Laura around today. Danny's with her."

"Thank God," Jessica said, her green eyes welling with tears. "I don't think I could take it if anything else happened to her because of me."

"Shhh." Alex folded her in his arms. "None of this is because of you. It's going to be okay now. But we need to get Joe out of here. Are you packed?"

"Yes. I just need to change." Jessica pulled away from him and glanced at her watch. "Theresa should be on her way back by now. She told me she'd have Joe back by 4:30 and it's a quarter after now. I'd better leave Danny a note too."

Jessica scribbled something on a notepad and disappeared into the bedroom. She emerged a moment later in a red T-shirt and faded jeans. Alex watched her twist her hair into a red ponytail holder, and wondered how anyone that strong could look so fragile.

Jessica caught him staring and grinned. The sight of that smile twisted his heart a little.

Jessica's smiles were too few and far between.

"All packed and ready to go, captain." She gave him a little salute. "As soon as Joe . . ." She paused at the rap on the door and gave Alex a wink. "Speak of the little devil."

She started toward the door, and Alex gently caught her wrist. He shook his head, and Jessica stiffened. Her gaze swung to the door, as if assessing the possible danger beyond it.

Alex winked at her, sorry to see the tight look back on

her face, and she nodded. He moved past her and looked through the peephole before opening the door.

Joe grinned and let go of Kacie's hand. He hurled himself at Alex's legs.

"You're back!" he shouted.

"Yeah, I'm back." Alex swooped Joe up in his arms, making him giggle. "How's it going, pal?"

From out of nowhere, Alex felt a stab of guilt. His brother's wife and his brother's son. He wanted them for his own.

"Hi, Jose," Kacie said cheerfully, and they all froze.

Alex shot Jessica a helpless glance over his shoulder. She forced a smile.

"Hi, honey, this is my friend Alex." She glanced at Danny's sister and whispered, "Theresa, I can explain . . ."

Theresa shook her head. "Danny explained—a little. I'm not sure this is good for her right now, though."

Jessica hugged her niece, and Theresa ushered the little blond girl out the door. Jessica followed them into the hallway.

A chill snaked up Alex's spine, making him twitch.

"What's the matter with you?" Joe asked with a laugh.

"Goose walked over my grave," Alex replied.

The little girl. She looked like Kaitlyn. Even their names were similar. Was that what had set his brother off?

"That sounds weird."

"Well, that's what Grandma used to say." Alex shrugged. "So, was the movie any good?"

"It was kind of girly." Joe made a face and pulled his gum out of his mouth. He tossed it in the garbage and said, "Kacie liked it, though. Lots of singing horses and stuff."

"I see." Alex ruffled Joe's dark hair. "And what do you like?"

"Monsters and swords. Dogs. Anything but singing horses."

Alex laughed. This kid was something.

"What's so funny?" Jessica shut the door behind her and lifted her eyebrows.

"You wouldn't understand," Joe said.

"Guy stuff," Alex agreed. He winked at Joe, who giggled back.

Jessica folded her arms over her chest and said, "Fine. Be that way." She stuck her tongue out at Alex as she walked by. "You guys carry the bags, then."

"Where we going?" Joe asked.

"Vacation," Alex supplied, before Jessica could say anything.

Joe's eyes lit up. "And you're going too?" Alex nodded, and Joe pumped his fist in the air. "Awright!"

"Go double check your room, make sure I didn't miss anything," Jessica told him, and rested a hand on Alex's shoulder.

A little surprised at her touch, he covered her hand with his. Alex wanted to take it as a sign, an indication that their problems weren't insurmountable, but he was afraid to get his hopes up. Before Alex could find words, Joe burst back into the room.

"Ready," he said.

Alex grinned at him and said, "Well, let's get out of here, then."

They drove up the coast for nearly two hours. Alex and Joe sang along with the radio. They even got Jessica to join in a couple of songs. He could almost believe what he'd told Joe, that they were just another family enjoying a vacation.

The fading sun painted the western sky with streaks of pink, purple, and orange. By mutual consent, they cut off the air-conditioner and rode with the windows down.

"Where are we going, anyway?" Jessica asked, peering at the map.

Alex grinned. "I haven't really planned that far ahead. Guess we'll drive until we find somewhere we want to stay. Where are we right now?"

"Entering Santa Barbara County."

"Alex!" Joe shouted. "Look over there."

From a quarter of a mile away, the tops of the tallest carnival rides could be seen against the skyline. The bright red and blue buckets of the Ferris wheel dipped and swayed as it made its rotation.

"Can we stop there? Please, can we?" Joe begged. "Oh, please, just for a few minutes."

Alex looked at Jessica. She frowned.

"Oh, please, please, can we, huh?" Alex said, batting

his eyes at her.

Jessica rolled her eyes, then smiled. "Oh, why not?" she said.

Alex followed the signs and gave a high school boy two dollars to park down a long row at the edge of a dusty field.

"This is great!" Joe exclaimed, and he bounded out of the car.

They were going to the fair.

Cole couldn't believe it.

In the past couple of days, Jessica and Alex had turned his world upside down. Had made him question his own sanity. And now they were going to the fucking carnival.

Cole watched his son run around to the front of the car and take Alex's hand.

How dare Jessica take something that so obviously belonged to him?

A rap at the window startled him. When he'd seen Alex turn onto the field, he'd pulled to the side of the road to avoid being spotted.

"Hey, mister." A pimply-faced boy peered in at him. "Everything all right? If you want to park, you need to go on down to the next sign."

"Okay, thanks." Cole forced his gaze away from Joe. He needed to stall for a moment until they were out of the parking lot. "Look." He paused to lower his sunglasses and extract a twenty from his wallet. "I'm a little worried about parking my Jag in that field. I don't mind paying more, but I wondered if there might be somewhere safer to park it."

The boy looked over the car. "Don't blame you," he said. "Wait right here."

As the boy walked to the gate to confer with an older man in a green plastic lawn chair, Cole craned to look for Alex and Jessica. He saw the back of Alex's head for a moment, then lost sight of him in the crowd going through the gate.

"Hey, mister." The boy jogged back to him. "You can park over there, in that driveway. It'll be fine there." He pointed to a faded blue house that adjoined the field. "My mom's home, and she'll make sure nobody bothers it."

"Thanks." Cole handed him the twenty and eased into the driveway.

This was perfect.

When he grabbed Joe, they'd have a clean escape route. They'd be roaring down the interstate before Alex could get his rental out of the crowded parking lot.

Chapter 16

Cole parked the Jag and hurried after them. When he entered the gate and scanned the crowd, the sight of Jessica sitting on a bench brought him up short. She wasn't looking in his direction, thank God, and Cole ducked behind a Future Farmers of America booth to watch her.

She waved, then turned her head aside to cough. Cole glanced past her to see Joe and Alex entering the animal barns.

Of course. Jessica's asthma would never allow her to set foot in such a place. A sense of relief stole over him. Apparently, Joe hadn't inherited that from her, either.

Cole eased around the information booths to get a little closer, carefully monitoring both his wife and the exit to the barns.

Jessica coughed again and stood. She walked straight

toward him, away from the barns. Hidden in the late afternoon shadows between a couple of booths, Cole didn't move. He lost sight of Jessica as she approached the first booth, but he heard her compliment the booth owner on her scrapbook display.

Cole rolled his eyes. Still wasting her time on foolishness.

He crept around behind another booth, anxious to catch sight of her again. He nearly went past her. The brown hair still threw him.

Jessica leaned against the flimsy wooden structure, just a few feet away. If she turned her head, she'd see him. Cole studied her profile, almost daring her to look around.

Instead of the anger he expected to feel—the anger he *wanted* to feel—a stab of longing shot through Cole as he watched Jessica smile at a stranger. For some reason, that smile cut him to the bone.

Smiles for strangers, smiles for his brother. Jessica had run out of smiles for him long ago. It seemed almost everyone had. Cole leaned against the plywood backing, horrified to find he was blinking back tears.

Ramseys never cry, he could almost hear his father shout. Cole squeezed his eyes shut.

This helplessness was suffocating.

Was he really the bastard everyone seemed to think he was? He wasn't sure. Wasn't sure of anything anymore. Nobody understood how he felt. No one cared. Couldn't they see he'd tried? He'd done what he had to do to survive. All his life had been one battle or another for control, and now he was losing.

More and more, Cole believed that Joe was his only chance for redemption. He would be a good father. He would take care of Joe and love him, and maybe Joe would even love him back. That's all he wanted.

Cole peeked around the corner again and was startled when he couldn't see Jessica. Following a brief surge of panic, he spotted her. She was walking back to the bench.

He had to go to the bathroom. Cole eased around the booths and entered the men's room, using his foot to push open the door. He grimaced when he walked inside, confronted by the smell of urine and sour sweat.

He bypassed the row of urinals and gingerly slipped into the furthest stall. Of course, it had no door. Why did the people who made these things assume men had no need for privacy? Careful not to step on the sodden mass of tissue in front of the commode, Cole awkwardly unzipped his pants. Stupid cast made everything harder.

The sound of his brother's voice stopped his urine in mid-flow. Cole didn't realize it for a moment, until he gradually became aware of his body's aching protest. He forced himself to finish his business, even as an icy sweat broke across his forehead.

"Those furry chickens were freaky looking," a child's voice commented, and Cole's heart stuttered when he realized it was Joe.

"They were, weren't they?" Alex laughed.

Cole's throat constricted as he listened to his son speak. Joe was so smart. Normal. The sweet sound of his laughter acted as a balm to Cole's jagged nerves.

We'll be okay together. We will, he told himself.

Cole heard the restroom door bang shut and after a few moments, he followed.

"What are we going to ride first?"

Jessica turned at the sound of Joe's voice. He looked so happy that she felt a stab of guilt. How often did Joe really look happy? He was always quiet, never difficult, as if he sensed the burden she carried. Her little boy had never really seemed like a little boy. She had a lot to make up for as soon this nightmare was over.

"Your choice. I'm game for anything . . . I think." Alex ruffled Joe's hair as they walked past the antique tractor display onto the midway.

A warm breeze carried mouthwatering aromas from the food court. Cotton candy, Italian sausage, and soft pretzels slathered in mustard. Jessica took a deep breath, recalling the county fairs she had attended as a young girl. Her grandfather always bought them each a special treat when they were leaving—a slick red candy apple for Laura and a still-sizzling funnel cake sprinkled with powdered sugar for her.

"Jess," Alex said. "You okay?"

"Yeah." She gave him a sad smile. "I was thinking about my grandfather. I wish Joe could've known him."

Alex wrapped his arm around her shoulder and kissed the top of her head. "I wish he could've known him too."

"Guess your weight, guess your age," a hawker called out.

"Hey, mister. Win the lady a prize?" another called.

They stopped to let Joe throw darts, and cheered when he burst a bright pink balloon, then a yellow one. He won a rather odd looking, lumpy white poodle and presented it to Jessica.

"Oh, this is the best present ever!" Jessica exclaimed, and hugged it to her chest.

"Gee, now you're making me look bad," Alex teased.

He gave one of the hawkers two dollars for three baseballs. He missed the first lob, and Joe snickered. Alex gave him a dirty look and proceeded to knock down the stacks of metal bottles with the next two tries. Joe laughed again because the bright pink pig Alex gave her was smaller than the poodle.

"I want to ride now," Joe announced. "How about the Mega Loop?"

Jessica cast a doubtful glance at the dancing yellow lights looming against the darkening skyline. "Oh, Joe, I don't know about that."

A train of cars swooped along the bottom of a circular track in ever-widening arcs until it made a complete circle and the passengers were upside down. The sound of their shrieks filtered down from forty feet above.

"Please, Mom, I'm tall enough," Joe pleaded.

"I'll ride with him. You can guard the pig and poodle," Alex said.

Jessica relented, and they went off to buy tickets.

The wind blew harder now, carrying with it the smell of approaching rain.

Better let him ride what he wants before the storm arrives, she thought.

Jessica watched them buy tickets and thought about how good they looked together. They got along so well.

A finger of apprehension touched Jessica, prickling the skin on her forearms. The feeling was sudden, powerful. She had to resist the urge to run to them, to beg them to get out of line. Looking around the midway, she saw nothing but throngs of smiling people. No reason for her heart to pound in her chest like a fist at a door. Jessica willed herself to calm down.

There is no danger here, she told herself.

But she couldn't shake the feeling that something was wrong.

The Mega Loop didn't fall from the sky. Joe didn't get sick. On the contrary, he was having a ball, and finally the knot in Jessica's stomach started to relax. She even rode a few rides with them, but begged out of the Scrambler because of her injured ribs.

Joe managed to make a friend as they made the circle. The little redhead with whom they had shared a car from the Scrambler ended up in the Ferris wheel line behind them.

"Mama, I want to ride with Freddie," Joe said. "You and Alex can ride by yourself."

"Nope, you're too little. I'm afraid you'll fall out," Jessica said.

"Aw, Mom, we won't stand up."

"Joe, I don't even think they'll let the two of you ride without an adult."

"I'll ride with them, ma'am."

Jessica noticed the girl behind Freddie for the first time. She looked about fourteen.

"I'm his sister. I'll watch them."

Joe looked pleased with the suggestion, and Jessica gave in. She and Alex took the next available car so they would get off before the kids did. They lurched a few feet and stopped.

"Quit worrying," Alex admonished when she craned her neck to watch Joe climb on. He stretched his arm across the back of the car and winked at her. "You know, lots of girls considered it a privilege to ride the Ferris wheel with Alex Ramsey."

Jessica snorted. "Oh, please. What's the big deal about riding the Ferris wheel with you?"

His blue eyes twinkled as he replied, "Wait until we get to the top, and I'll show you."

"My grandpa told me what to do to boys who wanted to show me things at the top of the Ferris wheel, so watch yourself, mister." She thumped her fist against her open palm, and Alex laughed.

The way he looked at her made shivers of a different kind run up her arms. With a flush, she remembered what it had felt like to be in those arms. To kiss him.

The car jerked, pitching Jessica forward. She grabbed the bar, then Alex's knee to steady herself as the ride began to move again. After a shaky start, its rotation smoothed out and Jessica leaned back against him. His arm tightened around her shoulder, and he murmured, "This is nice."

It *was* nice. Neither of them spoke as the wheel turned faster and faster. The gusts of air rushing against her face felt good. The big hand that caressed the back of her neck felt better. For just a moment, she let it all go. All the things that had happened in the past, all the things they had yet to go through. She held on to Alex and pretended none of it mattered.

Jessica had intended on giving Alex a hard time when they stopped at the top of the Ferris wheel, but instead she melted into his arms. Some things simply weren't worth fighting about. His mouth was warm and soft and tasted like Juicy Fruit gum.

She had missed him.

"I love you," he whispered. Jessica kissed him again.

They separated as the operator began letting off passengers. The ride jerked to a stop every few moments to let people disembark. Jessica leaned forward, anticipating it to stop on them, when the operator turned to speak to a fellow carnie worker.

"Oops," he said, as Jessica and Alex sailed by.

Instantly, Jessica's good mood evaporated. "Joe! He'll get off before we do." She twisted around in the seat to look for him.

"He'll be okay. He'll wait for us," Alex said, but he was looking too.

"Alex, I want off this thing!"

The panic Jessica had felt earlier slammed into her once more. Suddenly, she was terrified.

It seemed to take forever for them to circle around, but in reality it couldn't have been more than a minute.

Jessica's chest tightened, and she clutched the release bar. When the car stopped, she flung herself out of it as soon as the operator released the bolt, nearly shoving him aside.

"Joe!" she shouted. "Joe!"

She took off down the steps and pushed through the people lined around the side.

"Jess." Alex grabbed her shoulder. "He's right there."

He pointed to a nearby bench, where Joe, Freddie and Freddie's sister waited. Joe waved.

"Thank God!" she gasped and hurried over to him.

"What's wrong, Mom?"

"Nothing's wrong," Alex said quickly. "Hey, you guys ready to eat? I'm starving."

Joe waved goodbye to Freddie, and they made their way to the food court. Alex ordered a barbeque sandwich with coleslaw on top, and Jessica blinked when Joe ordered the same.

He hated coleslaw.

Joe followed Alex like an adoring puppy, and Jessica felt a small pang of panic. What if she and Alex didn't make it? How attached was Joe already? How attached was *she*?

Jessica ordered a hotdog, but gave up trying to eat after three bites. It was only nerves, but she couldn't shake the niggling sense that something was wrong. She caught Alex watching her a few times as she gazed into the crowd, but Joe's constant stream of questions kept him from asking what was wrong. Not that she could've explained anyway.

She wondered if it would be different when Cole was in jail; would she feel compelled to look over her shoulder for the rest of her life? Black clouds loomed overhead, all but promising rain. The wind picked up, and Jessica shivered, not knowing if the chill came from outside or within.

After they ate, they played Skee Ball under the glaring yellow midway lights. Joe regarded Jessica in horror when she asked if he wanted to pick up ducks.

"Kidding, kidding," she said, and threw up her hands in surrender. But part of her was sad that he *was* too big for that now.

"You used to love them," she said wistfully, remembering fairs of the past, when Joe would squeal in delight as his chubby baby hands grasped one of the pink or blue ducks from the endless blue circle they bobbed in.

"They're for babies." Joe crossed his arms over his chest. "I'm a big boy."

"Yes, you are," Jessica admitted.

"Joe!" Freddie came running up, startling her. "Wanna ride the Scrambler with me?"

Joe looked up at Alex. "Want to?"

Alex grimaced and patted his stomach. "I'm sorry, buddy, but that thing would probably kill me right now, this soon after eating."

"Maggie will ride with us. Can he, please?" Freddie pointed to his sister, and she waved.

Jessica looked up at the sky and frowned. "Joe, it's going to rain. We have to leave soon."

"One more ride and we'll go. Please, Mom?"

"What if it makes you sick?"

"I've never been sick on anything," Joe protested, his blue eyes pleading.

Jessica sighed. "Okay, but then we go. Alex and I will be right here at the gate, okay?"

Joe grinned, and the boys took off to get in line. Alex and Jessica trailed behind them.

"What's the matter?" Alex asked gently as he put an arm around her shoulder.

"I'm a little jumpy," Jessica admitted. They squeezed through the line and took a spot near the exit gate. Like most carnival rides, the entrance and exit were only a few feet apart. Joe wasn't going anywhere.

"It's going to be okay," Alex said as he turned to face her. He gripped the rail on either side of her, and she put her hand on the back of his neck.

"Promise?"

He kissed her nose. "I promise."

They watched the current passengers disembark, and waved at Joe when he climbed into one of the metal cars.

"I could ride anything too at his age, but that changed when I got a little older," Alex said with a rueful smile. "That would make me as sick as a dog."

Jessica's head ached, and she had to look away from the spinning tumblers. The ride next to them started up with a frenzied burst of rock and roll music, and Jessica wanted to cover her ears. Alex put his arm around her and continued watching.

"Where are we headed next?" Alex asked over the blaring music of the Himalaya. "Back to Tennessee?"

"I hate to leave Laura yet," Jessica said distractedly.

The Scrambler slowed, and suddenly she and Alex were surrounded by other parents waiting for their children to get off. She saw a flash of Joe's face before the car presented its shiny metal back to her on the far side of the ring. Children dashed past them, heading out the gate. Jessica edged closer, not willing to lose Joe in the crowd. She saw the top of Freddie's red head, but he was caught in the throng of people pushing out the gate.

She didn't see Joe anywhere.

The carnival worker opened the gate to let the next group in and Jessica grabbed his arm. "Wait! My son . . ."

Alex was already moving. He pushed through the exit and ran to the spot they'd last spotted Joe.

Jessica caught another glimpse of red hair. "Freddie!" she screamed. "Freddie!"

The little boy heard her over the blast of hip-hop music and hurried over.

"Joe! Where's Joe?" she shouted.

"His dad lifted him over the fence."

Jessica froze. She was suddenly struck deaf and dumb, unable to hear anything but blood rushing in her ears. Freddie mouthed "him" and pointed to a white-faced Alex, who stood in the center of the ride, shouting to the carnival workers.

Cole had her baby.

Some instinct took over, and Jessica took off running. She shoved her way through the crowd, screaming Joe's name.

Too soon, iron bands tightened around her chest, but Jessica grabbed her inhaler out of the bag and kept moving. Like a wild woman, she jumped on top of one of the tables at the food court and took a treatment, ignoring the startled protests of the table's occupants.

Her eyes darted over the crowd, and she caught a glimpse of the back of Cole's head a hundred yards away. He was moving fast, carrying Joe in his arms.

"Security!" Jessica screeched, but didn't see a uniform in sight. She jumped off the table and ran, feeling she was going to explode for lack of air.

Please, not now, Jessica thought desperately, sucking at the inhaler.

Cole was through the gate. Any second and he would be gone. There was no way she could catch him on foot. Frantically, she patted her pockets. There were the keys. Alex had handed them to her when he rode the Mega Loop.

Cole's pace picked up, and he was running too. He

ran past the field of cars. Jessica ran as hard as she could. Her head swam, and she stumbled around a parked car.

Tires squealed, and she saw the black Jag peel onto the highway. Her hand spasmed as she unlocked the rental car and threw herself inside. When the engine roared to life, she yanked savagely on the gearshift and crashed into an exiting vehicle. She put it in drive and floored the gas. Tears streamed down her face as she searched for the Jag's taillights.

"Oh, God," she whispered.

What if she never saw Joe again?

She fumbled in her purse and felt a little shock when her fingers brushed over the cool metal of the gun she had stolen from Cole's safe. She'd forgotten all about it; forgotten to buy ammo.

But Cole wouldn't know that.

Alex sprinted to the parking lot. A security guard ran alongside him, shouting questions. Alex had never been so scared in his life.

Another guard was talking to a couple in a red Honda Civic. The front fender was smashed, and the spot Alex had parked the rental car was empty.

Jessica.

"I need a cab. Get me a cab," Alex yelled. The security guard nodded and removed his cell phone from his pocket. Alex flipped his open too.

"Wally. I need to speak to Wally Davis."

The car he'd rented from Wally was equipped with GPS. Wally could track her.

"I'm sorry, but Wally isn't on duty right now," the receptionist's smooth voice intoned. "Can someone else help you?"

"Give me his number."

"I'm sorry, sir, but I'm not allowed …"

"Give me his number, dammit! This is an emergency."

Alex thought she was going to hang up, but she rattled off a number. He repeated it aloud as he hung up and punched it in.

Wally abandoned his meatloaf dinner and was on his way to the rental place when Alex hung up.

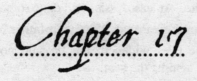
Chapter 17

"Why did my mama leave without me?"

Joe's soft question tore Cole from his thoughts, and he gave his son a reassuring pat on the knee as he sped down the interstate.

"You know your Aunt Laura is sick, right? Your mama had to go back to the hospital."

The lie rolled smoothly from Cole's tongue, but it twisted his stomach. He'd already lied to Joe twice in a matter of minutes, and he didn't like it. But it was the only way. Someday Joe would forgive him.

They had gotten away. Cole couldn't believe it. He'd missed his chance when Joe was on the Ferris wheel because of a loitering security guard, but fate had given him another.

Cole's sweat-soaked shirt clung to him. He turned up

the air conditioner, and smiled at his son. Joe gave him a tiny smile in return, and Cole's heart tugged. He was so innocent, so trusting.

"You look just like Alex," Joe said.

"Alex is my brother." Cole hesitated, then swallowed over the lump in his throat. "Do you know who I am, Joe?"

"No, sir."

Very polite. At least Jessica had done something right.

Cole cleared his throat. "I'm your father."

Joe's blue eyes widened, but he said nothing. He leaned back against the seat.

What? *What*? Cole thought, desperate for some reaction. What had Jessica told him? Was his son afraid of him?

"Mama said you were sick, and you couldn't take care of us," Joe said finally.

Cole's hands tightened on the steering wheel, but he forced himself to keep his voice level. "I'm better now. I'm going to take care of you."

"Are you going to take care of Mama too?" Joe asked timidly.

I wish, Cole thought. That was his one regret. He didn't have time to pay the bitch back for all the suffering she'd caused him.

"We're all going to be okay now." Cole ruffled Joe's dark hair. "We're going to take a little trip, just you and me, until things settle down. Your grandpa is helping me get things ready."

"Grandpa Mason?" Joe asked.

Cole winced. "No. Grandpa Earl." He hesitated. "Do me a favor, champ. Could you maybe not mention Grandpa Mason to Grandpa Earl?"

"Why?"

"Grandpa Earl is a little grouchy," Cole said, and was relieved when Joe smiled. "And he doesn't like Grandpa Mason all that much."

"I won't say anything." Joe mimed zipping his lips, and Cole winked at him.

The bleakness that enveloped Cole seemed to melt away in his son's presence. He was consumed by the need to know everything about this little boy: what he liked, what he didn't; what were his fears, what were his dreams. He peppered Joe with questions, and the hour-long drive to his father's house passed quickly.

Cole was laughing, actually *laughing*. God, he'd thought he'd never laugh again. His heart swelled with pride, and he found it amazing that two screwed-up people like him and Jessica could produce a child like this.

Some of his good humor evaporated when he pulled up in front of his father's dilapidated house, however. He hoped Earl wasn't drinking, but that was a pretty remote possibility these days. Especially since Earl had his hands on most of Cole's savings by now. Cole was under no illusion that all his money would be present and accounted for, but that was a price he was willing to pay. With no one else to turn to and no time to do it himself,

Cole had been forced to ask for his father's help.

Cole unbuckled his seatbelt and leaned over to unhook Joe. Together they walked into the junked-up yard, wading through the shin-high grass. Aluminum cans crackled underneath their shoes and Cole kicked aside an old pop bottle filled with tobacco spit. He grimaced and picked Joe up when the boy tripped over a rusty piece of twisted metal that might've once been part of a Chevelle. Even in this run-down section of town, neighbors griped about the state of Earl Ramsey's yard. Cole paid someone twice a year to clean it up, but it rapidly returned to its original state of disrepair. He didn't know what had happened to the kid he paid to mow the lawn. Scared off by Earl, no doubt.

Cole rapped soundly on the door and called loudly, "Pop, it's me!" before letting himself inside.

Cole was always afraid that Earl, in one of his alcoholic stupors, would think one of the crackheads next door was breaking in if he didn't announce himself.

Shoot first, ask questions later. That was Pop's motto.

Cole had offered to buy his father a house in another neighborhood, but Earl seemed content to wallow in his misery. Truth be known, he belonged here.

Cole made a sound of disgust as he watched a cockroach skitter over a cardboard pizza box on the floor. He took Joe's hand, not sure if he was comforting Joe or himself. Cole hated this place. It smelled of piss and vomit.

Earl lumbered through the kitchen doorway and

regarded them with bleary eyes. Cole could smell the Jack Daniels whiskey from five feet away.

Earl leaned forward to peer at Joe and nearly toppled in the process. "The boy's a Ramsey all right," he slurred.

He staggered forward, and Joe took a step back. Joe moved slightly behind Cole and pressed against his leg.

Suddenly Cole saw his father as Joe must see him.

Handsome in his youth, Earl Ramsey had gone to seed. Earl lifted the tail of his dirty white undershirt and scratched his distended belly. The sparse salt and pepper beard that covered his ruddy face was interrupted by a lightning shaped scar zigzagging down one cheek. Trophy from a barroom brawl. Earl looked like a man who'd spent a season in hell.

"What's the matter with him? Can't he talk?" Earl demanded, and took another lurching step toward them. "Is he not right in the head or something?"

Cole heard a snuffling sound behind him and realized, to his horror, that Joe was crying.

"Aw, hell!" Earl grabbed for Joe, who darted behind Cole, eluding his grandfather's clumsy grasp. "She's ruined him, Cole. He's a sissy."

Earl made another lunge for Joe, but Cole threw himself between them.

"Ramseys never, ever cry!" Earl shouted, and shook his fist at the little boy. "You need to whip him, Cole. Toughen him up."

"He'll learn. He's scared right now, but he'll be okay." Cole held up his palms in supplication. Earl frowned, noticing the cast for the first time. It distracted him, and he fell silent for a moment. Cole took advantage of his silence to speak to Joe. He crouched down and whispered, "Go upstairs right now, and let me talk to Grandpa. Then we'll leave, okay?" He pointed to the stairwell visible in the next room.

Joe nodded and rubbed his red-rimmed eyes. Then Joe caught him off-guard when he threw his arms around his neck. Cole hugged him tightly, surprised to feel tears of his own spring into his eyes.

Wouldn't that be a pisser? Earl would kill them both.

"Go upstairs," he whispered. "It'll just take a minute."

"You won't leave me here, will you?" Joe asked softly, and Cole kissed the top of his head.

"No. I'm not going anywhere without you." He gently slapped Joe's behind, and Joe bounded through the doorway. Cole heard his footsteps echoing up the stairs, and reluctantly faced his father.

"You shouldn't let him do that." Earl shook his head and removed a silver flask from his back pocket. "Boy will never amount to nothin', you let him get by with sh—"

"Did you get the money?" Cole interrupted, not wanting to hear his father's tirade.

Earl frowned. "Dammit, I knew there was something I had to tell you. I got the money from the safe, but the man at the bank wouldn't give me the rest. He said he couldn't clear out the account without you coming by personally to authorize it. And he also said that the cop had been by, asking about you."

Jesus. You'd think the old man might've mentioned it a little sooner.

"Where's the money from the safe?" Cole asked. "I have to get out of here, Pop." It wasn't much, but it would have to do.

"In the kitchen. I'll get it." Earl staggered off, and Cole started toward the window.

The front door crashed open and a crazed-looking Jessica burst inside, waving a gun at him. His gun.

"Where is he? Where's my son?"

Cole exhaled loudly. He didn't have time for this. He circled her slowly, forcing Jessica to turn her back to the kitchen to stay in front of him. Where was Alex?

"How does it feel, Jessica?" he demanded. "How does it feel to not know where he is, to not know if he's being cared for?" How do you like it now that the shoe's on the other foot?"

"Tell me where he is, or I swear I'll shoot you."

"Shoot me. You don't have the guts."

Jessica glared at him, her eyes dark with hatred. Cole saw movement behind her in the doorway and said, "Go on, kill me. Then you'll never know where he is."

Jessica glanced at the stairway, and he knew what she was thinking. She knew he hadn't had time to take Joe far.

Earl slipped through the doorway behind her. He held a skillet in his hands and, when Jessica opened her mouth to call out to Joe, he swung. The blow caught her squarely in the back of the head. Her eyes rolled back to show the whites as she crumpled soundlessly to the floor.

Cole pried the gun from her fingers and gave a snort of disbelief when he saw it was unloaded.

She really was crazy.

He tucked it in the waistband of his jeans and muttered, "Thanks, Pop."

Earl thrust a red and white Save-a-Bunch sack at him, and said gruffly, "There's your money. You need to take her somewhere, get rid of the body. I'll keep the kid and meet back up with you."

Cole paused, not sure what to do next. The only thing he knew for sure was that there was no way he could leave Joe with Earl.

Earl dug a set of keys out of his pocket. "Take the Buick. They'll be looking for the Jag. Get her."

Cole lifted Jessica in his arms and followed Earl through the kitchen into the attached garage. Earl opened the trunk, and Cole deposited Jessica inside. He felt a twinge of regret as he stared at her pale face. With a grimace, he shut the trunk and started back inside.

"I'm going to take Joe with me, Pop. They'll be looking for him here."

"The houseboat!" Earl exclaimed. "You can dump her in the ocean and head to Tijuana."

Cole mulled it over. It just might work.

The marina was in Chula Vista, a heartbeat away from the California/Mexico border. And Aunt Gina lived twenty minutes away in the next town. She could keep Joe while he disposed of Jessica. He didn't want his son to have to see that.

Earl gave him the keys to the boat, and Cole called for Joe. Joe hurried to him, giving Earl a wide berth.

As they pulled back onto the highway, Cole was a nervous wreck. If Jessica came to and started screaming, how would he explain it to Joe? What if the police were following him already? It was growing late, and traffic wasn't all that bad. Still, Cole found himself compulsively checking the rearview mirror, even though the night masked everything but the yellow glow of other drivers' headlights. Joe hadn't spoken a word since they'd left Earl. Cole patted his knee.

"You okay?" he asked, and Joe nodded. "He was pretty scary, huh?"

"I don't like that man." Joe's voice trembled, and Cole fought the urge to pull to the side of the road and take his son in his arms. As long as he was alive, Joe had nothing to fear from anyone.

"We don't have to see him again," Cole said automatically, then realized what he'd said. The thought caused a rush of conflicting emotions, of which the predominant one was relief.

He would be truly free. Now that he had his son, he could start over, forget the past. It was like a cloud lifting from his soul.

"The car hasn't moved?" Alex peered out the cabbie's

windshield, still talking to Wally on the cell phone. A soft pulse sounded in his ear, warning him that his battery was low.

"Not an inch. How close are you?"

"Should see it any minute. You said the corner of 3rd and Elm?"

"Yeah." Just as Wally replied, Alex saw the rental car. His heart sank. It sat alone on the curb. The driver's door hung open, and its windshield was smashed.

Alex paid the cabbie and jumped out in the misting rain to inspect it. His phone went dead, and he threw it at the car in frustration. The hub cabs and radio were already stripped. The thought of Jessica wandering alone in this seedy neighborhood made Alex's stomach curdle. He ran the rest of the way to his father's house.

Alex tested the door and found it locked. He pounded on it until he heard Earl bellow, "Keep your pants on, I'm coming!"

A red-faced Earl threw open the door and blinked when he saw Alex. "Well!" he exclaimed. "Look what the cat dragged in."

Alex gritted his teeth and shouldered past his father, ignoring his startled grunt. "Where are they?"

"Get out of my house," Earl said.

A small stream of spittle ran down the corner of his mouth, and he swayed precariously.

Three sheets to the wind, Alex thought with disgust.

Hard to believe he'd once feared this pathetic old man. Glancing around the chaotic living room, Alex caught a flash of gold against the stained green carpet. It was an earring.

Jessica's earring, the small gold hoops she'd worn to the carnival.

Fear threatened to swallow him. What had happened here?

He ran past Earl and searched the house. Alex found nothing until he walked into Earl's garage. The gleaming black Jag was parked inside.

Furious, Alex bounded back into the house. Earl was slumped in his recliner, drinking from a silver flask. Alex knocked it from his hand and hauled him to his feet by a handful of dirty undershirt.

"Where did he take her?" he shouted.

Earl merely smiled. "Take who?" he asked innocently.

Alex grabbed a discarded beer bottle from the end table and smashed it on the door facing. He pressed the jagged edge to Earl's throat hard enough to bring blood. The mockery left Earl's eyes as small beads of blood appeared. His father was a man of violence, and violence was what got his attention.

"You're too late," Earl slurred. "She's fish food by now."

"Where are they?" Alex demanded, and pressed the glass harder to his father's throat. Malevolence shone in Earl's eyes, along with some kind of sick excitement. A thin stream of blood snaked down Earl's neck to stain his shirt, and Alex felt queasy.

"At the marina. In Chula Vista. You're too late."

"The Jag, where are the keys?"

Morosely, Earl dug them out of his pocket and dangled them in front of Alex. "You'll never find them," he taunted.

"You're wrong about that, old man. You're going to help me."

Earl made a lurching move toward his recliner, and Alex spotted the stock of the shotgun sticking up behind it. He was lucky Earl hadn't thought of it while he was searching upstairs. Alex grabbed the gun and the box of shells beside it. Forcing his father into the garage, Alex threw him into the passenger seat of the Jag and slammed the door. He gave a sharp tug that sent the garage door flying upward, and jumped into the driver's seat.

"Cole's already killed her," Earl said. "Just looking to get rid of the body."

"You're lying." Alex clenched his teeth and struggled to stay focused on the road ahead. "You made him like he is."

"The hell I did." Earl leaned back in his seat. "You and your bitch of a mother abandoned us. We did the best we could, and besides, Cole turned out better than you did." Earl made a sound of disgust. "You choose some woman over your own flesh and blood. Your brother's *wife*, to beat it all."

Alex refused to take the bait. He wasn't going to defend himself to the old man. He sat ramrod straight in the seat and said nothing. Bored, Earl closed his eyes and turned away from Alex. Soon, he was snoring.

Alex turned the radio on to drown out the sound

and, with a frown, he tugged Earl's wallet from his back pocket. There was a thick stack of twenties still enclosed in the paper band. Cole's money, no doubt. Alex ignored the money and pulled the papers from the side enclosure. No driver's license—Alex was willing to bet Earl had lost that years ago—a tattered social security card, a couple of old lottery tickets.

"Bingo," Alex said as he unfolded a thin pink paper. It was a receipt from Mecklenburg Marina for yearly fees for slip 223. As he read the address, Alex saw the sign. Nearly there.

Alex turned off the four-lane onto a two-lane and soon found himself sitting at a traffic light. He didn't notice the absence of Earl's snores until it was too late.

A black and white sat on the side of the road. The officer was writing a ticket to some boys pulling a jet ski behind their pickup. Before Alex realized what was happening, Earl was rolling down his window.

"Help! Help!" Earl screamed. "He's gonna kill me. He's got a gun!"

The officer shot them a startled look, and Alex gassed it.

He jumped the sidewalk and cut off a garbage truck as he swerved back onto the highway. The officer was already moving toward his cruiser.

Alex raced toward the marina as the sirens began to wail.

Chapter 18

Cole pulled into the marina and wondered how he was going to get Jessica out of the trunk without anyone seeing. The indecisive rain they'd left in Los Angeles had no such qualms here. In Chula Vista, it was pouring.

Although that would deter many of the casual boaters, Cole knew some people lived at this marina year-round.

It hadn't been easy leaving Joe at his Aunt Gina's, but Cole had known she would take care of him. He'd hated lying to her. Gina was a good apple on a diseased Ramsey family tree. She hadn't hesitated when he'd asked her to watch his child, hadn't asked for explanations when he'd given none.

Joe had hugged him when he left, and Cole could almost feel the imprint of his little arms still. Joe had signed his name on Cole's cast, a heart with his name printed inside in careful, blocky letters. Looking at it strengthened Cole's resolve and warmed his heart. The force of his feelings for Joe took him by surprise. How could he love a child he barely knew?

As soon as he got rid of Jessica, things would be better. Joe would forget her.

Cole tooled around the parking lot until he found an empty spot tucked between a Winnebago and a Ford Explorer. Not perfect cover, but Cole wasn't going to complain. He sandwiched the boxy old Buick between them and yanked the keys out.

After a cursory glance around, he popped the trunk and hauled Jessica out. She was still unconscious. Her head rolled loosely on her shoulders, and he wondered if she was already dead. Pressing his fingertips to her throat, he detected the faint beat of her pulse.

"It didn't have to be like this, Jessica," Cole said softly. Shaking his head, he hoisted her to an upright position and threw one of her arms across his shoulders. She hung like a marionette with no strings.

Cole carefully affected his walk as they started down the wooden dock. After years of watching Earl Ramsey, Cole knew what a staggering drunk looked like.

"Come on, baby," he said, loudly enough to be heard should anyone be listening. "We're almost there." He kept talking to her, slurring some words and speaking at the carefree decibels of the terminally sloshed. Soon, the houseboat was in sight.

"Finally get some use out of the damn thing," Cole muttered.

He'd bought this boat twice for the old man, the first time when Earl couldn't make the payments and the second after he'd wagered it in a poker game. Cole just hoped the inside didn't look like Earl's house.

He scooped Jessica up in his arms and hurried toward it. They were both soaked.

A man emerged from the houseboat next door. His voice shocked Cole so badly he nearly dropped Jessica.

"Hey, buddy. Need any help?"

"Thas okay," Cole slurred. "I got her."

"Party hardy?" the guy smiled, and Cole winked.

"You got that right. I told the wife she should quit with the shooters while she was ahead, but . . ." Cole shrugged, and the man's grin widened.

"I know how it is. That's what I told my wife about the credit cards, but did she listen? Now the kicker is she's got the house, and I have to sell my boat."

Cole gave him a polite smile and started climbing onboard the houseboat. The man ran to help steady it. To Cole's irritation, he boarded behind them and rushed ahead to open the cabin door. Cole nodded his thanks and stumbled down to lay Jessica on one of the narrow beds. The man stood inside the cabin door, still talking.

Whatever he was saying died on his lips when Cole turned to face him. His eyes widened as he stared at Cole's chest. Cole glanced down to see a large bloodstain spreading across the front of his pale blue shirt where Jessica's head had rested.

The man turned to run, but Cole was faster. He

grabbed the Samaritan's leg with one arm and hauled him down the steps. The man's head bounced off the bottom step with a dull thud. Cole seized a handful of the man's hair. With one savage twist, it was over. The Samaritan's brown eyes gazed sightlessly at the ceiling.

Cole cursed and pushed himself to his feet. This, he didn't need. What was he supposed to do with two bodies? He considered moving both of them to the Samaritan's boat and simply leaving them, but someone might see the transfer.

His eyes lit upon the fuel container in the corner, and he formed a plan. He could burn them at sea. There was a little cove around the bend. He could douse the bodies in fuel, set the boat on fire, and hike back up to the freeway. By the time the police figured out the other body wasn't his, he and Joe would be in Mexico.

They could take the Samaritan's boat. The Samaritan was a man in the middle of a divorce. His relatives might assume he'd decided to take a trip and get away from it all. Stranger things had happened.

Cole dragged the man's body to the cot across from Jessica and stretched him out. Something about the stranger's unseeing gaze bothered him, so Cole covered him with a couple of blankets.

Cole released the boat from its mooring. He shoved it away from the dock with an oar Earl kept for that purpose. They drifted past the no wake zone, and Cole increased speed. The little cove was dead ahead.

Alex wasn't used to the horsepower of the Jag. He wove through traffic, pleased with the distance he was putting between him and the cruiser. Then he took a curve too fast, and the steering wheel was wrenched from his hands as the Jag began to spin.

It ping-ponged between the guardrails. Alex watched one of the Jag's wheels roll past in the left lane just before they crashed headlong into a concrete barrier. The shriek of twisting metal filled his ears, and the airbags deployed, knocking him senseless for a moment.

Alex wrestled his door, but it wouldn't open. He took his pocketknife and punctured the airbag, gagging when the sickly sweet chemical smell fogged the interior. Then he kicked the shattered remains of the windshield away. Fumbling for the shotgun, he climbed out. Cars stopped behind him, and people approached the car. They backed off when they saw the shotgun. Someone screamed. Alex started to run. He slipped down the embankment and ran for the docks. It wouldn't occur to him until later that he never spared Earl a backward glance.

As Alex ran down to the dock, he became conscious of a dull throb in his thigh, and glanced down to see the leg of his jeans darkened with blood. A jagged piece of glass had imbedded itself in his thigh. Alex gave it a savage wrench and gashed his palm in the process. Probably should've left it in. Blood streamed down his leg freely now, and squished in his shoe.

Cole was already gone.

Alex saw the empty slip and didn't know what to do next. He kept running down the pier. The day-use dock was just beyond the slips. A teenaged boy idled next to the dock in a red bass boat, waiting for his partner to back the trailer down to the water.

Alex raised the shotgun, although he didn't point it directly at the boy. "I need your boat!" he shouted. "It's an emergency."

The boy stared at him and raised his hands. "Hey, man, you can have it. Don't shoot."

He drew the boat closer. Alex jumped in behind him, and the boy hastily hopped onto the dock.

"I'm sorry," Alex said, then eased back the throttle and roared out of the no wake zone.

This was stupid. It was pointless. Alex had no idea what he was looking for, no idea how long Cole had already been gone. He didn't even know in which direction to go.

The endless gray ocean stretched before him.

Gasoline. Jessica smelled gasoline, but she couldn't open her eyes. Something banged to her right, and she had to stifle a scream when she felt the cold liquid splash on her legs.

Finally she managed to lift one leaden eyelid and watched Cole's back ascend the steps of the—what, a cabin? Were they on a boat?

Jessica sat up and had to grab the iron frame of the bunk above to steady herself. Her head swam crazily.

You can't pass out. You can't pass out, she told herself.

Black spots danced before her eyes, and Jessica stared down at her jeans. The legs were soaked with gasoline. After a moment's hesitation, she wriggled out of them and left them lying on the bunk.

Jessica shivered, clad only in a wet T-shirt and panties. Gripping the wall, she staggered toward the backdoor of the cabin.

While struggling with the metal latch, she heard a loud whoosh. A wall of hot air nearly knocked her down and the cabin burst into flames.

"Oh, God!" she gasped, and tore the door open.

The coolness of the rainy night took her breath away, a sharp contrast to the inferno behind her.

Jessica slipped on the back deck and crashed to her knees. Huge clouds of black smoke billowed from the cabin. She pulled the collar of her T-shirt up to cover her nose and mouth, and she began to crawl.

The smoke badly obscured her vision and she didn't see Cole until she was almost upon him. He was about to jump. If he got away from her now, Jessica knew she would never see her son again.

With a guttural cry of rage, she charged.

Cole looked up in surprise the instant before she crashed into him. They tumbled backward on the rain-slicked deck. She caught him off-guard, locked her hands around his throat. She squeezed as hard as she could, taking a grim delight at the panic in his eyes.

It was about time.

Jessica's triumph was short-lived, however. Cole

whacked her across the shoulders with his cast, knocking the air from her lungs. He caught her by the throat with his other hand and threw her like a rag doll.

She bounced off the rail and lay on the deck, trying desperately to breathe. Cole advanced toward her. Jessica could see the imprint of her fingers against his throat.

She pawed the deck, feeling for a weapon. Her hands closed on some sort of wooden handle. It was an oar. Grasping it, Jessica clamored to her feet.

"Come on, you bastard," she yelled over the roar of the fire. "Come and get me."

Chapter 19

Alex zipped past the marina and searched for any sign of them. Suddenly, he smelled smoke. He killed the motor and scanned the horizon. The clouds were so dark Alex couldn't see the stars, much less from where the smoke was coming. He started the boat and sped on, turning when the smell seemed to fade. Alex wandered into the cove. In the distance, he saw the muted orange glow of the flames.

Nearly blinded by the rain that pelted his face, Alex raced toward them.

Fire licked the top of the houseboat. The orange flames darted in and out of the thick black cloak that blanketed the boat. Alex was almost upon it when he saw the two combatants onboard. A half-clothed Jessica took a vicious swing at Cole with an oar.

The blow caught Cole in the side, and he staggered.

He grabbed for it and missed. Jessica drew it back to strike again, and Cole charged. They went down in a pile of flailing arms and legs.

Alex killed the motor and used the smaller trolling motor to draw close enough to grab for a rail. It took three tries, but he finally got it. He hoisted himself over, and shouted, "Stop it!"

Cole's head jerked up, and Jessica took the advantage to gouge at his eyes with her thumbs. With a bellow of rage, Cole slugged her in the jaw and seized her hand. Alex watched in horror as Cole stuck Jessica's fingers in his mouth and clamped down. Jessica shrieked, and Alex threw himself on Cole's back.

A loud explosion sounded inside the cabin. The boat pitched violently, nearly sending Alex and Cole tumbling over the railing.

"Jessica, get out of here!" Alex yelled. "Get off the boat."

Cole was on top, and he had the oar. The wooden handle pressed against Alex's neck, threatening to crush his windpipe.

A smaller explosion rocked the boat, and Cole lost his grip. Alex planted his foot on Cole's chest and shoved him backward.

Alex caught movement in his peripheral vision and turned to yell at Jessica.

"Get in the other boat. Now!" Alex heard the splash as she obeyed, but lost sight of Cole.

The boat gave a tortured shriek and seemed to fold

into itself. Alex started sliding and grabbed onto the rail. Somewhere in front of him, Alex heard Cole scream.

Still grasping the rail, Alex scrambled toward his brother. Cole lay trapped under a chunk of twisted metal. Flames danced all around him. He lifted something and pointed it at Alex.

It was a gun.

Their eyes met, and Cole squeezed his shut. He lowered the gun.

"Alex," he gasped. "For God's sake, go!"

"I'm not leaving you." Alex edged closer to Cole. He grasped at the metal that pinned Cole, and it seared his palms. Alex cursed, then tried again.

"I can't feel my legs," Cole panted. "I can't move."

The houseboat was almost completely engulfed. Alex saw the hopelessness settle in Cole's eyes.

Cole knew he was going to die.

Alex attacked the metal with a renewed vengeance, but it wouldn't budge.

"Get off here before the fuel tank blows!" Cole barked. When Alex ignored him, he stuck the revolver between Alex's eyes. "Now!" he shouted.

Alex felt like he was the one dying as he staggered away from his brother.

"Move!" Cole screamed. "I won't be responsible for you too."

Alex heard his twin's sobs and knew he was talking about Kaitlin. With a heavy heart, Alex climbed on the rail and stared at the churning water below.

"Take care of Joe!" Cole yelled. "He's at Aunt Gina's."

Alex jumped over the side into the black ocean below. He spotted Jessica and the bass boat through the haze. The rippling waves from the explosion had pushed them to the lip of the cove. Debris floated in the water around him, and the water was scummy with ash.

Alex swam hard as he could to her. Anxiously, Jessica leaned over the gunwale of the boat and reached for him. Just as their hands touched, the houseboat exploded.

The impact from the blast knocked Jessica from the boat and smacked Alex's head against the fiberglass hull. Even from fifty feet away, the heat seared him.

Alex dived under the boat and groped blindly for Jessica. He'd inhaled too much smoke and had to come up swiftly for a breath. Jessica surfaced beside him, coughing and gagging.

They helped each other back into the boat and stared at the flaming wreckage.

Suddenly, they were blinded by floodlights.

"This is the police!" someone droned into a megaphone. "Put your hands where we can see them."

Alex and Jessica slowly lifted their hands. Both of them were shivering despite the hot night air.

Burning. He was burning.

Cole crawled through the foliage, using his elbows to propel himself as he dragged his useless legs.

He had no conscious sense of moving, no sense of anything but consuming pain. His body acted purely on instinct, trying to flee from something it couldn't escape.

Even though the rough undergrowth scrubbed strips of flesh from his body, he didn't realize it. Like a snake, he crept up the embankment on his belly.

His palms touched cool, wet asphalt. Cole pulled himself onto the freeway.

An eighteen-wheeler barreled toward him.

One word broke through the red haze of agony in Cole's mind.

Kaitlyn, he thought, and lifted his head.

The driver saw the horrific thing in the road struggle to rise. He panicked when he realized it was human. He stood on the brakes, but the truck was too close to stop. Tires screamed against wet highway, and the big rig went into a slide.

It jackknifed. Like a scorpion, its tail whipped violently into the other lanes of traffic. The trailer smacked a gas truck, and the resulting explosion blew the trailer twenty feet in the air.

Cars slammed into each other, unable to avoid the catastrophic pile-up. Twenty-two vehicles were involved.

It was the worst freeway accident in Chula Vista history.

Emergency workers from three counties searched for survivors. Both truck drivers and a number of others were killed instantly.

One of the firefighters found the burned man with the

cast by the wreckage of the truck cab. She was surprised to find a pulse.

"Hey, we've got a live one here!" she cried.

Chapter 20

Jessica parked at the end of the gravel drive and got out. She hugged herself as she climbed the grassy hillside to watch the ceremony below.

It felt funny being at Cole's graveside service. Jessica was glad he was dead. She just hated it for Alex and Kate. They were both hurting.

The police had grilled them for hours after the explosion. Earl filed charges against Alex for kidnapping. He was also charged with stealing the bass boat, reckless driving, and evading the police.

Jessica, who wasn't charged with anything, pressed charges against Earl Ramsey for attempted murder. Earl's lawyer then met with Jessica's lawyer to plea-bargain. He would drop the charges against Alex if she would agree to reduce his charge to assault. Jessica accepted his offer.

Upon learning the details of the story, the owner of

the bass boat dropped his charges, but the police persisted in theirs. Alex paid a fine at the county courthouse and was released.

Earl Ramsey's allegations that Jessica had faked her death were dismissed for lack of evidence.

It was a legal nightmare.

Jessica hadn't spoken to Alex in two days. He'd been helping Kate make Cole's funeral arrangements. Jessica was worried about him. He seemed withdrawn, dazed.

Cole's body had been badly charred in the explosion. The investigators hadn't been able to extract DNA from the remains dragged from the ocean. There was some controversy, but based on Alex and Jessica's testimony, Cole had been declared dead.

The service was concluding. The crowd began to disperse, and Jessica searched for Alex. A sobbing Kate turned from the casket into Mason's arms. Alex wasn't there. Neither was Earl.

Kate and Mason slowly made their way up the hillside.

"Kate!"

Kate looked up and said something to Mason. She made her way over to Jessica, alone. They hugged each other, and Jessica said, "Alex isn't here?"

Kate wiped at her nose with a tissue. "Oh, honey. Alex is having such a hard time dealing with this. He . . ." She paused, giving Jessica a compassionate look. "He's gone back to Tennessee."

"What?" Jessica gasped. He'd left without saying a word?

"Please don't be angry with him," Kate pleaded. "He just needs a little time alone. He feels so guilty."

With no other recourse, Jessica waited.

After a month, she wondered if she would ever hear from Alex again.

Jessica was shocked when she and Joe inherited Cole's rather large estate. She didn't want it. Earl did, and contested it bitterly, but the probate judge dismissed his case.

Jessica considered hiring a construction crew to demolish the house she once shared with Cole. Then she thought about donating it to the fire department to use in training exercises. How she'd once longed to watch it burn. But in the end, Danny had supplied the best suggestion.

She donated Cole's house to a local battered-women's shelter. The house would be used as a temporary residence for women like her, women who were learning to live on their own for the first time.

Jessica donated the rest to various charities.

At last she was free. She even went back to being blond.

The only thing missing from her life was Alex. Jessica wondered where he was and what he was doing, if he thought of her. She'd told him the whole time that there was no way they could be together, and now she was scared he'd come to believe that too.

She spent another month in California with Laura, but soon grew restless. Los Angeles was no longer her home.

She and Joe boarded a plane and flew back to Tennessee.

Alex lifted the ax high above his head and had just started the downward swing when he saw her out of the corner of his eye.

Jessica appeared like a ghost through the trees.

Distracted, Alex glanced down as the ax made contact. The wood splintered, and the impact sent vibrations tingling up his arms. He was afraid to look up.

Afraid she wouldn't really be there. Afraid that maybe she would.

He'd dreamed of her last night.

Alex didn't dream much these days, because he made it a point to work himself to exhaustion to keep from it. But Jessica had found him anyway.

He dared a glance. She was still there.

"I followed the sound of the chopping," Jessica said, and took a tentative step in his direction.

"What are you doing here?" It came out harsher than he'd intended, and Jessica drew back.

"I was worried about you," she said softly. She looked around. "What are you doing?"

"Cutting firewood for the winter."

Jessica looked surprised, and Alex glanced around. He knew what she was thinking. He had enough wood split and stacked for the next ten winters.

"Diseased pines," he said abruptly.

"Have you been back to work?"

"Can't." Alex stood a section of wood on its end and raised the ax again. "My license is under review. Have to wait until the state makes a decision."

"Oh, Alex, I'm so sorry," Jessica said as he swung. She took another step toward him, and Alex felt the insane urge to run.

Jessica crossed over the wood. When she tried to hug him, Alex pulled away.

"I'm dirty," he said. Which wasn't a lie. His bare chest was covered with perspiration, dirt, and flecks of wood.

Feeling a little guilty for the hurt look in her eyes, he said, "Come on. If you don't mind waiting until I get a shower . . ."

"I'll wait," she said.

They trudged back to the cabin in silence.

"How's Joe?" Alex asked finally, as they climbed his front steps.

"He's okay. Glad to be home, though."

Alex held the door open for Jessica to enter. She passed close by him, and he had to close his eyes when he caught the sweet scent of her perfume.

"I'll be right back," he said hoarsely.

"I'll wait on the deck," Jessica said.

Alex scrubbed himself under the hot spray of the shower, wondering what she wanted. Wondering what he wanted.

Thoughts of Cole plagued him.

This whole thing was his fault. If he hadn't called Cole that day, his brother would still be alive. Joe would've never been kidnapped, and Jessica would never have been hurt. It seemed horribly wrong that he was still alive when he'd caused the whole mess.

Finally, knowing he couldn't hide in the bathroom forever, Alex exited the shower and toweled himself dry. He finger-combed his hair and smoothed a hand across his beard. Maybe it wasn't sticking up too badly. There was no way to check. Alex had removed all the mirrors from the cabin last week when the sight of his own face had become too much to bear.

He slipped on jeans and a faded flannel shirt, and padded barefoot down the hall. Alex paused in the living room, watching Jessica through the patio doors. She sat in the glider with her lovely bare legs tucked underneath her, staring down at the valley below.

Alex remembered the night they'd spent here and how it had felt to be in her arms. Then he wondered if he'd taken advantage of her.

"I finally get to see the sunset," she remarked as Alex slid open the patio door. Streaks of maroon, pink, and gold painted the western sky. The sun burned a brilliant orange as it slowly sank into the horizon. Alex sat on the swing beside her.

"So . . ." Jessica said, when Alex didn't respond. "How are you holding up?"

"I'm alive," he said, not realizing how sarcastic he

sounded until the words came out.

"That's nothing to be ashamed of," Jessica said quietly and took his hand. Alex wanted to pull away from her, but instead he stroked the top of her hand with his thumb.

"It could've been me," he said. "If I'd been the one with Kaitlyn—"

"It doesn't work that way, Alex. We could worry about different scenarios forever. If I'd never married Cole, if I'd just divorced him and took my chances. There's no such thing as what might've been."

Alex's eyes burned, and he turned his head.

"It's okay to have loved Cole. It's okay to mourn him too." Jessica hesitated and said, "It's okay to cry."

"Haven't you heard?" Alex said bitterly. "Ramseys never cry."

"Don't feel guilty because you survived, Alex."

She touched his face then, and the walls around his heart crumbled. Alex laid his head in her lap and cried. He cried until he felt weightless and empty. Cried until the storm inside him was finally quiet.

Epilogue

He opened his eyes in the hospital room, startling the pretty blond nurse who changed his IV bag.

"You're awake," she said, and smiled.

Something about her smile tugged at him, and he tried to smile back. His effort at movement caused a white-hot jolt of pain that snapped him out of his drugged stupor.

Something was wrong with his face.

"Are you in pain?" she asked.

He tried to answer her. Tried to say something, but his words emerged as a strangled croak.

"What's your name?" she asked. "They couldn't find any identification on you, and we haven't been able to contact your family."

She waited patiently but he didn't have an answer to give her.

He didn't know.

Don't miss Michelle Perry's next book!

IN ENEMY HANDS
Michelle Perry

How hard could it be to kidnap a pampered little rich girl? Especially if you're bounty hunter extraordinaire Dante Giovanni, who normally prowls the underworld in search of the most vicious criminals. Piece of cake, Dante thinks, when reclusive businessman Gary Vandergriff offers him a cool half million to bring home his estranged daughter, Nadia.

Enter Nadia.

His first meeting with her is stunning; both literally and figuratively. He foils an attempt on her life, and falls immediately under her spell.

It's not gonna be hard duty, Dante thinks, keeping her safe from the Mexican drug lord infuriated by her stepfather's expanding meth operation. He'll take her out of harm's way, no problem, get her back to her father, and enjoy the ride along the way.
Everything is great.

Until he delivers her into Enemy Hands.

ISBN# 1932815473
Jewel Imprint: Emerald
Coming 2006
$6.99

BLOOD TiES
Lori Armstrong

What do they mean?

How far would someone go to sever . . . or protect them?

Julie Collins is stuck in a dead-end secretarial job with the Bear Butte County Sheriff's office, and still grieving over the unsolved murder of her Lakota half-brother. Lack of public interest in finding his murderer, or the killer of several other transient Native American men, has left Julie with a bone-deep cynicism she counters with tequila, cigarettes, and dangerous men. The one bright spot in her mundane life is the time she spends working part-time as a PI with her childhood friend, Kevin Wells.

When the body of a sixteen-year old white girl is discovered in nearby Rapid Creek, Julie believes this victim will receive the attention others were denied. Then she learns Kevin has been hired, mysteriously, to find out where the murdered girl spent her last few days. Julie finds herself drawn into the case against her better judgment, and discovers not only the ugly reality of the young girl's tragic life and brutal death, but ties to her and Kevin's past that she is increasingly reluctant to revisit.

On the surface the situation is eerily familiar. But the parallels end when Julie realizes some family secrets are best kept buried deep. Especially those serious enough to kill for.

ISBN#1932815325
Gold Imprint: May 2005
$6.99

BREEDING EVIL

Liz Wolfe

Someone is breeding superhumans . . .

. . . beings who possess extreme psychic abilities. Now they have implanted the ultimate seed in the perfect womb. They are a heartbeat away from successfully breeding a species of meta-humans, who will be raised in laboratories and conditioned to obey the orders of their owners, governments and large multi-national corporations.

Then Shelby Parker, a former black ops agent for the government, is asked to locate a missing woman. Her quest takes her to The Center for Bio-Psychological Research. Masquerading as a computer programmer, she gets inside the Center's inner workings. What she discovers is almost too horrible to comprehend.

Dr. Mac McRae, working for The Center, administers a lie-detector test to the perspective employee for his very cautious employers. Although she passes, the handsome Australian suspects Shelby is not what she appears. But then, neither is he.

Caught up in a nightmare of unspeakable malevolence, the unlikely duo is forced to team up to save a young woman and her very special child. And destroy a program that could change the face of nations.

But first they must unmask the mole that has infiltrated Shelby's agency and stalks their every move. They must stay alive and keep one step ahead of the pernicious forces who are intent on . . .

BREEDING EVIL

ISBN#1932815058
Gold Imprint: Available now
$6.99
www.lizwolfe.net

SUMMER OF FIRE
LINDA JACOBS

It is 1988, and Yellowstone Park is on fire.

Among the thousands of summer warriors battling to save America's crown jewel, is single mother Clare Chance. Having just watched her best friend, a fellow Texas firefighter, die in a roof collapse, she has fled to Montana to try and put the memory behind her. She's not the only one fighting personal demons as well as the fiery dragon threatening to consume the park.

There's Chris Deering, a Vietnam veteran helicopter pilot, seeking his next adrenaline high and a good time that doesn't include his wife, and Ranger Steve Haywood, a man scarred by the loss of his wife and baby in a plane crash. They rally 'round Clare when tragedy strikes yet again, and she loses a young soldier to a firestorm.

Three flawed, wounded people; one horrific blaze. Its tentacles are encircling the park, coming ever closer, threatening to cut them off. The landmark Old Faithful Inn and Park Headquarters at Mammoth are under siege, and now there's a helicopter down, missing, somewhere in the path of the conflagration. And Clare's daughter is on it ...

Gold Imprint
June 2005
$6.99

For more information

about other great titles from

Medallion Press, visit

www.medallionpress.com